Hart, Carolyn G.

Death in paradise.

DATE			

Death in

Paradise

Also by Carolyn Hart

Henrie O

Dead Man's Island
Scandal in Fair Haven
Death in Lovers' Lane

Death on Demand

Death on Demand
Design for Murder
Something Wicked
Honeymoon with Murder
A Little Class on Murder
Deadly Valentine
The Christie Caper
Southern Ghost
Mint Julep Murder

A Henrie O Mystery

CAROLYN HART

AVON BOOKS NEW YORK

This is a work of fiction. Names, characters, places, and incidents either are the product of the author's imagination or are used fictitiously. Any resemblance to actual events, locales, organizations, or persons, living or dead, is entirely coincidental and beyond the intent of either the author or the publisher.

AVON BOOKS
A division of
The Hearst Corporation
1350 Avenue of the Americas
New York, New York 10019

Interior design by Kellan Peck
Visit our website at **http://www.AvonBooks.com**
ISBN: 0-380-97414-2

Library of Congress Cataloging in Publication Data:

Hart, Carolyn
Death in paradise : a Henry O mystery / Carolyn Hart.—1st ed.
p. cm.
I. Title.
PS3558.A676D448 1998 97-29701
813'.54—dc21 CIP

First Avon Books Printing: April 1998

Printed in the U.S.A.

FIRST EDITION

QPM 10 9 8 7 6 5 4 3 2 1

To Lou Aronica and Trish Lande Grader

Death in

Paradise

one

I struggled to breathe. If I'd come upon a cobra, hood flared, deadly tongue flickering, I could not have been more transfixed.

Yet, once my eyes saw the shiny white posterboard in its entirety, once my vision encompassed all of it—the cut-out pictures and story, the artfully pasted letters, the single stark sketch, and the taped plastic bag—a sickening acceptance washed over me.

The glistening cardboard had been folded in half to slip easily into the postal service's two-day, red-white-and-blue priority mailer. No cover letter, no note, no return name and address, simply the decorated posterboard.

I opened the envelope casually, standing by the walnut butler's table in my narrow entryway. I had no sense of impending drama, no inkling that my life would never be the same.

I unfolded the poster. There were six separate representations:

The first was my late husband Richard's obituary with the accompanying one-column news photo and the caption "Richard Lattimer Collins." A red pencil had underlined the words: Collins fell to his death at the remote cliffside home of Belle Ericcson on the island of Kauai. Ericcson is a legendary foreign correspondent whose credits include Vietnam, the Six-Day War and El Salvador.

I was swept by the hideous sense of emptiness I'd felt when I'd held a current newspaper in my hand, seen the story that spelled an end to the invincible joy of a happy marriage. I'd written obits in the course of almost a half century as a newspaper reporter. That's how young reporters started in my early days. It became a quick, automatic ordering of the facts of a life, typewriter keys clacking. I didn't realize then the pain of seeing a loved one's existence reduced to lines of type: . . . "Survivors include his wife of thirty-nine years, Henrietta O'Dwyer Collins; his daughter, Emily Collins Drake, and her husband, Warren; two grandchildren, Diana and Neal Drake. Collins was preceded in death by his son, Robert Lattimer Collins . . ."

The second consisted of cut-out letters and numerals in two straggly lines, forming the dates March 30 and April 1.

March 30 held no significance for me. April 1 was the day Richard died. I could never laugh again on April Fool's Day, a day meant for lighthearted games, silly teasing, elaborate jokes. Richard had loved April Fool's Day, and he and the children had outdone one another with straight-faced evocations of absurdities. "Hey, Dad, did you see that huge bird that just flew by? Big as a boxcar!" Richard looked inquiringly at Emily and Bobby. "Bird? What bird?" Emily grinned, "Why, Dad, it's a favorite bird of yours." "Really?" Richard craned his head, peered out the window. "Gosh, I don't see it." Then Bobby hung from the window, flapped his hand.

"Over there, Dad, over there." Richard peppered them with questions, but each time the bird flew by, he just missed it. Finally, he clapped his hands together and shouted, "There it is. It has to be. The bluebird of happiness. Right?" I heard the children's whoops of glee and Richard's dramatic declamations as if they were here beside me, close enough to hug, the three of them, Richard and Emily and Bobby. Then the happy voices subsided, plunged back into the recesses of my mind, there to be summoned but never again to sound in a careless present.

The third was a magnificent photograph of a steep cliff. Lush vegetation in every shade of green, from palest jade to darkest emerald, glistened in bright sunlight. Silvery falls splashed over sharp black rocks.

My hands trembled. The poster wavered. I didn't have to ask what cliff this represented, though I'd never seen the site where Richard died.

The fourth was a clip from an advertisement showing two gloved hands, palms forward, fingers outspread. The brown gloves had the rich sheen and texture of expensive leather.

The pulse thudded in my throat. Hands move at the direction of a mind. Human choice. Not chance. Not accident. I'd survived loss before. My foreign-correspondent father disappeared in the deadly melee of fleeing refugees and strafing guns after the fall of Paris in World War II. War is brutal and rapacious and incalculable, but its destruction is catastrophic, like a tidal wave or an earthquake. There is no individual to be held accountable. I could bewail the world, the human passions that result in bloody destruction, but not a single mind or pair of hands. Richard and I together mourned the death of our son Bobby in a car wreck. We grieved horribly, but it was an accident. No one deliberately snuffed out Bobby's young life. I blamed myself because I was the one who insisted we travel on the twisting mountain road to a fiesta. The brakes went out in the decrepit old truck that rammed us. But the driver's little girl was buried that next week, too. I could blame poverty, timing, my own willfulness.

But not a pair of hands.

The fifth was a sketch of a stick figure tumbling backward toward the jagged points of boulders far below.

The drawing was haphazard, almost childish, pressure unevenly applied to the thick black grease pencil. But no child had drawn that plummeting body. Before my eyes, the stick figure metamorphosed into Richard, my Richard, flailing toward bloody death.

The sixth was a sandwich bag taped to the bottom of the poster, beneath the scrawled boulders.

Through the slick plastic, I saw pieces of slate-gray cardboard. Whatever those pieces meant, I knew it would cause me pain.

More pain.

It was as if the intervening years vanished and I was once again caught up in the shock and despair of Richard's death, my mind arguing that it had to be a mistake, that the call would come, the phone would ring, and it would be Richard saying, "It's okay, honey, I'm coming home." As he had come home through the years from odd and distant places, a first-rate newspaperman and the man I'd loved above all others.

But there was no call, there was only emptiness, a world swathed in steel-gray, all color gone. I could see the vivid hues, but there was no warmth in my soul. I was alone.

I walked into my kitchen, carrying the posterboard in one hand, the mailer in the other. Thin March sunlight angled through an east window. I placed the posterboard on my kitchen table and ripped the bag loose, spilling out the cardboard pieces into a pool of sunlight. Despite the sorrow washing over me, lapping around me, a rising tide of misery, I understood what I saw. The uneven, oddly cut pieces of cardboard were a puzzle, a puzzle created just for me by a nameless, faceless, cruel correspondent.

I almost scooped up the pieces, crushed them into a wad of smashed paper. My hands came close to the table. Somehow I made myself stop. It would not staunch the memories—or the agony—to destroy these little pieces of cardboard.

I don't know how long I stood there, aching with loss.

The thin sliver of sunlight moved and now the cardboard pieces were dull, making them even more chilling.

What damnable message awaited me?

I started to reach down, hesitated. But I felt abruptly sure that I could touch these pieces with impunity, that there would be no fingerprints to smudge. The person who had so carefully and coldly created this hellish exercise would be far too intelligent to leave any trace.

I arranged the pieces.

They formed a tombstone. Black letters—R. I. P.—scored the granite gray. A thick question mark was scrawled on the tombstone, over the letters.

My eyes moved from the tombstone to the tumbling stick figure. But I didn't see the drawing. Instead, nausea clawing at my throat, I saw Richard's body—*felt* Richard's body—plummeting faster and faster, inexorably, the law of gravity bleakly enforced, to slam painfully into rough black volcanic rock.

Oh, God, the pain Richard must have known! And the hideous heart-stopping terror of falling out of control . . .

It takes so long—so eternally long—to fall.

That's how Richard's life ended, the brutal obliteration of a mind and body that had given me pleasure and delight through the years. His laughter was forever stilled. No more quick and clever thoughts, no more vivid, concise writing, no more passion or effort or joy.

My heart raced. I struggled to breathe. But through the

pain of imagining, remembering, reliving, I understood the point—the vicious, mind-bending point—of this ugly collection.

Richard was pushed to his death. Gloved hands shoved him over the edge of that faraway cliff.

Richard was murdered.

That was the meaning of this motley, cleverly contrived collection. Yes, there was no doubt of the message.

I slumped into a kitchen chair. My entire body shuddered. I wasn't prepared on this cold spring day to have an all too recent wound torn asunder. There is never an end to mourning. Yes, the soft warmth of the sun, a smile, a child's laughter can connect you once again to the miracle and wonder of life. But the joy, the deep welling of utter happiness, is gone forever.

Richard. Oh, Richard.

Tears burned my eyes. My head throbbed. A flush flooded my face. I felt as though I might explode as anger warred with sorrow, bubbled beneath the shock. Who had put together this macabre display? And why? Oh, yes, most importantly, why? Why on this March morning was the hard-won equilibrium of my life shattered?

I tried to sort it out in my mind.

It was Belle Ericcson who first called with the news of Richard's death. It was the only time I ever spoke to her, and she broke my heart. Now I couldn't even remember the sound of her voice, that sound was gone as much of my memory of that hideous day was gone, mercifully buried where old pain is hidden. At first, I'd refused to believe it, tried to deny it even after I talked to the police in Kauai. I can't now remember those days. They are a fog of misery. I was adrift in a limbo of despair for months. Some days I wept. Some days I worked furiously, and now I have no idea what work it was. Some days I remembered the past: Richard showing Bobby how to put a minnow on a hook, the touch of Richard's hands in the sweet deepness of night, Richard stroking a tennis ball to Emily. Some days I'd railed against the futility of it. Richard, my surefooted, graceful Richard, falling from a mountain trail.

But I never questioned that his death was anything other than what it seemed to be, a heartbreaking accident that took from us the kind of happiness that poets celebrate and lovers alone can understand.

Did life itself seem worthless?

Oh, yes.

But Richard would have me finish the course. No matter how long and hard and lonely the way.

Some realities are inescapable. There is no greater reality than death. I accepted reality. Richard was gone. Forever.

If, if, if . . . If he hadn't responded to the call from Belle Ericcson . . . If he had arrived on Kauai another day . . .

But no matter how the mind turns and twists, seeking respite, death is unequivocal, unchangeable, unrelenting.

So I mourned, spending an aimless, gray year, no longer finding excitement in covering late-breaking news. I'd spent a lifetime as a reporter, and much of that lifetime in tandem with Richard, willing to go where the news happened—at a trial, a hurricane, in war, in peace. Of late years we had accepted only occasional assignments, though we weren't quite retired. But we were talking of retirement, of spending days at art galleries, in traveling to exotic places, spending time with Emily and our grandchildren.

The year I lost him, I didn't accept any assignments. The world had lost its flavor. Without Richard, the old fire was tamped.

But I am too restless, too driven not to work. I needed work to fill the lonely hours. Finally, through a call from an old friend, I'd ended up on a quiet Missouri campus with a teaching job, a job that would end with this semester.

Throughout that time, I'd never questioned the circumstances of Richard's death.

The police detective I talked to—Kanoa, John Kanoa—had been gentle, but he confirmed Belle Ericcson's call. Richard had died in a fall from a canyon trail at the house where he had been visiting.

Ahiahi.

That was the name of Belle Ericcson's home high atop a remote cliff on the still unspoiled, as yet little developed island of Kauai.

Not that I'd ever seen Belle's house.

Not the house on Kauai. Nor the one in Dallas. Nor any of the others. The cities drifted through my mind like autumn leaves—London, Paris, Zermatt, San Francisco. She had a home, well-known architecturally, in each. It was odd that I knew this about Belle Ericcson. But through the years I had accreted little facts, unimportant facts, about a woman I'd never really known, a woman I'd carefully avoided knowing.

Oh, yes, I knew some things about Belle Ericcson, information likely familiar to the cognoscenti of popular culture. Belle Ericcson was rather famous in her own way, known as people know Barbara Walters or Judy Woodruff or Diane Sawyer.

Without thought or plan, I'd absorbed throwaway facts over the years: Belle's several marriages, her prize-winning exploration of the dumping of the mentally ill into the streets and alleys of America, the year she won the Powder Puff derby in her single-engine Cessna. And, of course, the great heartbreak of her life, a loss I understood only too well.

One of the wire-service stories about Richard's accident—but it wasn't an accident, was it?—had included a description of the remote, closed-to-public-view Ericcson home on Kauai and a translation of the name: Ahiahi—Evening.

All of Belle's homes had names. That's pretentious, isn't it? Or did I think that simply because I didn't like her.

Be fair, Henrie O. I could not in good conscience say that

I disliked Belle Ericcson. I didn't know her well enough to have an honest opinion.

Richard tried several times to bring us together. Belle came to Hong Kong and we were to meet for dinner at a restaurant high on a hill overlooking the city. I don't look back on that evening with pride. I tried hard throughout our years together to be honest or not to speak. That night I feigned a headache. That's the old excuse, isn't it? But I could not meet Belle. I was afraid. I knew that if I saw them together and surprised a look of intimacy, it would break my heart. And I could not say this to Richard because wouldn't I have then been accusing him of unfaithfulness?

I knew in my heart he loved me. I simply couldn't bear to know if he also loved another.

That can happen without any intention of disloyalty, especially under the circumstances of war. And that's how Richard and Belle met.

Years later in Washington, Richard asked if I would go with him to the National Press Club on a night when Belle was speaking. I simply shook my head.

He never asked again.

That constraint would last our lifetime together. Yes, I could have come to know her through the years, but I resented the claim she had on my husband. It was a claim I never understood, never discussed with him, never openly acknowledged. But there was a claim. It led him to the place where he died.

Richard murdered!

I trembled with a corrosive anger. My instinct was to destroy this communication. My heart thudded. I grabbed the poster. But somehow, through the haze of fury, the old instinct to know, to analyze, to understand began to steady me.

Wait. I had to understand what this meant. Not simply that it was about Richard. I had to determine—somehow—why it had been sent.

It meant Richard was murdered. Or it meant someone suspected that Richard was murdered. Or, level upon level upon level, someone wanted me to think Richard was murdered.

But it meant more than what happened to Richard. It obviously was intended to propel me into action. Because I had to know the answer. I couldn't simply shrug it away.

My unknown correspondent was counting on that.

I don't like to be manipulated. By anyone. And now someone had bulled into my life, plunging me into a frenzy of uncertainty and anger.

I flung the poster down, came to my feet, began to pace.

The phone rang.

I ignored it. After four peals, the answering machine picked up. ". . . heard about a job on a small daily near L.A. But no smog. Thousand Oaks. A ritzy community. Let me know if you want . . ." Dennis Duffy's brash voice continued. Nice of Dennis. He was the city editor of the University newspaper. I'd done him some favors in the past. He knew I was looking for a job.

But right now I didn't care about a job. I wanted to fling myself out of this house. I wanted to track down the unknown figure who had willfully plunged me back into heartbreak and pain. I wanted to grab that person, demand, "Who are you? What do you know? Who killed my husband?"

I was breathing hard. My chest ached as if I'd run a race. Questions caromed helter-skelter in my mind. I stopped, gripped the back of the chair. Hold on. Hold on, calm down. Uncontrolled anger is an enemy. I would not outwit the cold intelligence that created the poster if possessed by anger.

No. I had to be cold, too, cold and thoughtful and logical and smart. All right. I'd approach it as if I were writing an article. I would distance myself from the anguish churning within me, the anguish and ever-present sorrow, hold fast to the discipline I knew so well. Who? What? When? Where?

Why? and How? I would try to steel my mind even though anger and pain throbbed within me.

Oh, Richard, dear God, Richard, did someone take away from you bright days we could have shared? Nothing is more ordinary than a breakfast table and the smell of pancakes and the dark rich roast of brewing coffee. So ordinary, but that moment when shared is suffused with magic; that moment alone is sterile. We had so many more mornings—and nights—that should have belonged to us.

As if he stood beside me, I could hear Richard's voice: "Easy does it, Henrie O, easy does it." It was an echo from our past that steadied me.

Who, what, when, where, why and how. The familiar questions slipped through my mind like beads worn slick by years of devotion.

Easy does it.

All right, Richard, all right. I'd use the questions that worked for me, worked for us, throughout our years together. Using every bit of strength I possessed, I forced my mind to function as if this were an assignment. There would be time for blazing anger later, when I faced my unknown correspondent.

And, damn you, whoever you are, face you I will.

But first, first I had to find the source. That was always the objective. Find the source.

How was as intriguing a question as any, a good, concrete, specific place to start.

How?

I sat down and looked carefully at the exterior of the mailer. There was no return address. I squinted. A Chicago postmark.

I didn't get excited. It's quite easy to send a mailer to a postal station, requesting the postmaster to mail the enclosed, properly stamped envelope from that site. If this had indeed been done, there was no way I could trace it.

I dismissed Chicago from my mind. Richard's final days had no connection with Chicago. The mailer could have come from Anywhere, U.S.A.

More interestingly, the mailer came directly to me in Derry Hills. But that, too, was easy to understand. Anyone with a computer and a modem could obtain Richard's obituary from newspaper archives. I was listed as a survivor in the obituary. Once that was known, a little further effort would yield my present location. There are a number of directories and reference works that contain my current address. No, that told me nothing about the sender.

I understood how the mailer reached me.

When?

The postmark was dated March 21. Today was Monday, March 24. Richard had died six years earlier. What prompted the timing? Why should anyone sound an alarm now?

What?

The message told me that my husband was murdered. But it was more than that, much more. It was a prod, a device to move me. That made it doubly challenging, doubly enraging, not only its actuality, but its purpose.

Where?

I shook my head impatiently. Not where did the package come from. The where that mattered was the scene of Richard's death: Kauai.

Why?

That was the critical question. Why was the mailer sent? What did my unknown correspondent hope to achieve?

Obviously, the objective wasn't simply to upset me. No, my correspondent must want—desperately—to set into motion a series of events, culminating in . . .

The unmasking of Richard's murderer?

I scooped up the cardboard pieces of the tombstone, slipped them into the plastic bag.

No. If the objective was to punish Richard's murderer, if

that's what mattered to the shadowy figure who had so painstakingly created the poster, it could have been done much more simply. An anonymous tip to the police in Lihue would have been much more to the point.

So, justice wasn't the motivation.

But there had to be motivation, compelling, urgent, and intense, to account for this macabre display. Of course, this collection was purposefully gruesome. The better to rivet me.

Somehow, someone would benefit. It would satisfy an as yet obscure but definite design for me to come to Kauai. Because that had to be my ultimate destination if I responded to this call.

Who?

Somewhere, a hundred or a thousand or several thousand miles away, an unknown, anonymous creature must be wondering: Has it arrived? Has she opened it? What will she do?

"All right." I said it aloud. Crisply. I was talking to my . . . opponent? conspirator? nemesis? "All right. But there's something about letting genies out of the bottle, you know. I think I will come. I'm almost certain I will. But I will be prepared."

The sunlight is always thin in March and the earth is cold. I felt a chill. Surely it was nothing more than the sun slipping behind a cloud, the kitchen darkening as it did so. The posterboard was in shadow. I couldn't see Richard's photograph clearly. But the falling figure on the poster was clear and distinct and heartbreaking. I closed my eyes and pressed my hands hard against my face.

And still, I saw that falling figure.

two

The television film flickered on the screen. The *whop-whop* of a helicopter sounded, urgent and raucous, the ugly duckling of the air. The ungainly craft bumped onto the Tarmac. In a moment, the door swung out and Richard stood framed in the opening. Black smudges streaked his unshaven face. The residue of an explosion? Mud caked his Army-issue fatigues. His eyes had the emptiness of a man bone-tired and emotionally drained. He turned to grasp the hand of a slim, blond woman. She held tight to Richard as they clambered tiredly down the steps. She turned a haggard face toward the camera. Her too-large fatigues gave her a gallant, gamine air. On the runway they walked arm-in-arm, stumbling in exhaustion, helping each other.

And yes, I resented his arm around her, resented the bond they'd shared that I'd never fully understood, resented ferociously that Richard had died so far from me, so near to Belle.

It is an odd trick of age that there is a calming of old enmities—until you plunge back in time, assume again the emotions that you lived through. And perhaps thought safely entombed.

As I watched the flickering film, it was as though the years had sheared away and I was waiting for Richard to call from Saigon, praying for his safety, missing him with every fiber of my heart and body.

The voice-over droned: "Among the correspondents covering the Tet offensive were Richard Collins of Midwest Syndicated News and Belle Ericcson of the New York *Daily News*."

A line of heavily camouflaged trucks cut them from view.

I punched the "off" button. My eyes burned. I'd spent several hours in the Thorndyke University archives, studying television film from the Vietnam War, the war that had appeared nightly on America's television sets and plunged the nation into division, alienating the generations.

Vietnam was the war that James Reston of *The New York Times* remembered bleakly in his memoirs. Reston wrote, "From first to last, I felt that war involved so many lies, cost so many lives, and raised so many questions about the judgment of our officials that I hated to think about raking through the rubble one last time."

But Reston recalled the correspondents who covered that war with respect and admiration.

Yes, they were brave, and they told a reluctant America the truth, showing them in words and on film the bloody bodies of young American soldiers and the flayed skin of napalm-burned children and the villages turned to ashes.

Richard was one of the first to reveal the "secret" bombing of Cambodia. Belle was among the first to tell readers about the false body counts, the statistics created by the U.S.

Army to convince those at home that America was winning the war.

I punched the "eject" button, returned the cassette to its holder. The University archives contained almost twenty-six filmed reports that included Belle, five of Richard.

One of Belle's Vietnam stories vaulted her to the Pulitzer short list.

It took only a moment to call up the story. I nodded in appreciation as I read the lead:

"The ARVN major's gaunt face was empty of expression as he lifted the stubby revolver and shot the shackled Vietcong prisoner in the face."

Yes, Belle and Richard and hundreds of other correspondents found the truth and reported it, no matter how ugly, unpleasant, and grim. They told the stories of gallant American GIs, doing their best, fighting bravely, dying by the hundreds.

And Belle had style. Definitely I had to grant that Belle Ericcson possessed style and flair. And courage.

I stacked the videocassettes, remembering a war I hadn't covered.

I shrugged into my coat. The sharp March air was welcome when I walked swiftly down the library's shallow stone steps. Film always makes me feel headachy. But it wasn't simply the stuffiness of the small cubicle where I'd watched the past unfold that bothered me.

As I slid into my MG, tossing my notepad into the passenger seat, I wondered at decisions. And chance.

One cool spring day many years ago in Mexico City, Richard and I had tossed a coin in our apartment on Reforma, not far from the Angel. Richard had been offered a bureau spot in Hong Kong and I could easily string for the English-language newspaper there. The other possibility was a return to D.C. We wanted to leave Mexico after the car wreck that killed Bobby.

The coin came up heads—and Hong Kong.

When the war heated up in Vietnam, Richard headed for Saigon. I stayed in Hong Kong with our daughter Emily.

It was in Saigon that Richard first met Belle Ericcson.

Heads for Hong Kong.

Had Richard ultimately lost his life because of that long-ago gamble? I didn't know. I wondered if Belle Ericcson knew.

It was dark in the attic. I'd waited until after dinner to come up here. I knew why I'd delayed. This was going to hurt. All through the day, I'd moved swiftly, automatically, looking where I should look: the University film archives, my computer, the morgue of *The Clarion*, speeding through my fingers those old familiar beads, finding comfort in totting up facts. If you immerse yourself in facts, you keep emotion at bay.

I'd printed out a *Who's Who* bio of Belle Ericcson. The bio listed her nonfiction books, including her autobiography, *Belle on Belle*. I'd called a local bookstore. They were holding a copy for me.

I moved hesitantly in the cramped, dark space until I found the dangling chain and pulled it. I blinked in the sudden sharp light from the 200-watt bulb.

Yes, I was following every avenue. But this was going to be the toughest road.

I tugged the box free from a stack toward the rear of the attic, startling a daddy longlegs into flight. The box held Richard's daybooks from 1940 until his death.

In the year after Richard died, I'd donated most of his clothes to Goodwill. I'd kept a worn russet leather jacket that he'd treasured. It hung in my closet, wherever that closet might be—in an apartment, a rented house, wherever I went.

The jacket was too large for me, but I often wore it on

solitary walks, my hands jammed in the pockets that had known his touch, my shoulders caressed by the silk lining, now gossamer-thin, faded from gold to a delicate saffron. I'd kept his Washington Senators ball cap, his favorite fountain pen, a tartan muffler I'd bought for him in Edinburgh. In my jewel box was a set of cuff links in heavy Mexican silver. They were shaped like the old upright Smith-Corona typewriter. Our daughter Emily gave them to him on his sixtieth birthday. He'd first worn them to a dinner at the National Press Club.

Throughout my house, wherever I lived, were mementos of our years together: photographs, books we'd shared, trinkets we'd chosen.

I'd boxed up all of his papers, the thousands and thousands of words he'd written from his first story as a reporter in Paris, the March 7, 1940, meeting of American Undersecretary of State Sumner Welles with French Premier Deladier, to the last story he'd covered, a March 1991 interview with Ed Turner, the news wizard who made CNN a reporter's joy.

I opened the box. Dust drifted up, tickling my nose. I smothered a sneeze. I picked up the 1991 daybook. I stared down at the black softcover book.

Richard had held this book. His swift, certain hands had flipped open these pages. He'd written concisely, neatly, the little details of his days: interviews scheduled, story lines to consider, comments to remember—suppositions, declarations, weather—and had had no hint that his days were dwindling down.

I'd not looked in any of the books until today. Not because I didn't care. Because I cared too much.

I could not permit myself to cling to a yesterday that was beyond my reach. If I focused on what was over, I would not have the strength to face each lonely day. I'd deliberately immersed myself in the reality of the present, forced myself to look forward, not back. I'd taken another job, made new friends, enjoyed a romantic liaison.

But yes, I was tempted to pull out the volume for 1940. I'd like to search through Richard's elegantly spare sentences for his description of the moment when we met.

But I didn't need to read his words. The memory was indelible: a sunny day in Montmartre and Richard buying a balloon for the thin, dark-haired, dazzled daughter of his bureau chief. We'd laughed together and I'd thought him gloriously handsome, a young girl's dream of an older man. He was all of twenty-two.

I'd always thought him gloriously handsome: short hair with reddish glints like sunlight glancing on a Florentine villa; a broad, open face, a mouth that easily stretched into a smile; eyes with a glint of ebullient, rollicking humor. But a mouth that could be stubborn and stern when needed and eyes willing to dare the world for what was right and good and decent.

No, I didn't need to read his sketch of the day we met. It was part and parcel of my heart, a heart that ached anew when I flipped open his last daybook. Richard's small square printing was easy to read, clear and distinct.

I turned to the month of March.

I had not wanted, after his death, to read the entries for his last days, entries that would include Belle Ericcson. Yes, anger still flickered because he'd spent his last moments with Belle. I'd not wanted to think about that. Not ever.

Richard fell to his death from Belle's cliffside home on the island of Kauai six years ago on April 1.

It took every ounce of will to turn the pages.

But there were no entries for the last week in March. None.

How odd.

Richard had returned to Washington from Atlanta on March 20. I flipped back; yes, on March 21 a description of Ed Turner's wry humor and clear-eyed news sense and what a fascinating interview it had been. Richard noted dinner with an old friend from *The Times*.

I plucked one paragraph from the page: "Henrie O called. She'll be home next week. I love her."

I smoothed my fingertips over the words.

The last entry was on Friday, March 22:

Johnnie Rodriguez called. I could scarcely hear him although the connection was clear. Voice subdued. Hesitant. But determined. And sober. He said he had to tell someone the truth about the day CeeCee Burke was kidnapped. He asked me to come to the lake.

Oh, God, of course! Now I understood the dates on the poster.

April 1, the day Richard died.

March 30, the day one year earlier when Belle Ericcson's oldest daughter was kidnapped.

Kidnapping. It is like tipping over a stone and watching plump, white slugs quiver away from the light, like waking in the night to a banshee's wail, like opening a door and smelling death.

Kidnapping. As ugly a crime as ever occurs.

I should have known. I remembered well enough the days after CeeCee Burke's kidnapping when Richard went to Texas to be with Belle, her husband, Keith Scanlon, and her five remaining children.

But Richard and I never talked about that. Sometimes in a happy marriage there are subjects not broached. You cannot quarrel if you do not raise a question.

Richard knew I disapproved of his role after the kidnapping. But I would never voice that disapproval. He had to make his own decisions and sometimes those decisions could not be to my liking. And I could not—how could anyone?—begrudge a man going to a friend in time of terrible trouble.

Now I wished desperately that I had opened my heart when CeeCee Burke was kidnapped. I should have told Richard that I admired him. I might have disagreed with his action, but I admired him.

I wondered now if he would have told me of the call from Johnnie Rodriguez if I'd been at home when it came.

I'd never know.

But something within me—the part of me that looks with icy clarity at reality—thought not. I had not been there for Richard when CeeCee was kidnapped. He could scarcely be blamed for assuming I would not want him to pursue that case.

I turned the next few pages of the daybook.

There were no more entries. Richard had never written again in his daybook. But he had lived for another week—one week and two days.

Those empty pages spoke volumes to me. They told me that whatever happened to Richard in those following days was so explosive, so incendiary, he'd not been willing to commit it to paper.

I was sure of that because I knew Richard, knew his care with language. He was so aware that words once created had a life beyond the writer. He never committed facts to paper unless he felt certain of them. Certain of their truth.

Richard valued truth above all.

I shut the daybook.

I had returned to D.C. two days after Richard left. I'd found a brief note, saying he planned to spend a few days with Emily in Austin. Later, I'd always been glad he saw Emily, that she had a bright and happy visit as her farewell to her father.

I refused to be hurt by his deception.

Of course, it wasn't quite a deception. Merely a failure to tell everything he knew.

And that, again, was so very much a part of Richard. He obviously wanted to talk to Johnnie Rodriguez—and who was he? I would find out—and to evaluate what was said. And, of course, Richard didn't tell me about the call from Rodriguez because we'd never talked about the kidnapping, or about the time afterward that Richard spent in Texas, both at the lake and later in Dallas.

There was too much that we had never discussed. So he simply said in his note that he was going to visit Emily.

Richard: cautious, thoughtful, careful.

So I'd not known the purpose of his last trip, the true purpose.

I don't believe in presentiments. And yet, and yet . . . But surely it was nothing more than happenstance, Richard taking advantage of being in Texas and going to see Emily.

If he was troubled, his daughter had not perceived it. She would have told me.

But, again, I knew Richard so well.

If he'd learned something from Johnnie Rodriguez that shocked him, surprised him, he would take his time deciding how to respond.

I'd assumed that Richard had received a call from Belle Ericcson, asking him to come to Kauai. Perhaps that had not been the case at all. Perhaps Richard made the decision to go to Kauai because he learned something that Belle had to be told.

I hurried downstairs to my study. It took only a moment at my computer to link to *The Clarion*'s morgue and pull up the kidnapping seven years ago of CeeCee Burke.

in her bright blue eyes. I wondered if it was a long-buried resentment. Had she been jealous of Richard? The soc desk. I hadn't heard that phrase in years, but I remembered the old lingo. Yes, it was an exceptional woman reporter in those days who didn't end up writing society news. That's where Lou started. She ended as a lifestyle editor, and a very successful one. It had been easy to find an acquaintance who knew her and could arrange for us to meet.

Her avid, probing eyes settled on me. "What brings you to Dallas?"

What, indeed?

"I've been asked to do a piece on Belle Ericcson." I mentioned one of the popular weekly magazines that specialize in celebrity chatter. "And Dallas was her home base. Before the kidnapping." I listened to my smooth, pleasant words with a sense of shock at my capacity for deception. Inside, I seethed with dislike for this sharp-featured woman and her glacial, automatic charm. But wasn't I right on her level? She smiled and meant nothing. And so did I.

"Good luck. You'll need it." Her quick laughter was brittle and unamused. It was a taunt disguised by humor. It was clear she had no good wishes for me.

"Why?" I took a bite of steak, found it tasteless and knew the fault lay with me. Was my immediate distaste for this woman equally invalid?

"Oh, if you do the glossy, skin-deep stuff, you'll do all right. There's plenty of that kind of information around. 'Intrepid Belle Ericcson, prize-winning writer, accomplished pilot, generous philanthropist.' " The descriptive phrase, intoned in a deep, smooth voice, was an uncanny mimicry of a television announcer's soulful spiel. "Easier than making pie crust. I can do it in my sleep."

My quick, visceral response was anger. Who the hell did she think she was? And where did she get off, implying I would write fluff. My face hardened. My hand tightened on my glass of iced tea. Maybe it was luck, maybe it was the deep desperate need to discover what this woman knew, but I took a breath and replayed the words in my mind and caught the subtext.

Maybe, just maybe . . .

"You think Belle's public persona is phony?" I cut another piece of meat, tried to make it look as though I were eating. But I didn't care about food. Everything, all the everyday, ordinary actions were distractions, impediments. Yes, I would eat enough. And sleep. Dress and smile. Create conversation. But the goal—What happened to Richard? Why did Richard die?—thudded feverishly in my mind like incessant jungle drums.

"I did a piece on her for the Sunday section. It was like wrapping up a Christmas present—lots of tinsel, stars, stickers. Gorgeous bow. But when you open the box, there's nothing there." Dissatisfaction glittered in her eyes.

I shook my head when the waiter offered more wine. He filled Lou's glass. She took a greedy gulp as he moved away. It was she who'd chosen the wine, at my invitation, selecting an expensive French Chardonnay. And a very expensive entrée, quail in white wine. I'd chosen mesquite-smoked tenderloin. I couldn't come to Texas and not eat beef.

But expense didn't matter now. My last-minute plane tickets to Dallas and on to Hawaii were absurdly expensive even with the helpful senior discount. I don't like to waste money and I wasn't on anyone's expense account.

But money be damned.

The world be damned.

I was in Texas because I had to be. I was going to Hawaii. I would do what I had to do, go where I had to go.

Lou finished the glass, looked regretfully for the waiter.

I had myself well under control now. "You think there's more—or less—than meets the eye of the reader in stories about Belle?"

Lou took a last bite of quail, glanced again at her empty wineglass.

I caught the waiter's attention. More wine. An order for dessert, though nothing appealed to me.

"It's like fireworks," Lou said thoughtfully, holding the wineglass so that a stream of sunshine touched it with gold. "What's left after the hard, hot, bright glare? Twisted, dark pieces of wire, burned cardboard, a nasty smell. You know what I think?" She leaned her elbows on the table. Her bright, sardonic, weary gaze held mine. "I think there's a story there, all right. It's so perfect on the surface: brilliant and beautiful woman reporter with a fascinating family, three children of her own from her marriage to a gifted artist; widowhood; remarriage to a hard-charging newspaperman with his own three kids; melded family, high-society kids who provide appealing feature copy with lots of jokes and entertaining escapades. Sheesh. But I saw them in action here for cinco years and sometimes they didn't have on their party faces. I'd like to have been at Belle's Highland Park mansion when it was just family. Her third husband is a hell of a lot younger than she is. And CeeCee, the beautiful director of the Ericcson Foundation—now doesn't that sound like stellar Junior League? But she broke two engagements! To fine young men. And her latest fiancé, Stan Dugan, he'd probably never been inside a country club until he met CeeCee. A personal-injury lawyer." Lou's patrician nose wrinkled. "Ugly as sin. I imagine Belle was appalled. Yes, I think the right questions could flip some images fast. Who took care of Belle's kids while she was busy being Ms. Glamorous War Correspondent? Why did she marry two drunks in a row?" The shiny white hair quivered as she nodded vigorously. "God's truth. I had a friend who knew Belle and her first husband, Oliver Burke, in Tokyo. Burke was soused all the time. And the second one, Gallagher, was drunk as a lord when his car went into the Potomac. Find out which general she slept with in Vietnam." She shot me a sharp, quick look. "She knew Richard there. Didn't she?"

"Of course." I made my answer careless, as if it didn't matter.

Those hot blue eyes flickered with amusement and erotic supposition. "Belle was even more gorgeous then than now."

If I could have shoved back my chair and escaped, I would have.

Lou Kinkaid knew it.

"Richard thought very highly of Belle." My smile felt as if it were pasted to my face.

Her lips curved in malicious pleasure. "I'm sure he did. Most men did."

Damn you. Damn you.

I kept my voice even. "I've read a lot about Belle and her family." Read and made notes and studied and compiled. "It sounds as though they had a lot of fun. Until the kidnapping."

"Sounds that way." She drawled it. "But some questions never get answered. Why is her oldest son crossways with the world? And yet he's the only one who's stayed in Dallas. All the others blew town as soon as they got CeeCee buried. Coincidence? I don't think so. Belle handpicked a society girl for Joss, her youngest son, to marry. They didn't even stay married a year. They split right after CeeCee was kidnapped. Why did the foundation—the Ericcson Foundation, funded with Belle's millions—completely change direction after CeeCee died? She was the one who ran it, you know. And all the other siblings worked for her. One great big happy family . . . I don't think. Especially the stepkids, the ones who joined the crew when Belle married Gallagher. What do they really think about Super Stepmom? Gretchen Gallagher always looks like a thundercloud, especially when Stepmom's around. And Wheeler Gallagher's never had a real job." Lou looked again around the elegant dining room. "But Belle was a Dallas icon. I couldn't ask what I wanted to ask. What do you intend to ask?"

"Questions Belle has never heard," I said grimly.

Lou gave a small shrug that barely lifted her beautifully tailored jacket. She held up her wineglass. "Good luck." It was grudging but this time perhaps sincere.

The desserts arrived. She finished the glass of wine first—I'd lost count of how many—then spooned globs of a chocolate confection that looked darker than a Bavarian forest.

I ate peppermint sorbet. It was almost as tart as my thoughts.

The Greek Revival house glistened in the bright Texas sun. I drove the rental car into a modest parking lot screened by poplars. A small wooden sign at the foot of the broad steps announced: ERICCSON FOUNDATION.

The door opened into a broad central hall. To my right was a shiny walnut desk. A young woman with a pleasant face and ginger hair looked up and smiled cheerfully. "Good morning. May I help you?"

My shoes clicked on the wooden floor. "Yes. I'd like to see Mr. Burke, please."

Anders Burke was the older of CeeCee Burke's two brothers and it was he who was now director of the Ericcson Foundation.

"I'm sorry." She sounded genuinely concerned. "Mr. Burke is out of town and won't be back for a week. Perhaps I can help you."

I wasn't surprised. I knew where Anders Burke was. And all the rest of Belle's children, natural and adopted. They were on Kauai, gathering as they did every year in memory of their slain sister. They'd been there when Richard died. Did Richard go to Kauai because they all were there?

But I looked pettish, a wealthy woman irritated that her plans were thwarted. I fingered the heavy gold necklace at my throat. It was a great complement to my navy linen dress with matching gold buttons. "Oh, dear. I've come all the way from Lubbock to see him. I suppose I should have called first. I'm Isabel Rushton and I wanted to find out more about the foundation to see if I might include it in my charities."

She sprang to her feet. "Oh, I'm sure I can help you, Mrs. Rushton. And I'll have Mr. Burke contact you as soon as he returns. But I can give you a great deal of information about the foundation. I'm Ginger Cowan, Mr. Burke's assistant. And I'll be happy to show you our offices."

"Oh, yes, I'd like that." I looked around inquisitively. I pointed to the closed double doors across the hall. "Is that Mr. Burke's office?"

"No, ma'am." For an instant, she looked uncomfortable. "That was the office of our first director. At present that office isn't used."

I raised my eyebrows, a canny philanthropist scenting possible waste and inefficiency, perhaps compounded by unstable leadership.

Ginger plunged into explanations. ". . . and Anders—Mr. Burke—didn't want to take over his sister's office. I think it was just too hard for him. I know you'll understand."

"My, oh my, of course. That poor child. I remember now. As I recall, the kidnapping was never solved, was it? Of course, I understand." I had my hand on the brass knob to one of the doors. "But may I just take a peek?" An old lady with ghoulish tendencies.

"Of course, Mrs. Rushton." She hurried to join me.

I opened the door, stepped into an elegant room.

Ginger flipped a switch and a magnificent chandelier glowed to life. The turquoise hangings were as rich as a New Mexico sky, the gray walls cool as pewter. White linen slipcovers looked crisp on the occasional chairs. A shiny fruitwood desk was flanked by two tall french windows. But the room was dominated by a massive mahogany dining table covered with small plastic frames bright with color.

I walked to the desk. Each frame contained a miniaturized poster. It was easy to see at a quick glance the projects supported by the Ericcson Foundation.

RUN FOR THE ROSES
FIGHT BREAST CANCER

MAKE THE NIGHT SAFE
FOR WOMEN

ELECT LINDA MORGAN
PUT WOMEN IN
THE LEGISLATURE

There were dozens more, supporting political candidates and themes—drug-free schools, the anti-tobacco lobby, universal medical care—and each poster had the Ericcson Foundation logo in the lower right-hand corner, a bell emblazoned with a rose. CeeCee Burke championed causes dear to many women.

I picked up one of the plastic holders and felt the grit of dust. The line where the frame had sat was clearly visible on the table.

Ginger ineffectually brushed her hand across the line, leaving a smear. "No one comes in here very often. Let me show you the rest of the offices."

But I stared at the bright posters, frowning. "No one told me that the foundation was quite so *liberal.*" My tone indicated repugnance.

"Oh, Mrs. Rushton, please, all of this is completely out-of-date. The foundation is absolutely apolitical now. Mr. Burke has totally redirected the aims of the foundation." Ginger spoke fast. Her eyes shone.

"Indeed?" I looked at her suspiciously, a conservative dowager with pots of money available for the right programs.

"Oh, yes. Come. Let me show you." She urged me out of the dusty room, clicked off the chandelier, leaving the little plastic mementos shrouded in dusky neglect. She led me on a whirlwind tour, upstairs and down. There were brilliantly hued posters, but no miniatures now. They all proclaimed the same goal: protect our world, its environment and its animals. Save dolphins from shrimp nets. Release wolves in the Northwest. Stave off development of wetlands and the remaining tall-grass prairies. Stop the cruelty of medical research on helpless cats and dogs and monkeys who think and feel and suffer.

Coming back downstairs, I stopped and studied a full-length portrait on the landing. I didn't need the little bronze plaque at the bottom to identify Belle's daughter. But I looked at it inquiringly.

My young guide's face took on a subdued, somber cast. "That's Miss Burke."

I wondered who had chosen this photograph, had it enlarged to full length. It told as much about the selector as it did about CeeCee Burke.

"Mr. Burke's wife, Peggy, had it put there." Ginger stared up, her face puzzled, perhaps trying to understand the willfulness of fate.

So it was chosen by Peggy Burke, not by Anders.

CeeCee's head was thrown back, her long dark hair brushed back by a breeze, her face alight with happiness. She wore a plaid shirt and jeans and boots. An armful of Dalmatian puppies snuggled and licked and squirmed in her embrace. Bright sunlight glistened on a cottonwood tree and cottonwood puffs drifted on the summer air.

"Very nice," I said approvingly, but I struggled against the ache in my throat from that forever-gone image transfixed for one brief moment. It was a poignant reminder that Richard's death had been preceded by another.

I kept my face blank and walked on down the stairs. I played my part, making it clear that I was reassured about the goals of the foundation, but I wanted time to consider my course of action. I declined to leave my address and telephone number. "I'll be in touch, Miss Cowan. And I certainly appreciate your kindness today. I am very interested in Mr. Burke's commitment to nature." I accepted an armload of pamphlets. "Do you enjoy the foundation as much since it has so drastically changed its aims?"

She shook her head, smiled. "Oh, I didn't work here when Miss Burke was director. I knew Anders from animal-rights marches. He asked if I'd like to be his assistant. I've loved every minute of it. It's so wonderful to help animals."

I gave her a sharp, demanding look. "Is anyone here now who worked for Miss Burke?"

"Oh, no, ma'am." She spoke without hesitation, sure that her answer would please. "Not a soul."

I left the Ericcson Foundation, my hands filled with brochures and exhortations. I also carried with me a good many questions. But not the ones I'd revealed to Ginger Cowan.

The office was in a strip shopping center on a shabby stretch of Mockingbird Lane. Plate glass windows and a legend in bright gold letters: STANLEY JAMES DUGAN, ATTORNEY AT LAW.

The secretary looked up briskly when I stepped inside. She was a thin, middle-aged woman with faded blond hair, quick, intelligent eyes, and a tired, lined face. She wore good makeup, lightly applied. But her nose was shiny and the lipstick had worn to the edges of her mouth. Yes, she got up, started the day, put on makeup, but she didn't bother to freshen it up. Usually, I'd have wanted to know why. I'd have wanted to know all about her, what brought her to a solitary, high-stress job, what kind of home she lived in, whom she loved or hated, what her children were like, why her mouth drooped in repose.

Not now. Now she was simply an impediment, a challenge to be bested. But I knew I must curb my desperate impatience, the ravening hunger to gouge from this man or that woman the information I had to have. I had to resist the force of that unending drumbeat—What happened to Richard? Why did Richard die?—and maintain my composure. A desperate, anxious woman frightens people, shuts them up. I kept my words even, my tone level.

"No, I'm sorry. I don't have an appointment. Please give my card to Mr. Dugan."

"He's in conference. I doubt that he'll see you." The words were quick, bored, the patter of a well-trained gatekeeper.

I had to get Dugan's attention. I turned my card over, thought for a moment, knowing this was the only chance I might have. Quickly, I scrawled: "CeeCee Burke's murderer is on Kauai. Now." That was all.

It was enough. One minute later, I entered Stanley Dugan's office.

He stood behind a battered oak desk, a huge, homely, rawboned man. About six-seven. Small on a basketball court, overpowering here. His face looked as if it had been hacked out of hardwood by a nearsighted sculptor, the features oversized and a bit askew. And tough as rawhide. Shiny, thick-lensed glasses magnified cold gray eyes. All of a piece, except for his exceptionally well-tailored light wool suit. I'd have expected a rumpled, cheap suit. But it was a signal to me to remember that no one is all of a piece.

His big gray eyes scanned me like a laser. I saw the judgment: Money. Savvy. Doesn't look like a nut.

I wonder what he read in my eyes, because I wasn't missing much either. I knew I was facing a tough opponent.

Opponent. That's what I felt in this room, that I was going to engage in a mind to mind struggle with a powerful, determined, unpredictable adversary.

So it didn't surprise me when he attacked before I could say a word. He held up my card and it looked tiny between his massive thumb and forefinger. "What the hell does this mean?" His eyes were hard, suspicious, combative. He came around the desk, walked close to me.

I had to prove I wasn't horning in on a notorious case for money or sensation or malice. "Right now everyone in Belle Ericcson's family is at Ahiahi—and one of them killed your fiancée."

He took two big steps and was staring down at me, pressing so close I could see a tracery of tiny broken blood vessels in his ruddy face, smell talcum, feel the throbbing tension in his huge body. "Who? Damn you, who?"

"One of them. I don't know which. CeeCee Burke disappeared from Belle's lakefront home. One year later my husband—Richard Collins—went to Kauai because he'd learned who killed CeeCee." I knew this had to be true. Something that Johnnie Rodriguez told Richard revealed the kidnapper. If all went well, I'd have the same knowledge after I talked to Johnnie Rodriguez. "They said Richard fell to his death. I think he was pushed."

He flipped my card, glanced at the name. "Collins. The newspaper guy. Belle's pal." His eyes sought mine. "You got identification?"

I did. Driver's license. Social security card. Credit cards. Library card. Oh, yes, I had identification.

He riffed through the cards, handed them back to me, glared at me. "What did your husband know?"

"This last week, I looked through Richard's daybooks." That was true. But I didn't owe this man anything. I had no intention of revealing Richard's true entry, not until I talked to Johnnie Rodriguez. That had to come first. But I would say whatever I had to say to win information from Stan Dugan. "In his last entry, Richard wrote: 'CeeCee's killer will be at Ahiahi. I have to tell Belle.' " Yes, I made it up.

"Christ." It was an expletive. He grabbed my shoulders in a vise-tight grip. "Who? He must have said. Tell me who."

"I don't know. That's all Richard wrote. That was his last entry."

Dugan released me, turned away. "Someone at Ahiahi." His voice was harsh, full of the kind of anger I understood. "Goddamn. So that's why Collins came . . ."

I felt a quick shock. I'd not expected this. "Were you at Ahiahi when Richard died?"

"Yes." But his thoughts clearly were not in this room. "Someone at Ahiahi." His big hands clenched into fists.

Yes, he sounded angry. And vengeful. But he was there when Richard was murdered. I couldn't trust him. I couldn't trust anyone. Yes, he had been CeeCee's fiancé. But lovers can quarrel.

"Why aren't you at Ahiahi now?" I asked him. "They gather every year. To remember CeeCee."

For a moment, I didn't think he was going to answer.

Finally, his voice harsh, he said, "I don't do pilgrimages."

"But you went the first year." The year Richard died.

He ignored that. Instead, his eyes were once again hard and suspicious. "Why have you come to me? What do you want?"

"I want to talk to you about CeeCee." What did I want? I wanted to peer into his mind and heart. I wanted to understand him and through him to understand who CeeCee Burke was and why someone wanted to kill her.

I glanced swiftly around the office. I've been in a few law offices. Paneled walls. Hunting prints. Or drawings of barristers at the Inns of Court. Framed diplomas. Sometimes the Order of the Coif prominently displayed. Leather furniture. Fireplace. Oriental rug or two.

Not this one. Gray tiled floor, bleak white walls. Except for one wall.

My eyes widened. I saw more than I wanted to. My gaze jerked toward him.

The big lawyer gave a grim smile. "Not for the squeamish. Juries can't be squeamish about personal injury." He pointed at the jumble of color prints, pictures with lots of bright red blood. "Before and after photos. Before, you see a man or woman or kid when life was good. Happy faces. Weddings. Babies. Walking. Or running." He pointed at the snapshot of a smiling young woman holding a new baby. "Debbie Morales and Judy. Debbie was twenty-six, worked in the day-care center where her baby stayed. Single mother. Paid her rent on time. Damn proud to be off welfare. Rented a tiny apartment. Kept telling the landlord she was getting headaches and something was wrong with the heater. She and Judy had been dead for six days when they found them. Carbon monoxide. See that picture." He pointed to the next photo.

I didn't look.

"It was summer. Bloated and maggoty. Yeah, this wall tells it like it is. The happy pictures are before, before they got maimed or burned or crushed or killed. Juries see the pictures, they understand what happened. And, of course, there's my old friend Bob. He's a big help." He reached out to touch a yellowed, bony shoulder.

I stared at the bones. "Bob?"

He ran his fingers over the rib cage. "Bob goes to court with me. If you can show a jury—really show them—what got broke or burned or smashed and make them feel it in their bones or gut, the sky's no limit."

"You make somebody pay."

"Every time." His arrogance was startling. "It's the greatest game in the world—and I always win."

I believed him. And I wondered what that kind of confidence might do to a young man. It could engender a dangerous egotism.

Appraisal flickered in his eyes and I realized he was quick. Whip-quick.

"Yeah, lady, I'm the best. But my clients deserve the best. I can't give them back their health. Or their lives. But I can make the rich bastards pay." He waved his hand, dismissing the wall. "But none of that matters to you."

It mattered. It told me a lot about Stan Dugan. And something about CeeCee Burke.

"I want to know about CeeCee." About this I could be honest. Maybe the sincerity reached him.

"Why?" Now his glance was not so much suspicious as considering.

"You make the bad guys pay for hurting people. Do you want to make somebody pay for CeeCee?"

"Don't play games with me, lady."

Once again I was aware of his size and strength. One swipe of that huge arm could disable me. I wondered if my awareness was triggered by a sudden rush of anger toward me.

"My husband died at Ahiahi." I held his gaze until his eyes dropped.

He rubbed one cheek. "So how the hell will it catch CeeCee's killer—and your husband's, if you're right—to tell you about her?"

"If someone now at Ahiahi was responsible for her death, then it has to be because of who she was, what she was like, what she did and thought and felt. Not for the ransom, Mr. Dugan."

He looked across the room at another montage of photographs. I could just make them out, a motley collection of snapshots. Yes, these were pictures from his happy days. Before CeeCee Burke died.

"I want to know CeeCee, Mr. Dugan. And no one should

know her better than you. If you loved her, you will help me."

He didn't change expression. His face was still harsh and forbidding. But he pointed to a worn leather chair. "Sit down, Mrs. Collins."

I slipped into the seat. I realized then that my hands were sweaty and my knees were weak.

He walked over and picked up the montage of photos. Slowly, like sun breaking through clouds, his face softened. He stood that way for a long time. "CeeCee." His voice was a caress. "Jesus, she was one of a kind. She was beautiful and sophisticated. Not in my world. I spend time with people who've had a raw deal. Nobody's slick. Nobody's rich. Nobody's famous. CeeCee grew up in a world where everybody was somebody special, famous or rich or both. She wore perfumes that smelled like heaven and cost more than I spent on meals for a week. To CeeCee, fine food and expensive clothes and luxurious surroundings were simply to be expected, nothing to remark. I learned a lot from her. Purses that are considered works of art, carved out of fine wood. And china and crystal that exist just because they're beautiful. Steuben glass. French tapestry. All kinds of beauty. And CeeCee"—he cleared his throat—"she was like a piece of fine china, elegant and beautiful. But she wasn't just a pretty face. You know how tough good china is? That was CeeCee. Beautiful—and tough."

"How did you meet?" I knew there had to be a story here.

"Oh, it was pretty simple. She came into my world. I was preparing a case. She came to my office." For the first time since I'd arrived, his big, craggy face was alive with laughter and I realized how attractive he could be. "CeeCee looked around, looked it all over—the pictures, me, Bob. Then, straight-faced, she said, 'You give 'em hell, don't you?' I said, 'Damn right.' She said, 'Way to go.' "

I laughed. "So you liked her right off the bat?"

"I sure did. And I liked her even better after I took her depo. She was a passenger in a sports car that slammed into the side of one of those pickups with an exterior gas tank. Fried the pickup driver. The mother of two kids on her way to pick them up at school. You don't want to see those autopsy shots."

No, I didn't. But that comment was well calculated to evoke an emotional response. I must always remember in dealing with this man who he was and what he did.

"Hell of it was"—now Dugan's voice was harsh—"the driver of the sports car, Mr. Lance Whitney Cole the Third, ran a red light. He swore to the cops it was green. Another witness thought it was red. When CeeCee came to my office, I expected her to lie, to protect him. They'd been dating for about six months. So it blew me away when she told the truth. She was sorry she had to do it. But she did. He ran the red light. She saw it." He gave me a cool, level look. "You don't look impressed, Mrs. Collins. In most trials, liars are thicker than cottonmouths in a muddy creek in August. And here's this rich girl telling the goddamn truth. She was tough. She was the difference in the decision. I called her the day after the jury came in, said I wanted to buy her a drink. That was a Friday afternoon. We took a plane to Cancún that night. It was the greatest weekend of my life."

They say opposites attract. But that's rarely been true in my experience. If I now had a picture of CeeCee Burke, it was perhaps a reflection of this confident, assertive lawyer. He said CeeCee was tough. He was tough. He was also intelligent, aggressive, controlling, and impetuous. What did that tell me about CeeCee?

"When did you get engaged?"

He looked away and I knew he wasn't seeing his office or me. "That weekend."

So, yes, I called it right when I decided he was impetuous. And so was CeeCee.

"Do you know of any reason why anyone in the family would want her dead?" It was a bald, tough question.

His face hardened. "If I knew"—his voice was low and thick—"I'd have done something long before now."

I stood, picked up my purse. "Thank you, Mr. Dugan, for your time."

He said nothing until I was almost to the door.

"Mrs. Collins, are you going to Ahiahi?"

I looked back. His face was grim, all traces of warmth gone.

"Yes."

"If what you suspect is true"—he spoke slowly, emphatically—"you will be in great danger."

"I know." I turned away. But as I closed his office door and hurried through the anteroom, I wondered if he was warning me . . .

Or threatening me.

four

I reached the outskirts of Pottsboro. I doubted the main street—a straggle of small stores, a barbecue restaurant and several gas stations—had changed much in decades. And certainly not in the short span of years since the kidnapping.

I'd not found a phone listing for Johnnie Rodriguez. But I'd traced down an AP reporter in Dallas who had covered the kidnapping and learned that Rodriguez lived with his mother, Maria. I got her phone number and address. I debated calling. But I didn't want to frighten Johnnie. No, I wasn't going to take any chances. I was going to talk to him, whatever effort it took. And somehow, through threats or bribery or persuasion, I was going to find out what he told Richard.

I got directions at a gas station. Ten minutes later the rental car jolted to a stop at the end of a rutted, red dirt road in front of a small frame house.

There was no yard. Blackjack oaks crowded close to a

dusty path. I slammed the car door and the sound seemed overloud in the country quiet. Crows cawed. Far above, a Mississippi kite, its huge wings spread wide, rode a thermal draft.

Just for an instant I paused. Six years ago Richard heard the slam of a car door, felt a cool lake breeze, faced this empty path. It was as if he stood beside me, just for an instant. "Richard . . ."

Then a crow flapped past and the sense of Richard's presence was gone and I was left with a haunting feeling of unease. Richard walked this path and it led him to Kauai and his death.

I felt the faint warmth of the March sun and knew I did not want to die. Not now. Not yet. It's hard to be frightened. It's hard to find courage. "Richard . . ." I took a deep, ragged breath. I moved forward. Forced myself forward.

The house had a slovenly, unkempt air—paint peeling from the walls, untrimmed hydrangeas bulking up against the windows. A bicycle missing a front wheel lay on the sloping porch, along with a rusted bucket and an old car battery.

The sagging front steps creaked beneath my weight. Had this little frame house been so bedraggled, so forlorn when Richard came?

A thin, gray-striped cat bolted from behind a pile of firewood on the porch to block my way, hissing, ears flattened, tail puffed.

I heard a faint scrabbling sound and frightened meows.

"It's all right, little mother," I said softly.

I stepped around the cat.

The door opened. Grudgingly, slowly, with a mournful creak, as if it were an unaccustomed act.

There was no screen.

I looked into eyes as dark as my own, at a face wrinkled by time, dark hair streaked with silver.

We were probably close in age. But I'd been lucky,

blessed with good health and excellent medical care. And she had not. Her skin had the waxen look of illness, pernicious and irreversible. Her arms had so little flesh, the bones protruded. Her blue cotton house dress hung in swaths.

She was staring at me, her eyes puzzled. "I thought you were the district nurse."

"No. I'm Henrietta Collins. I know the Ericcson family." That was not true. "I'm here to see Johnnie Rodriguez." I tried hard to keep my voice even, undemanding, but I had traveled a long distance and all the way I kept thinking that if Richard had not come here, he might still be alive. And beneath my anger, fear pulsed. Yes, I was following in Richard's footsteps.

A claw-like hand moved to her throat. She opened her mouth, but no words came.

"Johnnie Rodriguez." I would not be stopped. My voice was harsh now. I couldn't help it. "I must talk to him."

Her head began to sway back and forth. "Oh, no. You can't, ma'am. You never can. Johnnie's dead. Dead and gone."

We stood at the end of a rickety pier.

Gulls squalled. The sun glinted on the huge expanse of lake. A gusty south wind tatted lacy white swirls across the blue surface. A speed boat thrummed past. Water slapped against the pilings. The air smelled like fish and dust.

The shoreline boasted vacation homes ranging from trailers perched on concrete blocks to elegant multilevel retreats. I noticed the surroundings automatically, my mind cataloging, the beads slipping through my fingers even while I was struggling with shock. Johnnie Rodriguez dead! I'd come all this way. I'd counted so much on talking to him.

Maria Rodriguez pointed down at the roiled water. "That's where I found Johnnie." Her face reminded me of a

Dorothea Lange photograph, misery and despair and mute acceptance etched in every crease and line.

"I'm sorry." The words drifted between us like wisps from a cottonwood. Sorrow freighted the air. Her grief and mine. "What happened?"

Her skeletal arms folded tight across her body. "Johnnie drank too much." She said it matter-of-factly. "The deputy said he must have fallen. He was too drunk to swim. So he drowned."

A matter-of-fact tone, but a tear edged down her sallow, wrinkled cheek.

The wind rustled her skirt, stirred my hair.

I looked back at the small wooden house where Johnnie Rodriguez had lived his whole life, then glanced at the end of the pier. How drunk would you have to be? "I'm sorry," I said again. "When did Johnnie drown?"

"Six years ago."

It wasn't the wind skipping across the water that made me feel chilled. I jammed my hands into the pockets of my coat. My fingers clenched into fists. "And the date?"

"April sixth."

Less than a week after Richard fell—was pushed—to his death.

If I'd had any misgivings about the truth of the poster, I could put them away.

She faced me. "Why did Miz Ericcson send you to talk to Johnnie?" She lifted a bony hand to shade her eyes from the sunlight.

I had the space of a breath to decide how to answer. It didn't even take that long. She'd made the jump, according me legitimacy because I said I knew the Ericcson family. That gave me a lot of room to maneuver.

Was I willing to play the lie? Of course.

But I phrased my answer carefully. "Johnnie was working for Belle Ericcson when her daughter was kidnapped. I'm trying to put together the recollections of everyone who was at the house that weekend."

She smoothed back a strand of lank hair. "Seems a funny thing to do. To want to remember the bad. Johnnie sure didn't like to talk about it. It upset him too much. And Miz Ericcson, they say she still grieves something awful. That's what I've heard. She's never come back, you know. She sold the lake house and the boat to a rich oilman from Amarillo. They say she went off to Hawaii and built a house up on a cliff and she's never come back to Dallas. Not once." She turned her gaunt face toward me. "I thought Miz Ericcson knew Johnnie was gone. You've come a long way for nothing. There's nobody here who was at the lake house that weekend except me."

"You were there?" I managed to ask in a casual, even tone.

"Yes'm." Her voice was tired but obedient. This was a nice woman, a sick woman, but she wanted to be helpful. "I got the call that Thursday to open the house, mop and dust and put on fresh linens and stock the kitchen. That was when I was still working, before I got sick. I had a big list, getting everything ready for Miss CeeCee's birthday party. The party was going to be Saturday night even though it wasn't really her birthday until Sunday."

Sunday that year was April 1. So April 1 was CeeCee's birthday. And the day that Richard would die one year later. No April Fool for the Ericcson family or for me. Not ever again.

I willed a pleasant expression on my face as I looked into dark, patient, sad eyes. "I understand CeeCee drove up from Dallas on Friday afternoon." I'd done my homework, pulled up every scrap of coverage about the kidnapping.

Those thin arms slid to her side. The blue-veined fingers of one hand plucked at the ruffled pocket of her dress. "They say she must have come then." Her voice was low and indistinct.

"You didn't see her?" I moved a little nearer.

"No'm. I finished up about five and I wanted to get home and fix Johnnie's supper. Johnnie lived with me. All my other kids got families. But Johnnie never married. Maybe . . ." She sighed.

"You went home," I said gently.

She looked up at a dazzling white house on the bluff. "I walked home. It's not even a mile if you go through the woods. Johnnie had the pickup. He'd been running errands all day, brought in fresh firewood and plenty of beer for the boat and he'd gone over to Pottsboro for barbecue. So, I left about five. And I locked up real good. I told them that." She looked up again at the house on the bluff.

I spoke as if the facts were so familiar and they were. I knew them by heart now. "CeeCee stopped in town for gas. It was just getting dark." The clerk remembered it clearly when she was interviewed by a television reporter. CeeCee paid for the gas and bought a bag of M&Ms.

"Josie Goetz was working at the station that night. She said Miss CeeCee seemed tired. She wasn't as cheerful and friendly as usual."

A crow cawed, sharp and strident.

Maria shivered. "Mighty cold out here on the water. I've got some fresh coffee made . . ."

We walked slowly—it was an effort for her—back to the house. She brought me a white pottery mug filled with coffee as hot and black as molten tar. She settled into a rocker, then made a hopeless gesture at the dust-streaked floor. "I can't clean no more. I used to keep everything neat as a pin."

Dingy crocheted doilies covered the arms of the easy chair and couch. Handmade wooden soldiers crowded the mantel, the windowsills, a pine bookcase, spots of color in the dim and dusty room.

She followed my gaze. "Johnnie made them. Pretty, aren't they?"

It was easy to see the same hand carved them all. Each blocky ten-inch-tall soldier stood on a two-inch base. The soldiers flaunted cockaded hats and brass-studded coats in vivid scarlet, cerulean, or tangerine.

Faintly, she began to hum "The March of the Toy Soldier," her voice sweet and soft, and I knew where Johnnie had gotten his dream.

"Johnnie loved toy soldiers. From the time he was a little boy." She picked up a Revolutionary War soldier with a musket. "He never learned to read real well, but all he needed was to see a picture. He spent all his free time carving. This was the last one he made. It was for Christmas." She held it out to me.

I put down my coffee mug, took the carving. Gilded letters on the base read: TO MAMA. I handed the soldier back to her.

Her smile was full of love. She put the carving down gently. "Johnnie was a good boy." The chair squeaked as she rocked. "And I know he never hurt Miss CeeCee." She fastened mournful, puzzled eyes on me. "Maybe it was meant, you coming here to ask about Johnnie. I been thinking. If ever I was to tell anyone, now's the time."

The moment stretched between us. I wanted to grab those thin shoulders, grip them tight, shake out the truth.

"Please tell me." I spoke as a supplicant.

Our eyes met and held and we each knew the other had a troubled heart.

She sighed and it was as light as the flutter of wings. "I growed up telling the truth. My pa said an honest heart was a gift to God. And I've grieved ever since because I lied about the night Miss CeeCee was taken. Johnnie was so scared the next week when the call come that the deputy wanted to see him and ask where he was when Miss CeeCee disappeared.

Johnnie said I had to tell them he was home that Friday night, like he always was. He promised me he didn't know what had happened to Miss CeeCee, but he was scared he'd be in big trouble if it come out what they'd done. They'd thought it was all in fun, but it was a trick. But they could never prove it, couldn't prove anything. He swore to me he didn't know anything that would help the police find her. And that was all he'd say—ever. But I know he didn't do nothing bad. Not Johnnie. So I said I was here Friday night and Johnnie and me had supper and he was working on a soldier and didn't go nowhere. And Johnnie had been working on a soldier, the parts were all out on his table. The deputy believed me because he and Johnnie went to school together and he knew Johnnie'd never hurt nobody. And Johnnie, he got out and searched till he was so tired he was ready to drop and he kept saying Miss CeeCee had to be somewhere."

Johnnie joined in the search. Yet, obviously he knew something of what happened on Friday evening. But if he searched, he must not have known where CeeCee Burke was. Or he searched to show he knew nothing.

I smoothed the doily on my chair arm. "So Johnnie said 'they'd thought it was all in fun'? They?"

"Yes'm, he did." Her tone was sharp.

Was this really what Johnnie had said? Or was this his mother's version to lessen Johnnie's involvement? Or had Johnnie lied to his mother?

They? Johnnie and who? "Did he say who he was talking about?"

"No'm. He never said." There was the faintest inflection on the last word.

"But you know?" I kept my voice undemanding, casual.

"Johnnie was working over there that day. It had to be that Mackey, that man who works for Miz Ericcson." The bones in her face sharpened, and for an instant she had the predatory look of a bird of prey.

That was a familiar name to me. Lester Mackey was Belle's jack-of-all-trades. Mackey had served her and her several husbands as a houseman, chauffeur and general dogsbody since Belle's early days in Japan.

"That Mackey! I never did like him." Maria Rodriguez's mouth folded in a stubborn, angry line.

"Why not?" I asked mildly.

Her eyes slid away from mine. "Whenever they come up from Dallas, he always had Johnnie hang around with him. And there was no call for it." Her bony face was both angry and anguished.

"If he hired Johnnie to work around the place—"

"He'd keep Johnnie late. And what for?" she demanded. "Can't work after dark. But he'd invite Johnnie to his quarters, show him art books." She stared down at the floor. "I didn't like it."

"But on the Friday that CeeCee disappeared, Johnnie was in and out of the Ericcson place working for Mackey. Is that right? And Johnnie didn't come home for supper?"

"No'm. He come in about seven and said he was sorry but he'd had to work late. He was kind of excited." She finally looked up, her eyes dark with pain. "But I thought it was just because that Mackey was down here. Johnnie always liked to hang around with him. Johnnie was in a real good humor, kept grinning to himself. 'Course this was before we knew Miss CeeCee'd been taken."

CeeCee Ericcson had stopped for gas in Pottsboro at a quarter to six.

No one ever admitted seeing her after that.

Lester Mackey later told police he'd found CeeCee's Mercedes a few minutes before seven o'clock on Friday night in the drive in front of the lake house. Mackey said the driver's door was open and the keys were in the ignition. CeeCee's purse lay in the passenger seat.

Mackey moved the car around to the garage. The house

was locked. He opened the front door, went inside, turned on the lights. He put the keys in a wooden tray on a side table. He said nobody was in the house. As far as he knew. He didn't go upstairs, but he said no lights were on.

It was dark by then.

Mackey later told police he'd had a few drinks so he went around to his quarters and fixed himself some dinner and watched TV and didn't think again about the car. He said he figured CeeCee had gone off to dinner with someone else in the family and they'd be coming in later.

It was a large family with members who came and went, of course, as they pleased. No one had any particular schedule that weekend, no set time to appear at the lake.

The alarm wasn't raised until Saturday afternoon.

Maria reached out for her coffee mug, stared down into the dark brew. "I was there when Miz Ericcson got the letter. On Saturday. It come in a mail truck."

Express Mail. The police traced it to a Gainesville Express Mail receptacle. It was processed shortly after 8 P.M. Friday. The return address was a downtown business, an insurance company. No one there had ever had any contact with CeeCee or any of the other family members.

On Saturday afternoon, Belle was carrying a pile of brightly wrapped birthday presents into the living room of the lake house when the mail truck arrived.

"I took the envelope from the postman." Maria hunched over her coffee mug. "One of the boys—I think it was Mr. Joss—said something about his mama never getting away from work. Miz Ericcson laughed and said she did too get away from work, and whatever it was, Elise could see to it. That was her secretary. So I carried the envelope over to Miss Elise. She said, 'I'll take care of it, Belle. This is your weekend to enjoy.' She opened it and pulled out a sheet of paper. Then her smile kind of slipped sideways and she made a gasping noise and said, 'Oh, my God. Oh, my God.' "

Maria put down the mug, the coffee untasted. "It got real quiet in the room. Real quiet. We all knew it was something awful. Miss Elise tried to talk, she opened her mouth and finally, her hand shaking, she took the sheet over to Miz Ericcson."

"Who was there?"

"Miz Ericcson's husband, Mr. Scanlon. He'd just come in the front door. He was carrying a big white cake box. Miss Gretchen was sitting on a bench by one of the windows, reading a book. Miss Megan was out on the terrace in a hammock. Mr. Wheeler and Mr. Anders were playing checkers. Mr. Joss was picking out a tune on the piano. He can play real well, but he was just doing one note at a time." Her eyes squeezed in remembrance, and now her voice was cold. "That Mackey, he was bringing in suitcases."

"And Stan Dugan?"

"Miss CeeCee's young man?" Maria shook her head. "No, ma'am. He wasn't there."

I made a note of that. It surprised me a little.

Maria Rodriguez shivered. "When it got quiet, everybody looked at Miz Ericcson. She'd been so happy. And she still had that armload of presents. She looked at the paper and her face got old right in front of our eyes, old and pinched. She looked at each one in turn and her voice was as cold as a blue norther. She said, 'This isn't funny. This isn't funny at all.' Then she looked around, like it would all be all right. 'Where is CeeCee? Where *is* she?' "

But CeeCee was nowhere to be found.

The note was quite simple:

IF YOU WANT CEECEE BACK ALIVE,
DO PRECISELY AS INSTRUCTED.
CALL THE POLICE AND SHE DIES.
FOLLOW INSTRUCTIONS.

So Belle refused to call the police. Or to reveal the instructions on a folded sheet of paper.

That came later.

"Miz Ericcson made each one of us promise not to say a word to anyone. But she asked me to go get Johnnie to help Mackey and the kids search around the place. They'd pieced it together by then that Miss CeeCee had come to the lake the night before, on Friday. Mackey told them about finding her car. I run home to get Johnnie. When I told him what had happened, he shook his head back and forth real puzzled. 'Mama,' he said, 'I don't understand. Listen, you wait here a minute. I got to see about something.' He jumped in the pickup and went off. He come back in about ten minutes and his face was like the ashes in the fireplace. 'Mama, I got to go over to the Ericcson place.' I asked him what was wrong, but he said he couldn't tell me nothing now.

"He didn't come home till late that night and then all he'd say was that they hadn't found no trace of Miss CeeCee and they all was wanting Miz Ericcson to call the police but she wouldn't and she was going to do what the letter said to do and she wouldn't tell anybody what it said. And she got on the phone and called some man to come and help her. And that made Mr. Scanlon mad."

Yes, Belle had called Richard and he'd gone to National to catch the next flight to Dallas.

"Did you ask Johnnie where he drove in the pickup after you came home to get him? Before he went to the Ericcson place?"

"No'm." She made no explanation, no defense. But the limp and sagging skin of her face was a study in fear.

Denial takes many forms. One is a refusal to ask questions that need to be asked.

I worried at her pallor. But I couldn't let her rest. Not yet. "When the deputy called, was that when Johnnie asked you to say he'd been home on Friday night between six and seven?"

She nodded wearily. "But the truth is he didn't come in until right after seven o'clock. I fed him then. But he did work most of the evening on the soldier."

Funny how you can pick up a little nuance. "Most of the evening?"

"Johnnie liked to walk out after dark. Sometimes late at night. He liked to find a place and stand real quiet and watch the raccoons. Sometimes a cougar'd pass by."

I waited.

She picked up the last toy soldier her son had made, gently touched the little wooden musket. "Johnnie thought he'd been part of a joke. Her brothers were big to play jokes. And 'specially since Miss CeeCee's birthday was April Fool's Day. Oh, they always had big jokes going on. Johnnie might have wanted to know more about it and maybe he went somewhere late that night to see what was happening. And he would've just stood quiet and watched. But I *know* he didn't see nothing terrible. He would've gone to the police if he had. Then Saturday when I come home and told him about that letter, he went back and Miss CeeCee wasn't there. And he didn't know what to do."

Somewhere nearby.

"Why didn't he tell the police?"

"He was scared." She pressed her hand against her lips to keep them from trembling.

"What do you think happened, Mrs. Rodriguez?"

She turned dark, haunted eyes toward me. "Just ten minutes. That's all he was gone Saturday afternoon. I think he went to where he thought Miss CeeCee was—but she wasn't there. And Johnnie was scared to death. Kidnapping!" She leaned forward, her face angry and vengeful. "That Lester Mackey, I never liked him. Talked so soft you'd think it was a rattlesnake slithering by. Not like a man. You talk to him."

The road was twisty but well-graded and the underbrush was thinned on either side. I pulled into a turnaround drive in front of the white two-story vacation home that had once belonged to Belle Ericcson.

The drive was empty except for my rental car. The blinds were closed. Nobody home. That wasn't surprising on a cool March weekday afternoon. It was nice for my purposes, though I couldn't expect to learn much after all this time.

I pictured a Mercedes curving up the drive, pulling to a stop, the door opening—

Although the house crowned a bluff, it was well screened from the road by a tall, thick hedge. It was extremely secluded here. The stucco home had clean, spare Mediterranean lines, a red tile roof and windows, windows, windows.

I followed a flagstone path along the east side of the house to the terrace that overlooked a private bay. Canvas covers shrouded the deck furniture. The patio umbrellas were tucked shut. A steep path led down the bluff to a boathouse and pier.

The terrace was in shadow, the late afternoon sun blocked by cedars to the west.

I walked across the flagstones, occasional leaves crackling underfoot. The floor-to-ceiling windows were masked by interior blinds, now closed.

I found a space at the end of one set of blinds and peered into the huge living room. The dusky, untenanted room gave no hint of the life and death drama it had seen.

I continued around the house and saw, on the west side, garages and separate quarters.

Anyone wishing to wait unseen could easily park on the west side of the house. Cedars screened a large parking area from the front drive.

Seven years ago CeeCee had arrived, opened the car door—and the kidnappers appeared.

There was no evidence of a struggle, no blood, her purse in the passenger seat apparently untouched.

Were the kidnappers armed?

Either armed—or armed with a story plausible enough to persuade her to come with them.

That was possible, of course, could account for the lack of struggle. A report of an emergency, an illness. *"Your mother's been hurt in a car wreck. She's in the hospital in Denison . . ."*

CeeCee had not—at that point—resisted.

The Mercedes—door open, keys in the ignition—was the closest link to her, made this driveway the last certain place she'd been.

The sun slanted through the blackjack, touched an early-blooming redbud. It was lovely and peaceful—and unutterably sinister.

Deputy Dexter Pierson drew in a lungful of smoke, coughed, and rasped, his voice hoarse and rough, "It stank. The whole damn thing stank. Worse than fish guts in August."

He glared at me pugnaciously from behind a paper-laden desk, his pockmarked face dangerously red. His office was small, four fake knotty pine walls and an old wooden desk. The grainy computer screen looked out of place.

"What do you mean?" I edged my chair a little closer to the open window and the small stream of fresh air.

His quick green eyes flickered from me to the window. "Yeah, smells like shit in here, don't it? I keep trying to quit." He stubbed the cigarette in an overflowing ashtray and the acrid smell of burning joined the fuggy odor of smoke. "Yeah. My wife says nobody smokes anymore but butts." He gave a whoop of laughter that ended in a cough. "Used to be the big clue, didn't it? A cigarette butt. Or maybe a button. Or a strand of hair. What was it in the Lindbergh kidnapping? A piece of a ladder? Well, nobody left anything around for us when they grabbed CeeCee Burke—if anybody grabbed her."

I looked at him in surprise. "Her car was found with the door open, her purse on the passenger seat, a ransom note came the next day. What else could it be?"

He clasped his hands behind his head, tilted back in his swivel chair, and stared moodily at a lopsided bulletin board decorated with a half-dozen yellowed Far Side cartoons. "We got crime around here. Sure. Guy gets drunk, beats his wife. Kids break into a store, steal cash and cigarettes and beer. We keep a close eye on some dudes, the ones who watch and see when the city people are gone, then break in and loot the houses. We smashed a pretty big burglary ring a couple of years ago. Every few years, we get a run of rapes. That don't happen too often. Country people have dogs and guns. But big-time kidnapping for ransom? No, ma'am."

He jolted forward in the chair, grabbed at his cigarette pack. "That whole deal was as fishy as a bass derby. I kept trying to tell the feds it didn't compute—but would they listen to a hayseed deputy? So"—he lifted his round shoulders in a sardonic shrug—"so screw 'em."

"I'll listen."

His red cheeks puffed in a pugnacious frown. "Okay. I got a theory. 'Course, I'll be up front with you. There's a big damn hole in it—because somebody picked up the ransom money and if my idea's right, that shouldn't've happened. But here's my take. She did it herself."

I suppose my face reflected utter surprise.

"I'll tell you, lady, suicide takes a funny tack now and then. A lot of times people'll go to a hell of an effort to make it look like an accident. I think that's what happened here. Because I been a deputy for twenty-two years and my brother's a homicide cop in Dallas, so I'm not the new boy in town when it comes to murder. Even if we're not talking murder and kidnapping. But I've never known anybody to be snatched—then murdered with a painkiller. Never."

"Painkiller?" I was learning one new fact after another. "But I understood her body was found in the lake, two days after she disappeared."

"Yeah. She drowned. But she'd had enough narcotic to drop an elephant."

"That wasn't publicly revealed."

"Nope. The sheriff sat on that. Thought it might be useful."

"Maybe the kidnappers fed her something with a narcotic. To keep her quiet."

"Lady, this wasn't just a tablet or two. She'd had a bottle's worth. No way it wouldn't kill her. And that's a weird way to kill somebody. Most kidnappers shoot somebody, crack 'em over the head, hell, bury 'em alive. No, the minute we got the autopsy report, I told 'em it was suicide. She dropped the Express Mail envelope in a slot on her way here. When she got up here Friday night, she set it up to look like she'd been kidnapped, then took a rowboat out on the lake, drank a bottle of wine laced with the stuff, waited till it spaced her out, then rolled overboard."

"Was a rowboat missing from the Ericcson dock?"

"As a matter of fact"—his voice oozed confidence—"there was a boat missing. It was found drifting near a public ramp."

"But the ransom money *was* picked up."

"Picked up? Maybe. Maybe not. Look at it this way, lady. The money was *gone* by the time cops checked it out." His tone was sardonic. "Listen, how do we know any of the crap the family told us was true? Did they call us in when they got the 'kidnapper's' note? Hell, no. We didn't even know there'd been this 'kidnapping' until a fisherman pulled her body up on Monday. She had on a silver bracelet with her name and it rang a bell with one of our troopers. He'd given her a ticket once. We ID'd her quick. We went out to the house and got this cock-and-bull story. I never did believe it."

"But the money." I wondered about Pierson's blood pressure. His entire face glistened like burnished copper.

"Yeah." His tone was grudging. "The goddamned money. Two hundred thousand in fifties and hundreds. In a shoe box. Miz Ericcson followed the directions. She got this dude out of the east to take the shoe box to the old cemetery in Gainesville. I mean, can you believe that? A cemetery! If they'd called us, we could have sewn it up tighter than a bulldogged calf. But no, they don't call anybody, they get the cash from a bank in Dallas and give it to this dude to deliver to the cemetery at midnight that Sunday."

I'd not known the details. As I said, Richard and I never discussed it. The news coverage didn't include information about the ransom drop.

When the story broke, Richard was identified simply as a friend of the family who had delivered the ransom.

"Midnight!" Pierson snorted. "Why didn't she throw in clanking chains and a buzz saw!"

"But the money was taken."

"Sure. Hell, yes. The dude tucked it behind the Beckleman mausoleum and the cops got there on Monday afternoon. More than twenty-four hours! Sure, it was gone. Anybody could have gotten it. Kids out there necking and they see this dude hide a shoe box at midnight. Or next day somebody drops out there to decorate a grave. Somebody in the family, for that matter. Those damn people. Nobody'd look at you straight."

"They didn't need the money," I said dryly. There are people to whom two hundred thousand is pin money. Belle's family members fit that description.

He shrugged. "Maybe not. But who the hell should be surprised when we check it out after the body's found and the shoe box is gone! Plenty of candidates. Maybe the dude who delivered the shoe box came back. Maybe he never left it."

"No." My answer was swift and harsh.

He looked at me sharply. His green eyes brightened. "Oh, hey. Collins. You're Mrs. Collins. That was the dude's name."

"Yes." My throat felt tight. Yes, that was the dude's name.

"So what's your game, Mrs. Collins?"

I gave him stare for stare. "My husband Richard came here six years ago to talk to Johnnie Rodriguez. Then Richard went to Hawaii to see Belle Ericcson. He fell to his death from the terrace of her home. On April first." I stopped, bent my head. It still hurt so damn much and the pain throbbed anew, as if Richard had just died. I took a deep breath. "This week I received an anonymous message saying he was pushed."

Pierson kneaded his hand against his red cheek. "And Johnnie drowned that year." His tone was speculative. "So, what are you going to do?"

"Go to Hawaii." Yes, I was going to go to Kauai and claw my way into Belle Ericcson's home, do whatever I had to do, fight whomever I had to fight.

Pierson shook loose another cigarette, lit it, but his eyes never left my face, calculating, bright, hard eyes. "You know something, lady? If I was you, I'd be damn careful."

five

The jeep squealed to a stop. I stared at the bar swung across the road and the stark sign:

NO TRESPASSING

I'd known the way would be barred. This was simply the first challenge.

I jumped down. The dark red dirt glistened greasily. The cane growing on either side of the narrow lane rustled in the light breeze. The cane was so tall, I stood in dusky shadow. Despite the languorous warmth of the air, I shivered.

I pushed the bar wide, jumped back into the jeep. When I drove past the barrier, I didn't stop to close it. Not because I was impatient. I kept going, driving faster and faster, red dust boiling from beneath the wheels, because if I drove slowly, I might turn back. I might not have the courage to persevere.

Fear rode with me.

Not only the bone weakening fear of danger. I knew danger awaited me at journey's end. Yes, I was afraid. But not simply of danger. I was tormented by a more complex fear, webbed like the silky strands spun by an industrious spider, a tendril of terror, a strand of anxiety, a wisp of apprehension, a thread of fright, all combining in a tremulous mélange of dread.

Oh, dear God, what was I going to learn at journey's end?

In the innermost recesses of my heart, I knew that I feared not so much learning the truth of Richard's death as the truth of his life.

What, finally, had Belle Ericcson meant to my husband? And could I bear to know that truth?

But I had to go on. A quick memory glittered in my mind, bright as a diamond: the softness of Richard's eyes on our fifth wedding anniversary; his eager smile as I unwrapped his present, a slim book of Millay's sonnets. I remembered, too, with a heart-wrenching clarity, the exquisite passion in our union that starry night.

Now the field of cane was behind me and the rusty red road began to climb, curving and twining, clinging to the edge of the rising escarpment.

Up and up and up. The cliff fell sharply away from the rutted roadway. Jutting up from the sides of the valley were trees and ferns so intensely green they glittered like sunlit prisms of jade, vivid enough to make the eyes wince and seek relief in the arch of softly blue sky.

I eased the pressure on the accelerator as I came around a curve. The road widened just enough for an outlook. Abruptly I braked, pulled to my right and stopped. I turned off the motor. My chest ached as if I'd run up that rising road.

No sound broke the quiet. I looked out over the valley to another ridge and beyond it to another and another. This was a Hawaii far removed from the bustle of Honolulu, wild and open, no sign of people or habitations, only rocky cliffs and emerald valleys.

Kauai is called the Garden Isle with good reason. It is pastoral still with an innocence and simplicity that I had to delve back to a child's memory of rural France for comparison: narrow blacktopped roads and cars traveling sedately; towns, not cities; sweeps of rolling land unspoiled by high-rises. Kauai has yet to be consumed by the tourism that has devoured Oahu. Travelers come here in search of breathtaking loveliness and peace.

But I had not come to Kauai as a tourist seeking its beauty: dazzling gold trees with blooms more yellow than butter, chinaberry trees with clusters of pale pink or soft-azure flowers, magnificent banyans with hundreds of aerial roots; or the endlessly fascinating and awesome sea, crashing with inhuman force against outcroppings of jagged midnight-black lava, eddying in tidal pools behind barrier reefs, running in swift and dangerous currents, sometimes gentle, sometimes deadly.

I came seeking vengeance, understanding, release.

As I stared over the tropical growth, overwhelming in its fecundity, my hands gripped the steering wheel so tightly my fingers ached.

Could I go through with my plan? Did I have the courage to plunge ahead to an uncertain and surely dangerous future?

It was an odd and singular moment. I'd spent a lifetime as a reporter, seeing much I would have preferred not to see, but always attempting to look with clear and non-judgmental eyes, speaking and writing as honorably as I knew how.

Now I'd left honor behind. I was prepared to lie, dissemble, employ every wile at my command. What would Richard have thought of me if he could see me now? My Richard, who was always straightforward and honorable.

Was it because of honor that he had never discussed Belle Ericcson with me?

Richard and I spent decades together. We knew passion and pain, joy and despair. I closed my eyes and for a moment he was in my mind as clearly as the last time I saw him, his face seamed with lines earned by a lifetime of effort and caring and loss.

That last view was such a familiar one, one of us departing or arriving. We'd done so much of that in our lives. I'd turned at the last moment before boarding the plane, looked back to see his steady, loving, generous gaze, his chiseled features, his ruddy skin with its age-won creases, his lopsided smile, ironic yet warm. His brown corduroy sports coat hung open. His shirt was a red-and-white houndstooth check. His chino slacks were crisp. We'd stopped on our leisurely walk through the airport at the shoeshine stand and his tasseled loafers glistened a cherry tan. His hand lifted in farewell, that broad, capable, strong hand.

I'd had no reason to suspect it would be our final farewell. Such an ordinary moment, but even then it was extraordinary because it was Richard and because he, standing there, meant so much to me, the center and heart and joy of my life.

Now Richard's face was always and ever in my memory, a talisman against despair and cynicism and hopelessness.

Faces tell everything you need to know. Do you see laughter or sourness, compassion or disdain, vigor or lassitude? And if the face lacks expression? That speaks, too.

Just for an instant, I felt Richard was so near, his broad, open face serious and intent, his quick eyes watchful, his generous mouth opening to speak.

To warn me? To admonish me? To salute me?

I opened my eyes and the illusion fled and with it all sense of comfort. Would Richard understand the course I'd set?

But I had to find out the truth. Dig it out, gouge it out, scratch it out, if need be. I couldn't leave unanswered any question about Richard's death. Even though I knew my arrival on Kauai served some purpose—dark or benign?—other than discovering what happened when Richard plummeted to his death.

Who wanted me here? And why?

Behind this pastoral scene there was a pattern I could not see. Perhaps I should turn back. I felt such a sweep of foreboding that I was shaken. I looked up. Once I reached the mountaintop, I would set forces into motion that I could not control. But control is always illusory. I knew that, could cling to that, but I couldn't ignore the fact that my actions would have consequences.

Take what you want, the old adage encourages, but pay for it. That philosophy requires arrogance. I'm not certain we ever know ourselves, but I think I can fairly insist I am not arrogant. No, I won't confess to arrogance. But I will admit to a passion for truth. And a bone-deep stubbornness. And a wild, unreasoning hatred for injustice.

Was Richard murdered? I had to know. I was impelled to follow this dark red, empty road because on that mountaintop I would find answers. I was determined, no matter the cost, to have those answers.

My hand shook as I twisted the key. Yes, dammit, I was scared, scared of what I might find, what I might learn, what might happen to me. The engine snarled to life. I jerked the wheel and gunned the jeep up that steep gradient. I leashed the speed as the curves sharpened. There were no guardrails. Not that a flimsy metal barrier could stop a plunge over the side and a sheer drop of more than a hundred feet.

Wind whipped my face, stirred my hair. Surely I was almost to the top of the ridge. I came around a curve fast.

It was almost the last curve I ever took.

A huge car loomed up in front of me.

I jammed my foot hard against the brake pedal, stomped the brake pedal. The jeep slewed a little sideways and bucked to a halt. A dark green Land Rover screeched to a stop only inches away. Red dust billowed around the cars. A pale face stared at me, the lips parted in a shout.

If we'd collided, the force would have propelled both cars over the edge. It had been a near thing.

The door to the Land Rover opened, then slammed shut, the noise harsh in the silence. A young woman jumped down and stalked toward me. "It's one way." Her eyes glittered with anger. "You're supposed to punch the intercom on the gatepost to signal you're coming up. And this is a private road. You're trespassing." She spoke in a crisp, decisive voice that was only a little breathless from the nearness of a crash. "I'll have to ask you to leave. At once." Raven-dark hair cupped an intelligent, confident face with wide-spaced gray eyes and an appealing snub nose. The swift breeze molded her white cotton top and linen skirt against her.

I knew who she was: Belle's secretary, Elise Ford. Even Belle's secretary was pictured in the newspapers in the aftermath of the kidnapping. I knew so much about all of them—and they knew nothing of me.

Except one of them. One of them knew me. The thought was like a trickle of ice down my spine. One of them knew a great deal about me. One of them had spent hours painstakingly creating a document to wrench me out of the present, propel me into the past.

I looked at Belle's secretary pleasantly, but I was scanning for character. At first glance all seemed in order, just the right amount of makeup, her clothing appropriate. Only one item jarred, an extremely expensive jeweled platinum watch. But perhaps Belle gave nice presents. Or Miss Ford had a well-heeled admirer. Or generous parents. Or an extravagant streak.

"I'm sorry, I didn't know about the intercom." I spoke

quickly, placatingly. "Belle offered to have me picked up at the airport, but I decided to rent a jeep. Awfully sorry if I've caused a problem." I smiled at her. "You must be Belle's secretary. I'm Henrietta Collins." I leaned out the car window to look past her. "Can you back up? Or should I back down to the outlook?"

She stared at me blankly. "You're expected?" Her questioning eyes noted my crimson hopsack suit and silver-and-turquoise earrings and necklace, looked past me at my luggage, sensible and sturdy black vinyl. "But Ms. Ericcson sees no one except by invitation."

I feigned equal surprise. Now I had to be convincing. The very rich live on a different plane, their privacy guarded in every possible way. I had to get past Elise Ford. "I know. So I'm very appreciative that she's invited me to visit her. It's very thoughtful of her."

She stood stiff and straight, like a sentinel. "Oh, no. There must be some mistake. I handle all of Ms. Ericcson's correspondence. This weekend is a family gathering."

"A family gathering?" I repeated blankly. "But . . ." I reached down to my purse and lifted out a creamy square of cardboard. I scanned it, then nodded. "Yes. I was asked to arrive today. Thursday, the twenty-seventh."

Elise Ford reached out. "May I?"

I handed the invitation to her, managing, I hoped, to look a trifle surprised, a little indignant.

She studied the card. It was quite tasteful, a thick square with a blue border. Belle's name was printed in raised blue ink. A coconut palm was embossed in the right margin. The secretary frowned, handed back the card. "Excuse me."

She walked back to the Land Rover and retrieved a mobile phone.

I shaded my eyes and listened hard without appearing to do so.

"Lester, Elise. I'm on the road and there's a woman—a

Henrietta Collins—who says Belle's invited her to visit. She has an invitation. But—" Her voice dropped.

I would have liked to have heard the rest of it. But I could guess. Was the stationery unfamiliar to her? The signature? That was no wonder. My local print shop had made the invitation. I'd signed it. Not, of course, in my usual handwriting.

She swung toward me. "Are you Mrs. Richard Collins?"

Oh, Richard, Richard. "Yes. Yes, I am." Yes, dammit, I still should be.

She spoke into the phone. "She says she is. All right, Lester. If you say so." She punched the phone off. "I'll back around. You can come up."

She swung up into the driver's seat, closed the door. Without a glance at the precipitous drop but with care and caution, she maneuvered the huge car around and roared away, up the mountain.

I followed in the jeep. I didn't mind the dust that swept back over me, almost obscuring my way. Another challenge met and bested. But this was just the beginning.

Yet another gate was at journey's end, a gate of bronze bars between twelve-foot whitewashed walls. Bougainvillea spilled over the walls, the crimson blossoms bright as blood. A semicircle parking area of red tiles fanned out from the walls.

I stopped the jeep next to the Land Rover. As I stepped down, the gate began to swing slowly inward. I glanced toward Elise Ford. She made no move to get out of the Land Rover. She looked past me toward the gate.

A tall, thin man in a checkered shirt and age-paled jeans walked out. He lifted a hand toward Elise. She nodded, backed and turned the big vehicle, and started down the mountain.

I walked toward him. We met beside a pink shower tree in full bloom, with masses of pink blooms.

"Mrs. Collins? I'm Lester Mackey. I work for Belle." His voice was soft and light with a mournful quality. It reminded me of a long-ago disaster and the voice of a mine official, telling me about the men blocked off by a deadly landslide. Soft and light and mournful.

Johnnie Rodriguez's mother had compared Mackey's voice to the whispery slither of a snake. But there was nothing snakelike about Lester Mackey. I was struck, in fact, by the anxiousness of his light blue eyes and the fine crinkle of lines fanning out from his eyes and mouth. This man had served Belle Ericcson for many years. I'd envisioned him as a kind of bodyguard. He didn't fit that preconception. There was nothing tough or hard about him. He had a sensitive face and graceful hands and that anxious, diffident look.

"I'm Henrietta Collins. Mrs. Richard Collins." I spoke crisply, a woman confident of her welcome.

Mackey nodded. "I understand there's some confusion about your visit." His soft voice was deferential.

I listened to his words, but I was gauging his eyes. I've watched eyes for a half century now. Lots of blinks? That's a liar. Dead and dull? That's despair. Shiny as marbles? Oh, watch out, that's a screen. Lester Mackey's eyes were shiny. I wondered what he was hiding.

"I called Belle. She's lunching in Princeville. She said of course to welcome you. She'll be back in late afternoon." The words were hospitable, but he kept darting quick, appraising glances at me as we walked toward the opened gate. Quick, appraising, shiny glances.

A middle-aged Hawaiian woman in a starched gray uniform waited for us, her plump face grave and dignified.

As we neared, Mackey said, "Amelia, this is Mrs. Collins. She will be staying with us."

Amelia smiled. "Hello, Mrs. Collins. Welcome to Ahiahi. I'm Mrs. Ericcson's housekeeper. If you will come with me,

I will show you to your room." Her voice had the sweet lilt of a native Hawaiian.

I looked toward Mackey.

"I'll see to your bags."

I wanted to talk to Lester Mackey. What did he know that he didn't want to reveal? It could have to do with Richard's death or with the reason Richard came to Ahiahi. More than ever, it seemed likely Lester Mackey and Johnnie Rodriguez indeed knew something about CeeCee Burke's kidnapping. But first things first. "Thank you, Mr. Mackey." I nodded to him and followed the housekeeper.

I've traveled the world, seen the Taj Mahal at sunrise, Saint Paul's in the fog, the Sphinx in a sandstorm. But when I stepped through the gate, I stopped and gazed in awe.

Paths of crushed shells wound through a fairyland of blossoms. Macaws flitted against the backdrop of cotton-candy-pink tecomas and lacy apple-green tree ferns and the delicate blue blossoms of the jacaranda. Sunlight glinted on porcelain Kyoto dragons. But the luxuriant tropical blooms were simply the setting for the jewel.

Pale violet clusters of rooms were strung along the canyon's rim like amethysts on a chain. Indoors and out flowed together so gracefully it was hard to discern boundaries. It was a house, but more than a house; the rooms independent, yet parts of a whole.

Beyond the flowering trees and a pond with the flickering brightness of fish colored more imaginatively than a tropical Gauguin, beyond the tiled flooring of the courtyard with its primitive depiction of volcanoes and thundering waves and swaying palms, beyond the open and unscreened windows and doors ran lanais overlooking the verdant canyon and the falls.

The falls. Always, ultimately, the eye was drawn to the falls as they arched and curved and thundered, down and down and down, the narrow, rushing water shimmering like diamonds glittering in a tiara.

If there was a more beautiful place in all the world, I'd never seen it.

Finally, I moved forward, catching up with the waiting housekeeper.

"If you please," she murmured, "here are some rubber slippers." She held out thongs.

"Of course." I sat on a sleek koa bench the color of almonds and slipped off my low-slung red leather heels and put on the thongs.

"Everyone leaves their shoes here." It was a gentle request. "If you don't mind," she added quickly.

I smiled and put my shoes along the edge of the tiled walkway that fronted the clusters of rooms. I noted a half dozen other pairs—tennis shoes, jogging shoes, dress shoes. Even though the clusters of rooms drowsed quietly in the sunlight, obviously there were others about. Somewhere.

Eventually, I would meet them. If Belle Ericcson permitted me to stay.

But I quite literally had my thong in the door. I wanted to get settled, to be ensconced in a guest room before Belle returned. It would be much more awkward to send away a guest in possession of a room. Though from what I'd gleaned about Belle Ericcson—and what I'd surmised over the years Richard had known her—I felt sure that Belle was tough enough to do whatever she deemed necessary.

"Yes, I'd love to go on to my room. I'd like to rest for a bit." It was surely a familiar comment from a visitor arriving from the mainland. Travelers reach Hawaii glassy-eyed and exhausted, so I'd flown to Honolulu on Wednesday and spent the night. I'd arrived on Kauai today well rested. I hoped to be fresh and quick and alert to face the most daunting challenge of my life.

"Yes, ma'am. This way."

I followed her along the walkway. We passed a series of wide-open rooms, the soft cream and pale blue furniture subtle spots of color, subservient to the vibrant hues of the canyon. It was breathtaking to realize that this portion of the house ran along the lip of the canyon. It was like being a bird atop a towering tree, unfettered, exhilarated, godlike.

Amelia's rubber slippers shushed softly against the tiled walkway as it followed the terrain in a series of steps and platforms. "Everyone has a separate suite, each with a lanai that overlooks the canyon." She slowed. "There are two suites available. The last one is the highest one. Mr. Mackey said I should tell you that the last one is where your husband stayed. Do you wish to choose it or the other one?"

There would be no trace of Richard in the suite. Nothing to show he had spent the last hours of his life there. But Richard had been there as he had never been in the house in which I now lived. Richard had been there.

I made my choice quickly. "The last one."

She darted swift glances at me as we climbed the last set of steps, reached the level of the last suite.

I realized when I stepped across the threshold that there was no door, no door at all.

The housekeeper saw my surprise and her lips curved in a suddenly merry smile. "Everyone notices! Here." She pointed at two buttons, one cream, one red, beneath the light switch. She reached out, touched the cream button, and a panel slid shut behind us. She touched it again and the panel opened, withdrawing into its recess. "When the panel is closed, you may push the red button if you wish to lock it."

We stood in a small, cheerful living area with white wicker sofas and chairs. The walls were also white. The only color came from the vividly patterned pillows, splashed with gold and carnelian and emerald. I was reminded of the macaws in the garden.

A sandalwood latticework jutted out from one wall to

demarcate the bedroom, also furnished in white wicker. The bedroom was open to its own lanai and the canyon.

I scarcely listened as the housekeeper demonstrated how to pull out louvered panels to close off the lanai. And, of course, there were ceiling fans in both the living room and the bedroom.

A quick tattoo sounded behind us.

"Come in," I called, but still I stood, staring out at the falls as a young woman placed my suitcase and carry-on in a corner of the bedroom.

I should have known Lester Mackey would not bring my cases himself. But that was all right. I would make an occasion to talk to him.

I smiled. "Thank you." She nodded briskly and turned away.

The housekeeper pointed toward an intercom on the nightstand. "If you would like anything—a snack, coffee, a drink—press it and one of the maids will come. And there is a small refrigerator in an alcove. It is well stocked, but don't hesitate to ask for anything that you would like to have."

"Thank you," I said again. "I'm fine. If you'll let me know when Ms. Ericcson returns . . ."

"Oh, yes, ma'am." Her quick footsteps pattered away.

I walked slowly across the floor, the lau hala matting soft beneath my feet. I stepped out onto the lanai and walked to the railing. It was a sheer drop of at least a hundred feet to the rocky valley floor.

I placed my hands on the railing, a wooden railing. I wondered if Richard had stood thus, if his fingers had felt the smoothness of the paint, if he'd been fascinated by the subtle variations in tones of green from the vines and ferns and trees that carpeted the hillside, if he'd watched the shadows lengthen in the valley as the sun slipped westward.

My hands gripped harder. Where had Richard fallen?

I would find out.

I swung away from the railing, found the little refrigerator in the alcove, fixed myself a tall tumbler of ice water.

But I didn't unpack. I must face Belle Ericcson first.

I settled on a comfortable wicker chaise on the lanai. Belle might return at any time.

I didn't know what I would say when I saw her. For the first time, I regretted the fact that we'd never met, not in all the years Richard had known Belle. I'd resented the phone calls across the years, from Belle to Richard. And from Richard to Belle. Yes, certainly, I should have welcomed a friend of my husband's. But there was something in the way he would respond to a call, dropping whatever plans we had to go to her side, that made me question the depth of their friendship. Or wonder, painfully, if it was more than friendship. Yet, I couldn't bring myself to ask Richard.

I could not do that.

He was always an honorable man. How could I accuse him of unfaithfulness? And it wasn't that I actually thought him unfaithful. I knew, knew beyond doubt, that he loved me. But between Richard and Belle there was a bond that exceeded friendship. And I was never willing to explore what that bond might be.

Now I wished I had not made that choice so long ago. Because everything hinged on Belle, on who she was and how she thought, on how much she cared for Richard, on her character.

Belle Ericcson, woman extraordinaire.

And my husband's lover?

I looked out at majestic beauty and steeled my mind and heart to think, not feel.

Belle Ericcson. If ever I needed to understand her mind, it was now. Of course, I knew a great deal about her as one knows about celebrities. I had some sense of her personality. I knew she was brave. It takes a gritty courage to cover wars.

Obviously, she was decisive, charming, intelligent. It took all of those qualities to forge the life she'd led.

As I waited for her to return to this spectacular retreat, I considered a quality I'd not expected. The more I had read about Belle, the harder I looked, the clearer it became to me that Belle Ericcson lived with élan. And that is no small achievement.

But I should remember that this was the public Belle. Even the tart-tongued Lifestyle editor Lou Kinkaid who knew every nuance of the social set in Dallas had more questions than answers about Belle.

What of the private woman? The woman who had known extraordinary success—and great unhappiness. Not even her autobiography truly revealed her.

When I'd made the decision to come here, to gain entrance to Belle's secluded retreat, I'd immediately set out to discover everything possible about her. I'd learned a great deal about the public Belle. And I'd picked up her autobiography on my way to the airport. I had to hope that every fact I'd gleaned would help me when finally—now in a matter of moments—we came face-to-face.

Belle's family history was as tangled and extravagant as golden necklaces heaped in a Middle Eastern souk.

Belle was born on the Fourth of July in 1935 in Seattle. Her father, Anders Ericcson, was a Swedish immigrant. Anders started off working as a lumberjack and ended up owning one of the largest lumber mills in the Northwest and marrying Abigail Joss, the daughter of a shipping magnate. Belle was an only child, and from the first, lovely and beloved, was showered with every attention and luxury.

A nanny recalled that Belle began reading the Seattle newspaper when she was four years old and shortly after her seventh birthday announced firmly at dinner one night that she was going to be a reporter.

Apocryphal? Probably. I'd vote for creative recall on the

nanny's part or poetic license by the author. Henry Ford's appraisal of history is not bunk.

In any event, Belle studied journalism at the University of Southern California and went on to Columbia Graduate School. And from there to the Paris *Herald Tribune*.

She met her first husband, Oliver Burke, in Paris. He was the third son of a British duke. Burke was an artist out of step with his own era. His paintings were as clear and precise as photographs. No matter that he painted with the lucent clarity of a shaft of sunlight striking a Gothic spire, he was forever dismissed as imitative, unoriginal, passé. Belle and Oliver were married in 1960 and their daughter, Charmaine Celia, was born in 1962. Their first son, Anders, was born in 1963.

In early 1964, Belle was transferred to the Tokyo bureau. Oliver obligingly gathered up his paints and came along. Their second son, Joss, was born in 1965. As American troops swelled to more than 300,000 in Vietnam, Belle took a plane to Saigon and Oliver stayed in Tokyo with the children.

She darted in and out of Tokyo, of course, seeing her family, but always she returned to the shifting, erratic, increasingly bitter and divisive war.

After the fall of Saigon, Belle and her family returned to Europe, living in Italy while Belle wrote a book about her war experiences. Oliver, a heavy smoker, died of lung cancer the next year.

Belle and her children came home to America and she authored a weekly column, "Fresh Eyes," from the perspective of an American returned to these shores after years abroad. It was an immediate success and soon was carried in almost three hundred newspapers. In 1977 she married Quentin Gallagher, a brawling, two-fisted reporter who shut down every bar he ever visited. A widower, Quentin brought to the marriage three children: a son, Wheeler, and two daughters, Megan and Gretchen. He also brought a cocky, flamboyant, fighting spirit and a penchant for one drink too many. Quentin died in a one-car crash with a blood alcohol level of .09.

Belle's household then consisted of CeeCee, Anders, Joss, Wheeler, Megan, and Gretchen. Belle celebrated her fiftieth birthday by marrying Keith Scanlon, a fortyish tennis pro she'd met at a health spa in Texas. She bought a Tara-style Southern mansion in Dallas's exclusive Highland Park. That became her primary home and jumping-off spot. She also bought the hilltop vacation home on the Texas shore of Lake Texoma.

Belle plunged into this new life with enthusiasm and became more Texan than most Texans. Stylized bronze armadillos graced the front steps of her Highland Park mansion. *People* magazine featured the armadillos on the cover and the artist soon had enough commissions to go from a Yugo to a Ferrari. Belle made white leather boots popular in the highest reaches of Dallas society, and she was a staunch supporter of Dallas and Fort Worth museums.

Like bees sticking to their queen, all of her children—natural and adopted—followed her to Dallas.

Whenever *Lifestyle* editors and tabloids across the country ran out of material, they always had recourse to Belle and her boisterous family.

One July Fourth, Belle's birthday party had drawn the rich and famous from across the nation to soar thousands of feet above the dusty Texas plain in brilliantly colored hot-air balloons.

The next September she sponsored a charity treasure hunt that ended with a socialite posting bail because she'd crawled up a rain spout to break into the mayor's home in search of his bedroom slippers.

The kids—as she called her children, whether Burkes or Gallaghers—were good copy, too. Quite close in age, they'd grown up convinced that fun was their own special province and they were endlessly creative in their enjoyments and in their efforts to one-up their siblings. Many of the stories were accompanied by photographs of the family, singly and in groups.

Belle was still lovely, with white-gold hair framing finely drawn patrician features and startlingly brilliant blue eyes. The most-often-used photo was the one that graced the jacket of her autobiography. Slim and elegant, Belle stood beside a huge globe of the world. She wore a cobalt-blue suit, a cream silk blouse and a single strand of pearls.

It might have been a bland photograph.

But it wasn't.

There was something in the vividness of her gaze, something in the lift of her chin, something in the way she stood that challenged the viewer, that said, "I'm here, I'm Belle Ericcson and I'm more alive than anyone you've ever known."

I'd also retrieved photos of the children. All of this material was in a zippered compartment of my carry-on. But I didn't need to get it out to remember. I remembered easily. Because one of the faces might belong to Richard's murderer.

And I would see all of them soon, very soon. If I got past my meeting with Belle.

I jumped up from the chair and walked to the carry-on and yanked up her autobiography.

A bookmark marked this passage:

I was bringing up the rear with another correspondent, Richard Collins of Midwest Syndicate. We were following a platoon from A Company, Fourth battalion, Twelfth Infantry, on a jungle trail north of Saigon, seeking an encampment of Vietcong. Suddenly machine gun fire swept across the trail and soldiers sagged to the ground, blood splashing against the brilliantly green ferns, flooding down into the dust. The attack came so quickly, there was hardly any sound except the clatter of the machine guns. A sunburned captain was hit three times as he tried to make radio contact for artillery support. Collins pushed me off the trail. A corporal with a machine gun held off the attackers. Collins and I were able to hide behind a well, then follow a path to an abandoned rubber plantation. We hid there for four nights, then returned to the trail and found our way back to an American outpost. Every man in our platoon was killed. Our escape was as fortuitous as the lives and deaths of thousands of GIs. Survival or destruction depended upon where you happened to be standing, which direction your patrol took, whether the artillery hit your helicopter or another. Since Vietnam, I've never had any sense of security—and I am haunted by the pointlessness of the deaths I saw. Why, dear God, why? They were so terribly, vulnerably young, those GIs. Every few weeks, I flew to Japan—a luxury unavailable to the ordinary troops in the field—and as I left behind the horror and despair, I often recalled the caustic comment of Mary Roberts Rinehart, the first woman to cover trench warfare during World War I: "Old men make wars that young men may die."

I closed the book, stared down at Belle's picture.

Richard was mentioned three more times in Belle's book. They'd been together the January night the Tet Offensive began and were among the last correspondents out of Tuy Phuoc. They were there when Marines fought through the streets of the old provincial capital of Hue. They covered the siege of Khe Sanh.

I was as impressed by what Belle left out of the book as by what she included. There were very personal, caring vignettes about soldiers: the stubble-faced eighteen-year-old from Dubuque who carried a small terrier with his head poking out of his backpack; the captain from Pittsburgh who died trying to help a pregnant Vietnamese woman escape from her village during a Vietcong rocket attack; the gray-faced major from Toledo waiting for the return of his helicopters, waiting and waiting; and acid-etched portraits of pompous brass in Saigon and "celebrity" reporters who dropped by Vietnam, then returned to the U.S. to parrot the Johnson war rhetoric.

But what was missing was Belle herself. Her chapters on Vietnam were a foreign desk's dream, clear, crisp, factual. But only occasionally, as in the passage about the platoon, was there a hint of her personal response.

And that was true of all the book. *Belle on Belle* was her report on the stories she'd covered, the people she'd interviewed, the history she'd observed.

Oh, yes, you can't read an entire autobiography and not have some picture of its author.

I knew these things about Belle: She was brave, tough, smart, charming, aloof, imperious. She didn't grandstand. And she didn't spend much time in bars.

Were she and my husband lovers? Her book didn't tell me.

Richard came home from that war bitter at the dissembling of our government, impressed by the courage of soldiers fighting a war they didn't understand, and convinced more than ever that reporters—with all their faults and mistakes—are essential to defend freedom.

And he came home from Vietnam with a lifelong link to Belle Ericcson. It was undeniable even though unstated. From that time forward, he responded whenever Belle called.

They'd been together a great deal in Vietnam. Was that their choice—or was it the randomness of a randomly fought war?

God, I didn't know the answer. I hoped—call me a coward—that I could meet Belle and still not know the answer. What I wanted from this place, from Belle, was the reason for Richard's death. I must know the truth of Richard's death.

I owed that—and so much more—to Richard.

And as far as Belle and Richard were concerned, whatever I learned, I had to balance it against the reality of a lifetime of love and trust and caring.

I heard the swift patter of footsteps.

I put the book on the bedside table, stood and faced the open door. I smoothed my hair, straightened my jacket and wished my throat were not suddenly so dry.

The housekeeper bobbed in the doorway. "Ms. Ericcson will see you now."

six

Belle Ericcson stood next to a waist-high cloisonné vase filled with a spectacular arrangement of yellow ginger, heliconia, and bird-of-paradise. Any other woman would have been diminished.

Not Belle.

My reaction wasn't simply an exaggerated response because she had been so much a part of Richard's life and had been, since the arrival of the shocking poster, the backdrop to my every thought. Belle had presence, that magical quality which marks presidents, prime ministers, movie stars, financial moguls. No one could enter a room where she waited and not be immediately brought under her spell, a spell as inescapable and pervasive and intoxicating as that deployed by any ancient goddess. Even in repose, she exuded vitality.

She was startlingly attractive, quite as lovely as all the photographs I'd found. But I was struck most of all not by her beauty but by her fragility. She looked as if she were sculpted in attenuated ivory, her bones refined to their essence beneath alabaster skin. Her elegant clothes clung to her.

I had a swift, eerie memory of Johnnie Rodriguez's wasted mother.

Yet, in astonishing contradiction, Belle emanated—without speaking, without moving—such a restless, relentless vigor that the very room quivered with energy. I felt exhilarated, intensely attuned, almost febrile in anticipation, and she had yet to speak a word. She had only to look across the room with her compelling gaze.

Her silver hair was drawn back in a chignon, emphasizing her deep-set blue eyes and high cheekbones. Her skin was lined and had the parchment-fine patina of age. This woman felt no compulsion to grasp artificially after the smoothness of youth. But it was her luminous eyes—as unforgettably, darkly blue as the Hawaiian waters—that mesmerized me.

And frightened me a little.

There was an emptiness in those eyes, a void, a longing, despite their intensity.

Her lips curved upward, but there was no more warmth than in the rosy brilliance of the crimson enamel in the cloisonné vase. It was the echo of a smile, a gesture once familiar and now foreign.

"Henrie O." Belle's voice was clear and high, like a silver bell rung as the shadows fall. I suddenly had a faint, ghostlike memory of hearing her say on that dreadful day, "I'm so sorry . . . Richard's dead." Then the memory was gone, like a flash of sunlight on chrome.

She walked toward me, a thin, graceful hand outstretched. It was not until then that I saw the cane in her left hand and her uneven, slightly halting gait. I was startled. An accident? Surgery? But such was her vitality that the cane and the limp immediately receded from notice. I was fascinated by her lovely, haggard, striking, unforgettable face.

The room—her study—was a marvelous backdrop. The walls were a pale, ethereal ivory, punctuated by brilliantly colored canvases. The pecan floors, sensuous as pools of honey, reflected light from globes inset in the ceiling. Chinese Buddhist temple hangings flanked a starkly plain marble fireplace. Crimson anthuriums rose regally from matching silver vases on the hearth. And, as I was beginning to expect in this cliffside home, there was the wide-open access to the lanai and the ever compelling vista of the robin's-egg sky and silvery falls and verdant ridges—breathtaking, spectacular, ever changing.

But the elegant woman in the orchid silk blouse and white silk slacks would always be the focal point.

She reached me, grasped my hand. "May I call you Henrie O? As Richard did?" Her touch was firm and cool and fleeting. The delicate scent of gardenia wafted over me.

"Of course." I returned her gaze. I could not return that ceremonial smile.

Those bright lips still curved, but there was no smile in her dark blue eyes. "And I'm Belle." She studied me.

I knew what she saw, a woman as dark as she was fair, my hair touched, too, with silver, my face lined with a lifetime of both joy and sadness. I don't claim even a particle of Belle's charisma, but I am lean and quick and still move with eagerness and energy.

I saw a quick flicker of approval in her eyes and I was surprised that it pleased me. That was even one more indication of the power of her personality.

"Now we meet." There was a shade more warmth in her voice. "After all these years . . . Richard spoke of you often."

I was not able to respond in kind. That was my doing. I was the one who had blocked that expression. But I could honestly say, had to honestly say, "Richard cared for you."

Her remote smile softened. "I valued him as the best friend I ever had. And now, finally, you and I meet." She led the way, moving carefully, the cane clicking against the golden floor, to huge rattan easy chairs on either side of the fireplace. As she eased down onto the oversized cushion, her eyes flickered toward the lanai, and the sharp planes of her face tightened.

It was like a rough hand squeezing my heart. Richard fell near here, I was sure of it.

I took the seat opposite her, but I gazed out at the turquoise sky and emerald canyon. "I've never known what happened to Richard," I said tightly.

Yes, I asked without preamble. It wasn't what I'd planned to do. But entering this room, meeting this woman, I knew I could not count on anything. She was formidable. I would not easily fool her. Or persuade her. My manufactured invitation was in my purse and I knew it wasn't worth the paper it was printed on. Belle Ericcson was neither simple nor credulous. I'd better snatch what I could while I could.

If my blunt opening shocked her, she gave no sign of it. "None of us know, Henrie O." Her face was somber. "We said good night about ten. The next morning, I thought he'd slept late. You know how tiring it is to come from the mainland. And when the mist burned off, oh, it was late morning, Wheeler looked down from his lanai and saw him. Richard was still dressed and his bed had not been slept in. He must have walked along the cliff path late in the evening. Perhaps he was returning to the main house for a book. We'll never know."

Belle clasped her hands tightly together. A bracelet of square amethysts in ornate gold settings glistened like the purpling sky outside. "I'm sorry." Her silvery voice expressed true grief.

"Thank you." I stared out at the steep, foliage-sheathed cliffs, beautiful and merciless, as nature so often is.

"It was doubly hard," she sighed, "because I'd been so

pleased to see him. And surprised. It was a wonderful surprise."

"You had not expected him?" I had to feel my way carefully here.

"Oh, no." Belle's reply was swift. "The children were all here. And Stan Dugan, CeeCee's fiancé. I ask them to come every year. That was the first year. I want them to remember CeeCee. But not in a sad way. I always want this gathering to be cheerful, as cheerful as CeeCee always was. I make sure it is a holiday, filled with golf, swimming, boating. Or simply relaxing. I'd played golf that afternoon with Joss and Anders and Wheeler. Richard was here when we returned." A quick smile quirked her lips. Her eyes brightened. "It was wonderful to see him. At first he said he didn't intend to spend the night, but I insisted. Now, of course, I wish . . ." Her voice trailed away.

"Did Richard indicate why he'd come?" I watched her intently.

She frowned and stood, using the cane to lever herself upright. She moved to a cut-glass decanter on a red lacquered table. "Sherry?"

It was hard to be polite, to welcome hospitality. All I wanted was answers. "Yes, yes, thank you." I forced the words, forced a smile.

She poured the wine, brought a glass to me. Then she stood, leaning just a bit on her cane, her expression thoughtful. She held her wine, but didn't taste it. "We had only a moment alone that evening. He came into the dining room and we went out on the lanai together. I asked him if he'd come to the island for a holiday. He looked at me and his face was very serious, very grave. He said no, it was a matter he might wish to discuss with me. But he wasn't yet certain. Then Gretchen and Peggy came out and we talked about their afternoon snorkeling at Anini. Everything after that was very general."

Richard didn't tell Belle what he knew—or what he suspected. Richard, always so careful and fair. He must have come with some knowledge, and yet he wanted to ask the person involved first. Had he made plans to see someone that evening, alone, in a quiet place?

I put my wineglass down and gestured toward the lanai. "Can we see where Richard was found from here?"

Slowly, she nodded.

"Will you show me?" I wanted to know. And I didn't want to know. But I had to know.

Shakily, I stood. For an instant, I thought she was going to refuse. She stared at me, her gaze probing. But I was Richard's widow. I had every right to want to see where he died.

Belle put down her glass. She walked slowly, the cane clicking. I followed her onto the lanai. The magnificent gold trees at either end of the lanai were in full bloom, their masses of yellow flowers shiny as butter. Hibiscus in a huge wooden tub were bright as a painter's palette, orange and pink, red and white. The breeze rustled a plumeria shrub with pale pink blossoms, and the most familiar perfume of the islands swept over me.

Our thongs shushed against apricot tiles. Belle reached the center of the iron railing. She looked over the railing. "Do you see the trail? Steps go down from each lanai to a trail that's been cut out of the cliff. It runs the length of the house. Other paths lead down to the pond beneath the falls. And there is a path up to the falls, but that isn't safe. I'm sure Richard was on the main trail. It is well lighted at night."

We looked down. I saw the trail, perhaps three feet in width at the most, clinging to the side of the cliff, a walkway with an eagle's view. It would take a good head for heights. And then I looked past the trail, down, down, down.

"The police thought he must have fallen not far from the steps to his lanai."

My lanai now.

"He was found near the kukui trees." Belle pointed far down the canyon to a stand of trees with pale green foliage.

I held tight to the railing, fighting off dizziness and such a surge of feeling—anger and despair and horror—that I was afraid for a moment I might fall. Or faint.

Thin, strong fingers gripped my elbow. Even through the pain, I was terribly aware of Belle's touch. She led me away from the railing to a wicker sofa.

Her words seemed to come from a long distance. ". . . still don't understand how it happened. Perhaps vertigo. Perhaps he slipped. We'll never know." Her face was bleak. "It must have happened quickly. He didn't call out. Or if he did, no one heard him." Her voice wavered.

I looked deep into her eyes. For an instant, those brilliant blue eyes were alive with pain and sorrow and anguish.

We told each other so much without words in that silent exchange.

I loved Richard.

Belle loved Richard.

We looked at each other and understood that this man had meant the world to both of us.

She settled back against the couch, folded her arms. Now her face was cool and aloof. The emotion I'd seen in her eyes—a softness, a caring—was gone as if it had never been. The gaze she turned on me was thoughtful, considering. "Is this why you've come?"

I'd been pummeled by emotion, but I couldn't afford at this moment to be affected by my sorrow and anger over Richard's death. I could not think about his terror and pain. Not now. Later I could weep. But now I had to control my feelings. I must be careful, without seeming at all to be careful.

When facing despair and destruction, Richard often found comfort in Hugh Latimer's exhortation to his companion as both were to be burned at the stake for heresy: Play the man, Master Ridley . . .

Play the man.

How hard it is to have courage.

"I hope I will find closure." Yes, indeed, that was my hope. And now, now came the lie. "I was so grateful to receive your letter inviting me to come this week. Every year the anniversary of his death has been very hard. I couldn't picture what happened. It had no reality. I only knew how it felt to see his casket lowered from an airplane. But now, I can see where he died. The cliff—what a terrible fall!" I closed my eyes briefly, then said determinedly, "But I needed to see it. I appreciate being able to come here."

Belle was quiet for so long I thought she wasn't going to answer. Those cool dark blue eyes studied me. Finally, she said, "I would not turn away Richard's wife."

Once again our glances met. This time I wasn't sure what I saw.

Her silvery voice was thoughtful as she continued, "But I must tell you, Henrie O, that I did not write to you."

Now I faced the greatest challenge.

I felt a sudden wash of sheer misery. I hated doing this. Belle had made me welcome as Richard's wife. I was accepting her hospitality, had, in effect, demanded her hospitality. But I'd begun the lie, and I had to carry on.

It had seemed, thousands of miles away, propelled by the message that Richard was murdered, the only possible way to gain entrance here. I'd gone to a great deal of trouble, taking time to find a letter from Belle to Richard, carefully copying her signature. ("Dear Richard, Thank you so much for the review of the new book on William Allen White. He has always . . .") A letter between friends, between colleagues. I'd simply plucked an envelope from his files, having no idea what I would find. I was so grateful that there was no trace of passion in that letter. I would not, could not read all the letters they'd exchanged. That was not my right. Not then. Not now. Not ever.

Oh, yes, I had my forged invitation with me. I'd even made certain it had fingerprints other than mine. Just in case. How? I'd dropped it out of my purse at the grocery and the woman standing behind me picked it up, handed it to me. At that point, it was a cerebral exercise, a coldly calculated, carefully devised game.

Now I struggled to maintain my composure. Was it any wonder I looked uncomfortable? "You didn't write to me? But I have the letter. I can show it to you." Indeed I could. If I had the stomach for it. "You . . . the letter invited me to come, to arrive today and spend a week. I don't understand."

"Nor do I." She studied me intently and now I saw a reserve, a question. Not suspicion. Not yet.

"You didn't . . . Oh, I'm sorry. I'll leave at once. I'm so sorry . . ." I started to rise.

"No." She reached out, caught my hand, her touch again cool but firm. "You mustn't leave. I am delighted to have you at Ahiahi."

"Belle, I wouldn't dream of—"

"No, you must stay. There's no more to be said about that. Come." Once again she was a hostess with a determined smile. "Let's go inside. We've left our sherry there."

I suppose I should have felt triumphant as we walked back into the lovely room. Instead I felt weary, tired, empty. Yet I knew I had to remain alert. It would be so easy to say the wrong thing. I don't know when I've ever felt more alone, more uncertain.

Oh, Richard, have I gone at it all wrong? She cared for you. Should I have told her the truth? Should I tell her now?

But I had arrived under false pretenses. Wouldn't Belle toss me out of her home? Even if she understood the desperate reason for deception?

And I *had* to stay here. I would never know the truth of

Richard's death unless I plumbed the secrets of this mountain hideaway. What happened to Richard six years ago was locked within the heart of someone here at Ahiahi.

I steeled myself and faced her. We stood near her desk.

But Belle wasn't looking at me. She held the glass of sherry in her hands and gazed down at an elegant antique globe. "You've come such a long way. Just as Richard did." She lifted her head. "It was such a lovely surprise to come home that day and be told he'd arrived." Her elegant face was impassive, but her eyes watched me closely.

So now Belle wondered about the reason for his journey. I knew why Richard came. Richard had responded to Johnnie Rodriguez's call. Richard had talked to Johnnie. Whatever it was that Richard learned, it brought him here to see Belle.

But if I told her what I knew, I would have to tell her everything.

If only I knew Belle better, could gauge what effect my revelations might have.

"I didn't know Richard was coming here," I said carefully. That was true at the time.

"He wasn't"—her choice of words was equally careful—"in Honolulu on a story?"

"Not to my knowledge."

"I see. I thought . . ." she shrugged. "But it doesn't matter. Very little matters anymore." She put down her sherry and reached out and gently touched the cold sculpted cheek of a marble bust of a young woman.

I glanced at a face forever young, at lips forever tilted in a buoyant smile.

"My daughter, CeeCee." Her composure almost held. Then, catching her breath, Belle leaned down, pressed her cheek for a moment against the cold marble. "Damn whoever did it. Damn them."

"I'm sorry."

She didn't answer.

I had to ask. "Them?"

Her head jerked up. Her eyes blazed with a dark and fervid anger. I understood that anger, the awful anguish of unjust heartbreak. Life is not fair. Evil flourishes. But there is something in our souls that will not accept this.

"Whoever it was that took CeeCee and killed her. The police didn't find anything. No trace. Nothing, nothing, nothing."

Nada, nada, nada, the deputy had rasped.

And there I stood, watching this mother grieve—and I knew something. I didn't know what Richard had discovered, but I knew more than Belle. I knew that Richard came to Ahiahi because of something he had learned from Johnnie Rodriguez, something that had to do with the kidnapping and death of CeeCee Burke.

If Richard indeed was murdered because of that knowledge, it meant—it *had* to mean—that CeeCee's kidnapper, CeeCee's murderer had been here in Belle's secluded island home when Richard arrived.

And Belle had no idea of this.

None.

I saw it clearly then. I had to speak out. My plan, to insinuate myself into this house, to watch and observe and learn as much as I could, no longer seemed defensible. Not in the face of her grief.

I had not looked past my own grief. Now I had to think of Belle. My lips parted—

She lifted her head and her smile was so gallant I wanted to cry. "Please forgive me. I know you understand. It's always harder this time of year. So hard." Her voice broke. She blinked away tears. "I'm sorry. I'll see you at dinner." She turned and walked unevenly away, her cane clicking against the wood.

I almost called out to stop her. But this wasn't the moment. Let Belle regain her composure. And let me regain mine.

I walked slowly from the study onto the lanai. Did I dare tell Belle the truth? Could I show her the anonymous message I'd received? And tell her how it had led me to discover Richard's stop in Texas before he came to Ahiahi? Could I insist that Richard's death meant someone in her family or on her staff had kidnapped and killed her daughter?

Why should she believe me?

Because Richard was dead.

That was the terrible, awful, unmistakable proof.

But Belle could insist that he'd fallen and either I had created this absurd story for who knew what deranged purpose or I had been used as a tool by someone wishing to destroy her family. And I had to remember that I was here to serve someone else's purpose, a purpose I knew nothing about.

I wanted to do the right thing.

It's frightening how difficult it is sometimes to know what is right and what is wrong.

I had come to Kauai to discover the truth of Richard's death. That still was my goal. And my only hope of discovering what happened on the cliffside trail was to be here at Ahiahi.

I stood on the lanai, miserable, uncertain, but clinging to my purpose. I'd known this was going to be hard. I hadn't known how hard it would be and how Belle, the woman I'd feared, the woman I'd been jealous of, how appealing she would be. No, I can't say I felt a liking. But I was intrigued, fascinated, charmed as I suppose everyone had always been with her. Yet, I couldn't let Belle's personality prevent me from pursuing justice.

All right. I was here. And unobserved. I would take this time to explore. I wanted to talk to Lester Mackey. As soon as possible. And at this moment, there was no one about, no one to notice if I quietly surveyed Ahiahi.

The blossoms in the gold tree rustled. But that couldn't account for my sudden uneasiness, the sense that this lovely scene hid malignity and evil. The beauty was everywhere: blossoms, bright birds, trees and ferns shockingly green; the sumptuous rooms curving along the rim of the cliff; the iridescent sheen of the huge greenish-blue Chinese pottery vases on pedestals near the steps leading down from each lanai.

And then I saw the shadows. Two of them. The huge, irregular shadow of the gold tree shifted against the smooth surface of the lanai, the blooms and leaves softly rustled by the breeze. The other shadow was thick and long and motionless, unlike the wavering, breeze-stirred image of the tree. Then the long shadow moved.

Stan Dugan walked out of his hiding place. His craggy face was somber, hostile.

"What are you doing here?" I demanded, my voice sharp because I felt a thrill of fear as the big, quiet man approached. We were alone on this lanai and the cliff fell away from the railing, down, down, down.

"I'll ask you that, too, Mrs. Collins. You didn't tell Belle that somebody killed your husband." His eyes once again were cold and suspicious.

"You listened to our conversation?" I knew that, of course. I was scrambling for a response that would satisfy him. I had to keep him from revealing to Belle what I'd said to him.

He didn't bother to answer. He didn't have to. And my uneasiness increased. Why would he skulk in the shadows, eavesdrop?

"I have no proof." I eased away from the railing, back toward the study.

He jammed his hands into his trouser pockets, rocked

back on his heels. Was this how he examined a witness? "Where's the famous daybook?"

"I don't have it with me."

"Gee, that's a hell of a surprise. I'd think you'd have it. Or a copy. Or something. But maybe that's all fiction. Maybe you made it up." His raspy voice was full of disdain. "Could it be because that's all bullshit and you're here because you write true crime books?"

Dugan had moved fast, built an excellent dossier on me just as I had all of Belle's family. But why did he care about me? And why was he angry? Or was his outrage simulated, a cover for fear?

"I'm here because I'm going to find out what happened to Richard. Why are you here? It's a last-minute trip, isn't it?"

Those big owlish eyes gazed at me.

I pressed my attack. "What did you tell Belle when you arrived unexpectedly?" I'd never expected trouble from him.

His mouth twisted in brief amusement. "You're pretty good, lady. A good offense and all that. Yeah, you're right. I lied to Belle. But so did you." He gave me a considering, thoughtful, cold look. "I wonder what will happen . . . if one of us tells Belle the truth?" He turned away, and with his long, swift stride was gone before I could answer.

Why had he come? Of course, if he cared for CeeCee, truly loved her, my accusation would bring him. But he'd been here when Richard died. I had to remember that fact.

I'd felt I was balancing on a tightrope ever since I arrived at Ahiahi. Now I felt as if I were balancing on a frayed tightrope that could easily unravel.

I looked down the lanai. Stan Dugan was long out of sight. Yet I still had a sense of an inimical presence. I looked all around the lanai. Then I glanced over my shoulder and just glimpsed a flash of white.

Someone had stood on the far side of the entryway to

Belle's study and watched me. Ahiahi with all its shrubberies and rooms that flowed into each other offered easy concealment.

Had the unknown watcher listened to Belle and me, then overheard my sharp and odd exchange with Stan Dugan?

Danger. I felt it sharply. I wanted to find another human being, talk to someone, do something to dispel the atmosphere of evil. But I had to take advantage of this moment alone, explore Ahiahi while I had the chance.

I walked along the lanai past the study and found a library. Farther on, I glimpsed individual lanais to the separate living quarters. I turned back, passed Belle's office and reached the huge living-dining-room area. The lanai curved as the rooms followed the contour of the canyon. Succulent smells indicated the kitchen. I took a glimpse through the wide archway and saw a cheery woman bustling about with several helpers doing her bidding. This domestic scene was normal and right, and the feeling of danger and discord eased. I was in a beautiful home and walking in its public areas in broad daylight. I was all right.

I turned up the flagstone passageway between the dining area and the kitchen and reached the garden side of the house. To my left, nestled among hibiscus shrubs, were several cottages. No waterfall view here. No doubt this was where the staff lived.

I passed a gardener snipping a hedge with huge rosy blooms. "Hello."

"Hello, ma'am."

"Which cottage belongs to Mr. Mackey?" I smiled.

He nodded toward the first.

Again inside and out flowed together. A Mexican creeper bloomed along the wall of his lanai. I walked to the open doorway, looked into a spare and sparsely furnished living area. "Mr. Mackey?"

There was no answer.

Reluctantly, I retraced my steps. But now I knew where to find him. I took the path back between the kitchen and the dining area. This time I passed one of the huge vases and hurried down the steps at the end of the lanai to the narrow path that had been gouged out of the mountain slope. I saw a steep path down the slope, ending, I supposed, at the pool formed by the splash of the waterfalls. Belle had mentioned a similar path beneath the study.

If I followed the path to my left I would eventually fetch up beneath the lanai to my suite. I looked to my right. The cliff jutted out here. The path curved out of sight.

I picked my way carefully along the cliff face. As I came around the curve, I looked up to see yet another lanai, the last one. I was deep in shadow. A slim, imperious figure stood near the railing.

"... want you to find out everything about her. Everything. What she's been doing these past years. What kind of person she is." Belle's light, clear, bell-like voice carried clearly.

It was hard to breathe. I put my hand against the rock face, felt the crumbly soil.

"Yes, Belle." This voice was young, deferential.

"Right now."

"Yes, Belle."

Belle moved away from the railing. But I could still hear her voice.

"... something's going on, Elise. She's here for some purpose I don't understand. Check and see when she arrived. And where she came from. And tell Keith I want to see him as soon ..."

The words faded.

I turned away, walked back along the path.

I didn't need a primer to tell me who Belle was talking about. So my story of a letter hadn't fooled her.

My time at Ahiahi might be measured in hours. Not only

was Belle suspicious of me, there was Stan Dugan to fear. It would only take a word from him and I would be ousted.

But I was here for the moment.

I'd work as fast as I could.

seven

Torches on the lanais above me suddenly glowed as well as small lanterns spaced every few feet along the path. It was easy to see my way, even though dusk was falling and much of the canyon was in dark shadow. I passed the last lanai, noting notched steps up to my own suite. The path rose steadily higher. In another twenty feet, I came out near the top of the ridge.

Great swaths of topaz and coral streaked the darkening sky as the sun began to slip behind the mountain. The falls were glistening strands of silver pulsing down the cliffside, sounding like the rustle of thousands of birds lifting into the sky.

The path forked. One way led to the left alongside a tall lava-rock wall adorned with crimson, pink, and yellow bougainvillea. I continued straight ahead, following a dusty upward ribbon. I watched the way carefully. Belle had said a

path led to the falls and it was dangerous. But this path seemed fine.

A hawser-thick rope was anchored waist high to the side of the cliff. My foot kicked a loose stone and it spun over the edge of the trail, beginning its hundred-foot fall. I didn't look down. I grabbed the rope and welcomed the harsh prickly feel of its fibers.

The trail led out to a point. The cliff rose sheer on my left. The trail curled around the point. A verdant semicircle awaited me. Straight ahead, the falls tumbled in splendor down a jagged rock face. To my left, the canyon wall curved inward, offering a deep, shadowy recess. And in the wide ledge was a single grave enclosed on three sides by a low wall of lava rock. The open side faced the canyon, forever overlooking the falls and the trees. The view of the falls and the darkening canyon surpassed everything I'd seen before. It was the kind of beauty that touches your heart, as ineffable as a baby's smile or the peal of a church bell in solemn farewell.

Bright red blossoms dotted the twisted gray branches of an ohia tree that shaded the bronze marker. It was not an especially pretty tree, but it was particularly, distinctively Hawaiian. In olden days the ohia was sacred, used only for carving temple images and war gods.

Flagstones led through an opening in the wall. I reached the grave, looked down at the marker:

CHARMAINE CELIA BURKE

APRIL 1, 1962–MARCH 30, 1990

ALOHA

The wind rustled the glossy green leaves of the ohia and the quickly cooling late afternoon air touched me with a chill. I looked past the grave. The path continued to the top of the cliff where the stream rushed forward to the falls. A sign barred the way, stark crimson letters on white:

DANGER
DO NOT PASS
SLIPPERY ROCKS

"Don't even think about it," a cool voice advised.

I swung around.

The wind ruffled bright red hair, molded a white cover-up to an athletic body. "Occasionally a smart-ass trespasser ignores the warning, thinks he'll be okay if he stays away from the falls, strolls by the stream. But those rocks"—she lifted a freckled hand, pointed to the dark, gleaming, wet rocks—"are slick from the water. Step on them and you're history."

I glanced at the swift-running water, watched it thunder over the rocks, plummeting in a swirl of mist and splendor far below to a boulder-ringed pool. "I wasn't thinking about it," I said pleasantly. "I was thinking how lovely it is here, what a beautiful site for a grave."

She hunched her shoulders and stared at the ohia tree. "If there are spirits, CeeCee's perched on a low branch, feet dangling, looking out over the valley and planning a party." The voice was light and mocking. "She dearly loved parties. She'd have the best-looking surfer up here, some guy who could handle the waves on the north coast, and the handsomest ukelele player. Probably have to shanghai him from some club on Maui. It's too tame here. Believe me, the sex scene's all on Maui. Banana shakes and kiwi fruit are the standard here. And early to bed. Lamentably, usually alone. But she'd have managed. There were never any flies on CeeCee when it came to attracting hunks. Damn shame she's not here. Trust me, Belle's way past the hunk stage."

I read the dismissive summation in bright hazel eyes: And so are you, lady.

I met her glance steadily and her mouth quirked in a quick grin. Perhaps she read the summation in my eyes: Not on your life, kid. But she was clearly a young woman with an attitude and a lively disregard for convention. I wondered if this was her usual demeanor. I recognized her as Belle's youngest stepchild, Gretchen Gallagher. She was about my height. Late twenties. She looked at me boldly from a bright, quizzical, oddly defiant face. Her swim cover was a bright white with a bird-of-paradise appliqué. She carried a red-and-green-striped beach bag.

"I'm Gretchen Gallagher." It was more of a challenge than a greeting.

"Henrie O Collins."

"I'm on my way to the pool." Her glance was speculative, as in, "And where the hell are you going, lady? And who the hell are you?"

"Pool?" I supposed the tall lava-rock wall where the path forked was part of an enclosure for the pool, creating a barrier against the wind that fluttered the tree branches here on the unprotected ridge. And perhaps Belle had enclosed the play area so that this remote grave site would remain eternally calm and peaceful.

"On the other side of the wall. Pool, tennis courts, even a picnic pavilion. You can't miss it if you come from the garden."

"I didn't pass the pool. I came up the path from Belle's study."

"I saw you on the trail." She spoke casually, but her eyes were sharp.

And wondered where I was going. And who I was.

I waved my hand toward the falls. "I've been exploring."

The young woman glanced down at the grave, then at

me. "Did you know CeeCee?" It was a polite way of asking why I was standing at her stepsister's grave.

"No."

"So you didn't come here to visit CeeCee's grave?"

"No. I didn't know the grave was here. And I don't want to intrude if—"

She gave a quick, humorless laugh. "I'm not into grave vigils. I'm going to take a quick swim before dinner." But she wasn't completely satisfied. "Belle invited you for this week?"

I wasn't going to explain about the letter. I'd leave that up to Belle. "Belle and my husband Richard were good friends."

"Richard . . . Oh. Richard Collins? The guy who fell . . ."

"Yes."

"I'm sorry." Her voice was contrite. "I didn't mean to be rude. But we've been hounded so much, the last few years. Actually, it's nice to have a new face here this week. We're all getting a little tired of the annual wake." The animation fled from her face. She looked grim and resentful.

"Wake?"

She pointed to the bronze marker. "You know about CeeCee." It wasn't a question.

"Yes."

"Well, she was nuts about Kauai. So after she . . . she died"—even this casual young woman wasn't going to be flippant about murder—"Belle decided to bury her here. Because CeeCee'd camped here and said it was the most beautiful spot in the whole world. But Belle's not content to get the land and have a grave. She builds a house and stays. And every year we all come. Belle says it's to celebrate CeeCee's birthday. But it isn't exactly damn festive."

"No," I said quietly, "I wouldn't think it would be festive."

"So, are you into wakes?" It was a cocky demand.

"They serve a useful function." She was too young to understand. "The wake is to help the living."

"It doesn't help me. I mean, CeeCee's been dead for years now. Why can't Belle let go?" She scowled.

"Perhaps because she doesn't know what happened to CeeCee. Or why."

"But she's never going to know!" Gretchen's voice was querulous.

For an instant, I felt like an ancient priestess, an oracle. Perhaps that's why I spoke so confidently. "The truth has an odd way of coming out. Sometimes years later. Someone will remember something. Discover something."

She drew her breath in sharply. "Do you know something?" she demanded. "Did your husband tell you something?" She peered through the dusky air as if I possessed some secret that might make a difference.

So she not only knew who Richard was, she was well aware of his part in the aftermath of CeeCee's kidnapping.

"Richard never talked about the kidnapping." Certainly that was true.

Steps gritted on the rocky path. "Gretchen, hey, Gretchen, where are you?" A muscular young man in tennis clothes came around the curve. I watched him with the same pleasure I would have taken in observing the smooth stride of a panther. He moved with exquisite grace and power. And he carried with him a masculine magnetism that would attract any woman—red hair damp with exertion, sloe eyes that exuded confidence, full, sensuous lips.

She looked at him fondly and her face remade itself, the pettish discontent dissolving into affection. "Mrs. Collins, my brother Wheeler. Wheeler, this is Mrs. Collins. Belle's invited her to visit. Maybe it's going to be a real house party this year."

"Hello, Mr. Gallagher."

"Wheeler, please." Those full lips spread in a lazy, appealing smile. "I heard voices. It's nice to have a visitor."

I wondered suddenly if Belle realized how difficult the annual gathering was for the siblings, at least if the reaction of these two reflected the feelings of the others.

"Do you know Kauai, Mrs. Collins?" Wheeler asked.

"Not well."

"I'm just the man to remedy that." His voice had a soft Southern sound.

"We'll give you a guided tour you won't forget," Gretchen said eagerly.

"I doubt anywhere could be lovelier than here." I spread my hand toward the falls and the dusk-shrouded canyon.

But they stood silent and both stared down—just for an instant—at CeeCee's grave.

"It's getting dark," Gretchen said abruptly. "I think I'll head for the pool."

"You know how Belle is about being on time for dinner." Wheeler's voice was pleasant, but there was an underlying edge.

"I'll be good." But her voice was irritated.

He reached out, patted his sister's arm, a big brother encouraging good behavior.

Wheeler shepherded us back toward the fork in the path. Huge night lights glowed from the corners of the sports compound. I glimpsed two courts through an arched entryway and heard the *thwock* of a tennis ball expertly struck.

"The pool's just past the courts. With another grand vista." Gretchen shrugged away the magnificent scenery. "If you like to spend a holiday stretched out on a chaise longue, you've come to the right place. Though there's plenty to see on the island. We'll plan an outing tomorrow. Did you know the Nurses' Beach in *South Pacific* was filmed on the north shore? I can take you there if you like."

"I'd like that very much."

"I'll see you at dinner then." Gretchen veered off toward the sports area.

Wheeler ambled alongside me. "If you like a challenge, there's always the Na Pali."

Richard and I had holidayed on Kauai many years before and climbed the rugged Kalalau Trail along the magnificent Na Pali cliffs, perhaps one of the last bastions of untouched majesty in the world.

I'm in good enough shape for my age. But, no, I couldn't tackle the Na Pali now. Crumbly soil, deep ruts and tangled roots made the hike a difficult and sometimes dangerous challenge. I can wrap my arthritic knee and still manage a slow jog and a couple of sets of doubles with players of my era. But not the Na Pali. "Perhaps I'll have time for a helicopter tour."

"Better go by raft," Wheeler said. Then he added quickly, "Sorry. Not trying to tell you how to spend your vacation, but Belle's really down on helicopters. She thinks the noise is an intrusion, a kind of ecological trauma. Anders is big on that sort of thing. And there have been some crashes, too. Oh, here we are."

The path sloped down suddenly and we came into the garden. Now we could see the clusters of rooms perched on the rim of the canyon. Lights glowed here, too, indoors and out, the living areas spotlighted like stage sets, the garden's colors softly illuminated. The mélange of colors was richer than a rainbow: the purples of bougainvillea, glory-bush, and orchid trees; the oranges of silk oak, hibiscus, and kou; the pinks of oleander, pink shower tree, and pink tecoma, and the majestic whites of plumeria, oleander, and angel's-trumpet. Near the front lanai, the jacaranda blossoms looked like festive lavender bouquets bunched on their delicate feathery leaves. The fragrances mingled, scenting the night air like a sweet and spicy perfume.

"I'm staying here." I gestured toward the first and highest suite. "What time is dinner?"

Wheeler glanced at his watch. "At seven-thirty. But everyone gathers about seven for a drink."

"I'll see you then. I'm looking forward to meeting everyone."

We parted with smiles. But I knew my eyes were cold. Yes, this would be a memorable evening. I would study the inhabitants of Ahiahi carefully indeed. I wanted to look hard at each and every one of them.

One smiling face masked a murderer's soul.

In my absence, a maid had unpacked my cases. I opened the closet and chose my black rayon-crepe dress with small white seabirds. I liked the oversized collar and ribbed sleeves. Dressy but resortish. I put the dress and lingerie on the bed. I slipped into the pale apricot terry-cloth robe hanging in the bath. I was leaning over to turn on the bathwater when I paused.

I turned back to the closet. Yes, my clothes were there. And I'd found my lingerie in the top drawer of the wicker chest. My purse sat on the chest.

But I didn't see my briefcase.

My carry-on and suitcase were in the corner. I checked. Both were empty. I tried the other drawers in the chest. Shorts, slacks, tees. No briefcase. It took only a moment to be certain. The briefcase was not in the suite.

My first impulse was to plunge out of my room, search. But I knew that was foolish. Wherever my papers were, they would not be easy to find. And I didn't dare invade the rooms of the other guests.

Or Belle's quarters.

The sense of menace I'd experienced on the lanai outside Belle's study was back in full force. I'd been right to feel an inimical spirit was near. It had been very near.

I walked to the open doorway, pushed the cream button. When the panel was shut, I pressed the red button. I moved to the lanai and pulled shut the louvered panels, slid the bolt shut.

Safe. And stuffy. I turned on the ceiling fans.

I checked the time. Twenty minutes to seven. I was bathed and dressed in ten minutes. Then I opened the door and the panels. I walked out on the lanai. I leaned against the railing, looking up at a sky spangled with stars so bright they looked like diamonds nestling against black velvet.

Anyone in the house could have gained access to my suite through the open threshold or through the lanai. Obviously Belle had not considered security a problem when building Ahiahi. After all, only her family, her guests, and her employees had entrée to this cliffside haven. The main entrance was barred to all outsiders and the rugged canyon and mountain ridges were inaccessible except to exceptionally hardy trespassers.

The theft of my briefcase meant that someone—one of a small number of persons—was very curious indeed about me. Could it be Belle herself? After all, she'd told her secretary to find out everything about me. Immediately.

Or the case might have been taken by my unknown correspondent. Or by someone else for some unknown purpose.

But, whatever the reason for the theft, the disappearance of the briefcase put me in a difficult position. It hadn't occurred to me to copy the poster about Richard. Now there was only my word that I'd ever received it. I could not prove its existence. And if I confessed to Belle that I'd forged a letter to gain entry here, why should she believe my tale about a poster?

Moreover, the briefcase contained my research about Belle and her family. What would anyone—especially Belle—make of that?

It didn't matter to my quest that the research was gone.

I had good reason to retain every fact, every nugget that might help me strip away the mask of a killer. I have a reporter's memory for detail. There was plenty of information available about Belle and her family, and I'd retrieved it.

I'd found dozens of photos of CeeCee that were carried after the story broke about her kidnapping: CeeCee dancing, riding her quarter horse, playing tennis, at a cotillion. But the one I liked best was an unstudied shot—obviously a photo taken by a friend—of CeeCee sitting by a fire. Dark hair cupped her narrow face. Her expression was thoughtful, pensive, and intense. Such a young face—unlined, carefree—and yet even in repose there was a clear indication of determination. Yes, I had a sense of CeeCee's appearance, even perhaps a tiny gauge to her character. I felt sure she'd been a complex young woman. There were other photos—CeeCee dancing after midnight, her face dreamy and sensuous—that seemed to confirm Gretchen's drawled comments.

I'd found photographs of them all, taken when they were society darlings, before heartbreak intruded.

Anders leading a march against cruelty to animals. Pointing toward a poster of a struggling cat strapped to an operating table, Anders had shouted, his narrow face twisted in disgust, his dark eyes glittering. Anders was as dark as his dead sister. But where her face had been thin and elegant, like Belle's, his features were almost unnaturally sharp and gaunt.

Joss dancing in the chorus line in a fraternity skit, a straw boater riding atop his curly blond hair, his good-natured face split by a huge grin.

Wheeler at a track meet, plunging through a tape, the winner in the 440. Bright red hair curled above a freckled, flushed face stretched in gut-wrenching effort. Strong, swift, confident, I would guess he excelled at many sports. His manner reminded me of a long-ago tennis player, Alex Olmedo.

Megan sweeping down a runway, elegant and aloof, in a swirling silver-beaded short evening dress. She was by far the most photogenic of all the Burkes and Gallaghers. A brilliantly successful international model, she split her time between New York and Paris. Tall, leggy, and blond, she looked more like Belle than her natural children. I wondered if she looked like her own mother, Quentin Gallagher's first wife. That would prove the old adage that men always marry the same kind of woman.

Gretchen jabbing a pitchfork into a mound of hay. Denim coveralls flopped on her thin body. She was more attractive in person than in photographs. The press hadn't managed to come up with very many of her. Perhaps she'd resented the notoriety.

The tabloids had loved it—six brothers and sisters, rich, good-looking, with an appetite for excitement and a history of immensely complicated rivalry.

Sometimes the teasing had gone too far.

Late one night a few years before the kidnapping, Wheeler had convinced Joss that the yacht on Lake Texoma had been hijacked. Joss jumped overboard without a life preserver, and it was touch and go whether he'd be found before he drowned.

Anders was especially gifted at computer snooping. He managed to get into Gretchen's college records and alter her transcript to all Fs, which she discovered when she applied for an internship with *Texas Monthly*.

Not to be outdone, Gretchen sent the uncompromisingly prim (and brunette) fiancée of Anders an altered photograph of him in bed with a buxom blond showgirl.

For Belle's fifty-fourth birthday, Joss arranged fifty-four pink plastic flamingos on the front lawn, causing sheer anguish on the part of their Highland Park neighbors. Joss had definitely taken to his new Southern background. Many of the flamingos had extra decorations: golf clubs, tennis rackets, ballet slippers, and Hook 'em Horns pennants. Joss was attending the University of Texas at the time.

Megan seemed to be the only one who apparently hadn't been involved, at least publicly, in some kind of hoax on her siblings.

CeeCee, of course, was always the target of great fun because of her April 1 birthday, and there was constant competition in the family for the most outrageous joke to play on her.

Joss was considered the all-time winner the year he placed CeeCee's name on several hundred religious-tract mailing lists and she was inundated with exhortations to bathe in the Blood of the Lamb from as far away as Zimbabwe. For months, earnest-faced women in plain blouses and dark skirts arrived at the Highland Park house hoping to talk with Sister Charmaine.

But on March 30, 1990, the laughter ended.

Yes, I knew a great deal about those who were here at Ahiahi. But not yet enough. Not nearly enough.

This would be unlike any puzzle I'd ever pursued. It was far too late to be concerned about alibis on the afternoon Richard fell or the purported whereabouts of Belle's family and staff when CeeCee disappeared. No. That had been the province of the police at the time, and it was too late by years to pinpoint comings and goings. My task was far more difficult and subtle and discreet.

I must cleverly and carefully pierce the social pretenses of those who were staying at Ahiahi. I must discover the truth of their souls.

I've always been good at features. Those are the stories that focus on personality rather than fact. Now it was time to use every scrap of skill I possessed for stakes far beyond any I'd ever imagined.

eight

Torches flared along the cliff railings. The flames were reflected in the shiny glaze of huge pottery vases that sat on pedestals at the top of the steps leading up to the lanais. I stood in the shadow of one of the Chinese vases on the lanai by the living-dining area. More light came from a long, narrow reflecting pool. Beams angled up through the water, luminous as moonlight in a tidal basin.

Identical wicker furniture, lamps, and sculptures were clustered the length of the living-dining area and on the lanai, the outdoors mirroring the indoors. The interior walls were covered with hand-painted tapa bark, decorated with designs that reminded me of stylized butterflies. There was an eclectic mix of Polynesian, Japanese, and Chinese artworks, including Tahitian fertility-god carvings, silk screens of Japanese calligraphy, and a Chinese scholar's rock on a teak base.

White wicker chairs with emerald-green cushions surrounded a huge pink marble dining room table. The odd combination of marble and wicker created a saucy air, like an elegant seaside hotel coupled with a jaunty carousel.

Voices melded in desultory conversation. I looked from face to face. Most of them I had yet to meet. But all their faces were familiar from my lost collection of clips: Belle's athletic husband, the surviving children and stepchildren, Anders Burke's wife. I had met Belle's man-of-all-work Lester Mackey and her secretary Elise Ford. And, of course, Stan Dugan, CeeCee's fiancé.

One of them was my enemy, mine and Belle's. One of them had killed Richard and kidnapped CeeCee. One face belonged to a murderer. I knew it. Belle did not. Once again I was swept with misgiving. But for this moment, I had to play the hand I held.

Belle stood near the reflecting pool, next to a bronze alligator with heavy-lidded malachite eyes. One hand tightly gripped the head of her cane. Her pale ivory dress had a rosy sheen in the crimson light from the torch. She was speaking in a low tone to her husband.

Standing near them was Elise Ford, alert and attentive, still the perfect secretary despite the social setting. She looked like a demure kindergarten teacher in a navy blue linen shirtwaist dress. I wondered if she was as circumspect as her choice of fashion indicated. Or if she simply liked plain and simple clothing. Or if it was her instinct to avoid notice. I wondered, too, if she'd discovered anything about me yet. More than likely she had. Computers with a modem make gathering information quick and easy.

From my vantage point I could see everyone. I noted the occasional sidelong glances toward Belle, the unnatural awareness of her on the part of her family and guests.

Her husband, Keith Scanlon, had a look of professional charm: bright eyes, plump cheeks, a broad smile. He was tanned and muscular, the epitome of the sporting man in his vivid Hawaiian shirt and white tropical trousers. He, too, was attentive and alert—and tense. The hands clasped behind his back gripped each other tightly even though his face was determinedly genial. Was it the purpose of this gathering that stressed him? Or the presence of Belle's family?

Anders Burke paced on the far side of the pool, talking rapidly and intently. He was as dark as his mother was fair. His narrow face was an exaggerated version of hers, his cheekbones too sharp, his chin too pointed. His eyes blazed with fervor. He gestured excitedly.

Watching Anders, an indulgent smile on her face, was Megan Gallagher, the middle child Belle had acquired from her short marriage to Quentin Gallagher. Megan looked like the model she was in a shirred pink-and-beige satin jacket and champagne satin trousers. One beautifully manicured hand toyed with an enameled button shaped like a recumbent lion. Her oval face was smooth, pretty, and empty. I was reminded irresistibly of a porcelain doll. Anybody home?

Peggy Burke, Anders's wife, watched him, too, her face creased in an uncertain frown, like a mother hen whose chick is perilously near the barnyard cat. She looked prim and unfashionable, her rose silk dress too vividly flowered and ill-fitting, but her passion for her husband was nakedly clear in that watchful gaze. And I never underestimate the power of passion.

Joss Burke, Belle's second son, sat at the grand piano near the fireplace. Strains of Cole Porter drifted on the night air. He played very well indeed. I wasn't surprised. I'd retrieved a half dozen pictures of him involved in student musicals while he was at the University of Texas. Absorbed and withdrawn, he stared down at the keys as if he were alone in the room. He wore a candy-striped shirt and white trousers. All he lacked was a white straw hat and a cane. And a smile.

Gretchen Gallagher leaned against the piano. Her short

black-and-white polka-dotted dress had a flouncy two-tiered skirt, perfect for a night of dancing. She sipped at a drink, her freckled face discontented. And mournful. Did the music—"Night and Day"—stir melancholy memories?

Wheeler Gallagher was busy at the bar, his sloe eyes intent, his sensuously handsome face remote, his red hair glistening like flame. His pale green Oxford shirt and white tropical trousers were a perfect foil for his coloring. He poured a jigger of amber whiskey into a tumbler, a commonplace act made special by the fluidity of his movements. Some men have extraordinary appeal; some men don't. Wheeler definitely did.

The last guest—the other surprise guest besides myself—was Stan Dugan.

I'd found out a lot about him before I visited his office. Dugan came from a working class background, making it through college and law school on scholarships and by holding down jobs that ranged from driving a cab to bartending. Tonight he combined a highly fashionable collarless dress shirt with Levi's and alligator cowboy boots, part Brooks Brothers, part rebellious outsider. He sprawled in a big easy chair sipping a drink, his owlish eyes studying his hostess and his fellow guests.

Lester Mackey stood alone in a shadowy niche next to an antique Venetian lantern, one hand loosely gripping the bright red lamppost. The eye was drawn to the ornate ironwork around the glass and the flickering glow of the candle. He was so slender and self-effacing, my glance almost passed him by. Was it deliberate that he chose one of the few areas in the room where his face could only dimly be seen?

It has been my experience that those who least seek the limelight often have the most interesting stories to tell, stories they are reluctant to yield.

Out of all this assemblage, I was abruptly the most curious about Lester Mackey, perhaps because I knew so little of him. I knew he'd been a military driver for Belle in Vietnam, had joined her household when his tour of duty ended, and had worked for her ever since. And I knew he had a soft voice and Johnnie Rodriguez's mother disliked him.

He seemed lost and lonely standing in the shadows, not a part of the evening, yet I had the sense he was utterly absorbed in this family gathering.

Just as I stood and surveyed the collection of guests, so did he, his eyes moving slowly from face to face as mine had. But he knew them all well. They had been a part of his life for decades, everyone but Stan Dugan.

I watched these people carefully because I was suspicious of them, seeking to discover a killer among them. What caused Lester Mackey to watch with equal concentration?

Lester Mackey. I had to talk to him.

It should have been an elegant and enticing party. Soft-footed maids glided in and out of the room, bringing dishes for a magnificent buffet along one wall. There was even an ice sculpture of a humpback whale.

The dining room table wasn't set, so I assumed the guests would sit in smaller groups at the tables scattered about the lanai. The reddish glow of the torches was supplemented by a full moon that bathed the lanai and the reflecting pool in silver. The small tables should encourage easier conversations.

I didn't think the casual seating would accomplish its goal. Wariness permeated this gathering. It was apparent in the carefully schooled faces, the uneasy glances, the bland conversations:

"... wish they'd rebuild that hotel. Don't you know it's full of rats and ..."

"... most of the hurricane damage is gone except ..."

"... interminable flight. Each time I swear I'm going to stop over in ..."

"... thinking about moving to Paris. It would be ..."

I looked again from face to face, all with social masks intact. Or nearly so. Anders looked gauchely intense. But I suspected that was his customary manner. Belle's husband was oddly ill at ease for a man who'd spent his life in a country-club setting. But there was no hint in any face of a marauding tiger. That's what I was looking for—the quick, feral willingness to destroy.

I'd traveled thousands of miles in response to a challenge. Someone wanted me at Ahiahi for an unknown purpose. And now I was here. I'd been uneasy ever since my encounter with Stan near Belle's office. When he left, I'd had such a strong sense of danger. When I returned to my room and discovered the briefcase was missing, I felt even more threatened. My feeling of discomfort increased as I stood watching, despite the beauty of the surroundings and the ostensible party setting. There was a dark purpose to my presence. I had to thwart that purpose. But I had no guidelines. Whom should I talk to? How could I learn the right facts quickly enough? Which might be the weakest link in this tension-filled family?

I stepped out onto the lanai.

Belle saw me at once. "Good evening, Henrie O." She clapped her hands. "Everyone, please." It was abruptly quiet, every eye on me. "I want to introduce Henrietta O'Dwyer Collins. You all remember Richard Collins, my old friend."

Keith Scanlon's eyes narrowed, his customary bonhomie was gone for an instant, supplanted by a flash of dislike. I knew instinctively the dislike was of Richard, his memory of Richard, the man Belle had turned to when CeeCee disappeared.

Belle's secretary looked at me curiously.

Anders flicked a dismissive glance toward me.

Peggy plucked at her husband's sleeve while flashing a bright smile.

Gretchen nodded, but her face still looked forlorn. And wary.

Joss studied me with cool blue eyes and lightly sounded introductory chords.

Wheeler lifted his glass, a cheerful gesture, but his eyes were thoughtful.

Stan Dugan watched me like a hawk spotting a mouse.

Megan glanced down at her perfectly manicured nails.

Lester Mackey's face was still in shadows. He stood very still. Unnaturally still.

Belle's light voice carried clearly. "I want everyone to give Henrie O a warm welcome. She'll be with us this week."

There was an instant of silence. Nothing was said of CeeCee's birthday. Or of Richard's fall.

But their images overlay the sumptuous room like the shadow of shifting leaves dappling a forest clearing, intangible but inescapable.

"Come, I want you to meet everyone." Belle was at my side. "My husband, Keith." Her hand lightly brushed his arm.

Keith Scanlon grinned and pumped my hand, seemingly with genuine warmth. "Do you play tennis, Mrs. Collins?"

"Yes. At a relaxed pace." No longer did I dart around a court. But I still had fun.

"I have a tennis academy. Near Poipu Beach. A lot of retirees play and they're always looking for a sub. You'll have to come down one day and I'll find you a game. Clay courts." He was like a cocker spaniel offering a ball.

I smiled. "I'd love it."

Belle gave him a fond glance.

As we moved away, his smile vanished. Belle was a step ahead of me and didn't notice.

"You've met Elise Ford," Belle said carelessly. "If you need any help"—Belle's glance was suddenly searching—"Elise can find out anything about anyone."

"Really. That's a useful skill."

Elise smiled pleasantly, but her gaze was avid.

Belle paused by the shadowy niche. "And you've met Lester. I don't know what we would do without Lester. He keeps us all in order."

Lester Mackey nodded at me. "Good evening, Mrs. Collins."

I wished the light were brighter. I wished I could see his face clearly. But Belle's hand was firm on my elbow. We stopped in front of Stan Dugan.

He came to his feet and suddenly everyone else in the room seemed small. "Hello, Mrs. Collins." His voice was deep and agreeable enough, but it had an underlying challenge in it.

I shook his massive hand. "Hello." So we were going to pretend we'd not met. That suited me. But I had a gut feeling I'd better not count on his silence. Could I pretend astonishment, deny having talked with him? How many lies could I tell with any hope of success?

Belle gave his muscular forearm a quick squeeze. "Stan and CeeCee were engaged."

Dugan's face was determinedly blank. Was the reserve there because he distrusted me? Or was it deeper, a reflection of continuing grief for CeeCee? Or did he resent Belle's tying him to a past that had ended?

"Stan's a trial lawyer. That's how he and CeeCee met." We moved toward Anders and his wife. "My son Anders."

There was pride in Belle's voice, but concern in her eyes.

Did she worry about what Anders might do or say at this moment? Or was her concern deeper, a mother's recognition of a child at peril for some reason?

Anders brushed back a lock of dark hair. "Hello, Mrs. Collins. Your husband worked for the wire services." His tone was almost contemptuous. Wasn't that odd for the son of one of America's most famous foreign correspondents?

"Sometimes. And so did I," I said lightly. "And for assorted newspapers. And we freelanced. What do you do, Anders?"

He looked at me proudly. "I fight dragons, Mrs. Collins. Not a game your husband played. Or you either, I guess." His gaze was pitying.

Dragons? What did this boy know about dragons? Richard escaped from Nazi-occupied France, but he parachuted back with American troops to cover the invasion. I could respond with a lifetime of Richard's achievements, but that wasn't—at this moment—the point.

"Everything's different now," Anders continued. "Back in the old days, the press was pretty much a toady to corporate America. But now environmental issues get the attention they deserve."

Ignorance can be amusing. I wondered if he'd ever heard of the greening of America, if he had any inkling of how powerful the press had been in convincing at least one generation that war was wrong and people were more important than profits. Or, more profoundly, if he grasped the inconstancy of the public. And the press. This year's darling can well be next year's pariah, and it is also true of causes. One year the press worries about the plight of loggers, the next it trumpets the possible extinction of a rare species.

I met his gaze. "I told the world about a lot of different kinds of America, Anders. And so did my husband. Jonas Salk. Birmingham and Bull Connor. Watts. The Challenger. Habitat for Humanity. The good and the bad." I refrained from pointing out that his mother's private fortune was very much the fruit of corporate America. And asking whether he liked being a rich woman's son with all the privileges that provided. I was still on my company manners. For the moment.

Anders gave me a condescending smile.

I smiled pleasantly in return though I understood exactly

how much pleasure it must give a terrier to take a rat by the throat and shake it.

Belle's gaze lingered on her son. She almost spoke to him, then, with a tiny shake of her head, she turned to his wife. Peggy's face mirrored Belle's uneasiness. Anders worried the women who loved him. Belle said briskly, "And this is Peggy, Anders's wife." She patted Peggy's hand. "CeeCee introduced Peggy to Anders."

"I'm so glad to meet you, Mrs. Collins." Peggy's voice was high and fluttery. I had a sudden picture of her at fifty, anxious and awkward. She wouldn't be much changed.

"And what do you do, Peggy?"

She looked surprised. And pleased. "I have an antique shop, Mrs. Collins."

So Peggy loved old and beautiful artifacts. And money, of course. Antiques require money.

I smiled and tucked another fact into my collection. Later I could sort through what I'd learned. But slowly, piece by piece, I was beginning to find out who these people were. And remembering—always remembering—that one of them was a murderer. I managed to keep on smiling.

Belle and I reached the piano. Joss still played softly.

Belle's face was suddenly pinched and weary. " 'September Song.' CeeCee loved it." She reached out, touched her son's shoulder. "My son Joss."

He dropped his hands to his lap. "Hello, Mrs. Collins." He started to rise.

"Please don't get up," I said quickly. "You play very well."

"Thank you. I enjoy it. I'm glad you do, too." He had all the charm his brother lacked.

"Joss is an actor," Belle said without expression.

I glanced at her. There was a definite tightness to her mouth.

"Sometimes." His good-humored mouth curved into a

wry smile. "Resting, at the moment. But available. I do soaps, television movies, big screen, stage. Whatever. I'm for hire."

I smiled in return. "It's a tough life."

Belle touched his shoulder. "Joss is also a wonderful writer. I'm trying to persuade him to come here. I can't think of a better place for a writer to live."

"Not this writer, Mom." He said it nicely, but his voice was determined. The blue eyes that gazed up at her held a mixture of defiance and sadness.

"Nobody who's alive would want to *live* here." Then Gretchen clasped a hand over her mouth.

Belle drew her breath in sharply.

Wheeler came out from behind the bar. "Stuff a sock in your mouth, sis. And no more Mai Tais. How about you, Mrs. Collins? Let me fix you an island special." He grinned at Belle. "Gretchen and I met Mrs. Collins at—" He paused for just an instant. "—near the tennis courts this afternoon." He waved toward the bar. "One of my dad's legacies. I can mix drinks better than a licensed bartender. Coco locos, fog cutters, scorpions. Name your poison."

"I'll take pineapple juice." I stepped to the bar. "How about pineapple juice and ginger ale. With a squirt of orange juice and a squeeze of lemon."

"Coming right up. I can even garnish it with an orchid." He opened the refrigerator, picked out containers of juices.

"Wheeler, I have a lei for Mrs. Collins. On the top shelf of the refrigerator." Belle smiled, but there was so little life and pleasure in that smile.

"Sure. Here we are." He lifted out a lovely plumeria lei and handed it to his stepmother.

Belle slipped the fragrant wreath over my head. "Aloha." Her musical voice made a lovely word even lovelier.

"Thank you." I touched the cool petals. Welcome to paradise.

"There's a lei for Megan, too." Belle held out her hand.

He handed his stepmother the second lei, and Belle smiled her thanks.

Wheeler swiftly splashed juices into a tall frosted glass.

Megan sauntered gracefully toward us. "For me, too?" There was a childlike pleasure in her voice as Belle dropped the lei lightly onto her shoulders. "Thank you, Belle."

"Of course." Belle brushed back a strand of Megan's lovely hair.

They stood close together, the young woman and the old, and I was once again struck by their resemblance—both fine-featured, both silver-blond, both tall and willowy.

Belle slipped an arm around her stepdaughter's thin shoulders. "Megan is our exotic creature. She's a model and spends her time in New York and Paris."

"That sounds very exciting." I smiled.

Megan's perfect brows arched. "Oh, people think so. But it can be very tiring. And I get *so* hungry."

"Then eat," Gretchen said crisply. She was standing near the buffet. She picked up a shrimp ball and poked it into a pink sauce.

Megan sighed. "I never get to eat. Carrots. And club soda. But they pay me very well."

There was an odd silence.

Belle looked at her in concern. "Megan, you aren't starving yourself?"

For an instant, something dark and angry stirred in the model's deep blue eyes. "Of *course* I am, Belle. All models starve." She held up one slim arm and it was simply a bone sheathed in skin, a Picasso-like rendition of a limb.

Belle stepped back, looked Megan up and down. "I won't have it. You certainly don't have to do that."

"I don't have to. But I will." Her vivid eyes flicked around the room, pausing just for an instant on each face in turn. "I"—and there was a marked emphasis on the pronoun—"don't have to ask anyone for anything. Ever."

Belle started to speak, then, her face stiff, turned away.

Wheeler looked amused. He darted a sardonic glance at his sister, then picked up a swizzle stick and twirled it in a tall frosted glass. "Here you are, Mrs. Collins."

There was a sudden babel of conversation.

A tiny smile of satisfaction curved Megan's perfect lips.

I looked at her with more interest. Yes, indeed, somebody was home. That would teach me—once again—never to succumb to first impressions. Or be swayed by stereotypes.

Anders gave a hoot of laughter. "Looking for a halo, Megan? They're in short supply around here. But you have a lei. That may not please you, though. Did you know plumerias were first planted around cemeteries? So plumeria's called the graveyard tree. And white means death, too."

Belle was shaking her head. "It's the Japanese who associate white with death, Anders. Not Hawaiians. Plumerias are very popular for leis."

Megan reached up and stroked the delicate blooms. "I don't know about you, Anders, but I'm not superstitious."

"Don't tease Megan," Peggy said quickly.

"Oh, I'm not teasing," Anders said softly.

Megan crossed to her stepbrother and swiftly dropped the lei over his head. "It's just the thing for you, Anders. Enjoy it."

Anders reached up. His hand closed tightly around the blossoms, crushing them, then he shrugged.

"That's enough, you two." Belle waved toward the buffet. "Come now, let's have dinner."

And what a delicious dinner it was: dainty steamed meat dumplings, egg rolls, and shrimp balls to dip in plum-brandy sauce; sea bass with pine nuts; spareribs with black bean sauce; bean sprouts and peppers; cauliflower with water chestnuts and mushrooms; and baked papaya.

I filled my plate with a sampling, not too much of any one food. I was more interested in the company. I took my time finding a seat, pausing to admire a spectacular flower arrangement with a half dozen bird-of-paradise flowers. So I ended up at a table with Joss, Anders, and Peggy.

Joss set out to charm us.

"... could have happened to somebody in a situation comedy. But this was real life!"

Peggy and I looked expectant.

"Not very real," Anders muttered. He made a little pile of water chestnuts, then began to eat one after the other, crunch, crunch, crunch. The sweet-scented lei still hung from his shoulders.

Joss smiled at the ladies, ignored his brother. "I was on 101 and the traffic was snout to butt and we kept stopping. And stopping. I tried to make a couple of calls, but the static was busier than a porno site on the net."

Peggy's eyes widened.

Joss grinned at her. "Kitten, it's a big bad world out there." His drawl was deliberately provocative. "Anyway, there I was, stalled. I don't like to waste time. So I decided to work on my lines for an audition the next day. Can't get in trouble for that. Right?" He paused for dramatic effect.

Anders rolled his eyes. "Joss, don't you ever make yourself want to puke?"

But Peggy and I watched attentively. We were a good audience.

Joss flipped up the collar of his sports shirt, mussed his hair so that a thick blond strand fell across his forehead, jutted his face forward.

It was generations ago but I wondered if Joss had ever heard of Richard Widmark, once the Hollywood king of menace. There was that same aura of horror about to happen, made doubly horrific because of Widmark's gentlemanly appearance, as befitted a one-time English professor.

"I got you now. You won't get away from me. Not ever," Joss growled. "See this knife?" He raised his hand and a knife glittered. It was only a table knife, but he seemed a deadly figure of menace. It was the look in his eyes, the tautness of his muscles, the way his fingers gripped the knife, held it aloft, as if at any moment it might flash down in a violent arc.

"Ooooh," Peggy shivered.

Joss's face was suddenly transformed, a merry gaze, a brilliant smile. "Nice, huh?" His satisfaction was open and charming.

"Very good. But on the freeway—" I prompted.

"Never again on the freeway. Believe me. There I was. Practicing. Not bothering anybody. And there's this gorgeous gal in a red Porsche, stopped right next to me. And you know what she did?"

"Called the cops on her mobile phone." Anders sounded bored.

That didn't bother Joss. "Damned if she didn't," Joss agreed. "Guess her model was pricier. No static. Anyway, the next exit a shitload of cop cars came on and I spent two hours at a substation asking them for Christ's sake to look at my script! But all they wanted to talk about was the bone-handled hunting knife I'd been brandishing." He leaned forward, his scowl pugnacious, jabbing a forefinger. " 'All right, buddy, explain this knife. What's this knife *for*?' " He straightened his collar, returned the knife to his plate. "Can I help it if I like good props?"

"And good food and good whiskey and *no*-good women," Anders muttered, pushing back his plate. He'd eaten very little. All the water chestnuts.

Joss scooped out a spoonful of mashed papaya. "Anders, go soak your head. It might improve your outlook on life. We're all sorry for the little kitties and doggies who don't have homes, but somehow we bear up."

"At least I know what real life's all about." Anders's voice was hard-edged.

Joss clapped his hand to his heart. "Oh, poor me. Lost in the canyons of Hollywood, adrift on a sea of celluloid."

"And enjoying every minute," I observed.

He grinned. "You bet I am."

"Now, Joss, it's fine for you to do what you want to do, but you have to admit that Anders's efforts for animal rights have made a huge difference," Peggy said earnestly. "Why, there was an article all about him in *Time*."

I finished my last bite of cauliflower, savoring the faint seasoning of soy sauce. It seemed to me that Peggy's comment didn't need an answer. Instead, I looked at Joss. "How long have you lived in Hollywood?"

Just for an instant, fine lines creased the corners of Joss's eyes. He looked much older. "Several years."

The maid deftly removed our plates and offered us coffee. I shook my head.

"Several years," Anders mimicked. He put two heaping teaspoons of sugar in his coffee. "Now you can come closer than that, bro. How about you dumped Janet and hit the road the week after CeeCee died."

Joss's eyes were cold and hard. "You never quite have your facts right, Anders. For the record, Janet dumped me. And it's been a while."

Peggy squirmed in her chair, bent close to me, and whispered, not very adroitly, "Janet was Joss's wife."

Anders watched the steam rise from his coffee like a diviner studying a portent. "Yeah, after CeeCee died, everybody got to do what they wanted to do, go wherever they wanted to go. Belle had a guilt trip. She'd pretty well kept us around in Dallas—working for the foundation. Of course, she meant it for the best. But after CeeCee was gone, Belle let everybody do what they wanted to do. Joss headed straight to Hollywood and Gretchen to D.C. and Megan to New York and Wheeler to Seattle."

I had most of them pretty well assorted in my mind at

this point. Joss was an actor, Gretchen a writer, Megan a model. "What does Wheeler do?"

For the first time, Anders looked genuinely amused. "Oh, he has a sailing sloop and takes out charters. Tough duty, right?"

"And you, Anders?" I asked.

"I stayed in Dallas. Somebody had to take over the foundation. I was elected." He tried to sound casual, but he couldn't suppress his satisfaction.

"Anders." Peggy's voice was anguished.

Anders ignored his wife, just as he ignored anything that wasn't connected to the passion of his life, protection of animals and the environment.

There was no trace of the charming, ebullient Joss when he looked levelly at his brother. "You're a fool, Anders."

Anders looked dourly from Joss to me. "Am I?" He shoved back his chair, stood. He raised his voice a little. "I thought Mrs. Collins might like a little truth in packaging. Even if it isn't her usual beat."

The other diners looked toward us.

"What is your usual beat, Mrs. Collins?" Elise Ford's voice was smooth, polite. She stood near our table, a shawl over one arm.

"I'm between projects right now."

The silence lasted just an instant too long and I was aware of a wave of malignity. I looked searchingly at each of them in turn, but all I saw were inquiring expressions.

Elise raised an eyebrow. "Do you intend to write another true-crime book soon?" She lifted her voice. The words carried clearly across the lanai. She reached Belle, held out the fleecy white wrap.

Belle slipped the shawl around her shoulders. She, too, looked toward me, her face clear and cold in the moonlight like marble statuary in a garden.

So Elise had indeed been busy this afternoon. I supposed

Belle now had my entire dossier. Had that seemingly innocent question been planned by the two of them?

I pushed back my chair and stood. "I've written one true-crime book. Several years ago. But at the moment I'm between projects. I'm looking forward to learning more about this lovely island. And getting to know all of you." I smiled. "It's been a fascinating evening. Good night." I didn't mind leaving the party early.

Let them wonder if there was a fox in the chicken coop.

nine

I wasn't going to bed. I had other plans. It took me only a few minutes to reach my room and change into a navy pull-over—the mountain air was crisp and cool—and dark slacks and sneakers. I waited on my lanai, watching the shadows of the valley change shape as clouds drifted across the moon. I wanted to plunge into the night now, to wrest facts from fancies, but I had to be patient and give Lester Mackey time to reach his quarters.

I felt pressed. It was like driving on a torturous mountain road with a heavy truck crowding too close behind. A sense of imminent danger flashed deep in my mind like a beacon on a foggy night. I felt an unaccustomed lack of control, although I am old enough and, I hope, wise enough to know that any semblance of control is illusory. At best, we can control our responses to a world often chaotic and fortuitous. But I am also old enough and wise enough to heed inner warnings. I wondered whether my fear—and fear it was—

sprang from my awareness of the undercurrents swirling about the dining room or from that wave of malignity I'd sensed so keenly at the last. Uneasiness consumed me, yet I was in a wild hurry. I had to discover the hidden design before it was too late.

Too late for what?

Why, why, why was I here?

I paced like a caged beast until the swaths of light falling from the lanais into the valley one by one disappeared. Finally, it was dark and quiet, only the torches on the lanais flickering against the velvet of the night.

I felt as though I'd burst free from chains when I climbed down the steps from my lanai to the narrow path.

I always travel with a pocket flashlight. I carried it with me, but the intermittent lighting along the path and the wands of fire from the torches gave sufficient illumination. I was glad. I didn't want a bobbing light to attract attention. It would be difficult to explain this late-night excursion.

I stepped carefully. In hiking parlance, this was an exposed trail. A misstep could be fatal.

I reached the path beneath the dining room. I stopped still when I heard the music. I supposed it was Joss, once again at the piano. Now he played "Star Dust." I was transported across the world to a nightclub in Hong Kong when Richard came back from Vietnam. We danced, his arms tightly around me. I rested my head on his shoulder. I didn't want the moment or the music ever to end. I could feel the beat of his heart through his jacket, steady, strong. Alive.

A bird cawed, for an instant drowning out the song. I looked down. But I couldn't see the drop in the darkness. Or the kukui trees where it all ended for Richard. Somehow I moved forward. I hated to leave behind the familiar notes. I wanted to cling to them because they brought Richard back, if only for a moment.

I felt dreadfully alone when I curved around the bluff. I

reached the stairs leading up to the kitchen area and edged up the steps. No torches flared on this lanai. I slipped quietly up the passageway, alert for any sound or movement. I darted into the garden, sought refuge in the deep shadow of a koa tree. I paused, smelling the sweet fragrance of its pollen, and looked around the shadowy garden. The only movement was the rustle of the shrubbery in the breeze.

I stepped cautiously on the crushed-shell path, moved around a thicket of bamboo. Lester Mackey's quarters were straight ahead. His lanai was softly lit. I saw a dark shape in a chair. A cigarette glowed. The acrid smell overlay the sweet scents of the garden.

I reached his lanai. Mackey was slumped in a wicker chair. Beside him on a small table was a half-full whiskey tumbler and a pint bottle. I didn't wait for an invitation. I pulled a wicker chair close to him.

The moon spilled out from behind a cloud. The silvery light smoothed out the anxious lines in his face, made him look young, and I knew I had a glimpse of him as he'd appeared when he and Belle first met.

"You go back a long way with Belle." My tone was easy, friendly.

"Yeah. Yeah, I do." His tone was guarded.

"You were her driver in 'Nam?"

He stubbed out his cigarette. "I don't talk about 'Nam."

A cloud slid over the moon. It was suddenly dark, but not a comfortable dark.

I pressed. "Why not?"

He splashed more whiskey in his glass. "Are you a fool, lady?"

"Were you wounded?"

He took a deep drink, held the glass. "I don't talk about 'Nam."

"What did you hate? The Vietcong?"

"I'd take the Vietcong over—" He stopped abruptly.

"What happened to you?" Something ugly, something dark, and he carried the scar within him.

He drank again, emptying the glass. "You writing a book?" The words were ever so faintly slurred.

"Not right now." Equivocal. Deliberately so.

"Everybody thinks you are." He picked up the pint, emptied it into the glass.

"People can think what they want to." I hoped it worried the hell out of them.

"A book about CeeCee's kidnapping." There was no mistaking the tension in his voice.

"Richard came here to talk to you about what happened to CeeCee." I spoke with utter authority.

Once again Mackey was rigidly still, just as he'd stood in the shadows at dinner. But he wasn't going to escape me.

"There's more to what happened at the lake than has ever been revealed." God, how I wished his face were clear again in the moonlight. "Richard told you what Johnnie Rodriguez said."

The evening breeze rustled the shrubbery.

"No, he didn't." His denial was swift, harsh. "He asked me if I saw anybody that night at the lake when I found CeeCee's car. That's all."

So Richard indeed talked to Mackey before he died. It was like winning the pot at poker. I'd come all this way, wondering, hoping, uncertain. Now I knew. Richard had faced this man with the knowledge he'd gained from Johnnie Rodriguez. Whatever had happened existed in the recesses of this man's mind.

I was close, so damned close. "What did you tell Richard?"

"I saw nobody." But Mackey pressed his hands over his face for a long moment. When his hands dropped, he gave a ragged sigh.

He was lying to me. I was sure of it. I wanted to grab his thin shoulders, shake them, demand the truth.

"But Richard told you he'd talked to Johnnie Rodriguez, didn't he?" I demanded.

"No. He didn't say anything about that." The answer again was swift. And such a lie. Richard came to Kauai because of what he'd learned from Johnnie Rodriguez. Lester Mackey and Johnnie Rodriguez were together that evening between six and seven o'clock, the time when CeeCee Burke disappeared.

I've asked thousands of questions, listened to thousands of answers—from cops and crooks, from politicians and movie stars, from ordinary people and not-so-ordinary people. I've been lied to a lot. I won't say I can always spot a liar, but I knew Lester Mackey was lying.

"You *said* you found CeeCee's car. What really happened, Mr. Mackey?" I punched on the flashlight.

The beam caught him for an instant, sharp as a pinned butterfly, his pale blue eyes squinting in protest, his thin face strained and wary, a trace of tears on his lined cheeks. All right, dammit. He still grieved for CeeCee. Or too much whiskey made him tearful. But he was a liar and I was going to know the truth. I kept the beam on his face. "You and Johnnie Rodriguez hung out together."

He crooked his arm in front of his face, shielded his eyes. "He worked for me."

I lowered the light, just a little. "Johnnie's mother didn't like it. Why?"

He made no answer. His eyes fell.

"Was Johnnie handsome?" I asked gently.

"It wasn't anybody's business." But he didn't look at me.

"No. I don't suppose it was. You and Johnnie. Except that night it's my business. It's everybody's business. You and Johnnie together. What did you see? What do you know? It was still early—six o'clock, wasn't it?—when you said you found CeeCee's car. What did you and Johnnie do between six and seven? Where were you, Mr. Mackey?"

"We were getting stuff ready for the party. Just like we always told everybody." His voice was blustery, but thin. He frowned. "Johnnie's mother. You talked to her? And to Johnnie?"

The night air was cool, but his second question was even more chilling.

"Oh, no. No, I didn't talk to Johnnie."

"Why not? He'll tell you. Same as I have." But he watched me so closely.

"I'd talk to Johnnie if I could, Mr. Mackey. Johnnie knew something about the kidnapping. I know that. But I can't talk to Johnnie." I waited, stared at him. "Johnnie's dead, Mr. Mackey. They say"—I spoke quite clearly—"that Johnnie was drunk and fell off his pier. He drowned."

"When?" Mackey's voice was deep in his throat.

"A couple of weeks after Richard fell from the trail here."

The breeze rustled in the trees, a forlorn and lonely sound.

"Johnnie's dead. Richard's dead. Tell me what you know, Mr. Mackey. For God's sake, tell me!" It was a demand and a plea.

"Johnnie . . . I never thought . . ." He pushed to his feet, turned away.

"Mr. Mackey—"

But he kept on going.

As I watched, he entered his quarters and the louvered shutters closed. The sound of the bolt was loud. And final.

I walked slowly along the path, reaching the garden in front of the house. It was late enough now that the house lay quiet, the dining room empty, only an occasional light left on in the string of lovely rooms. I walked softly, noiseless in my sneakers.

Sibilant whispers sounded over the silken rustle of the wind-stirred shrubbery. I stopped, listened. Why should anyone whisper? Whispers indicate stealth. Whispers also indicate private conversations. I hesitated. But I was not simply a guest enjoying a holiday weekend. So I stepped even more lightly and cautiously came around a bend in the path.

There were no lights here, but in the silver glow of the moon I saw a man and a woman standing close together in a heavy shadow near a clump of ti shrubs. Body language shouts. Both leaned forward, their bodies as tense and hostile as boxers squared off in a match. She spoke, her whisper a whistling hiss. He kept shaking his head, bullish, impervious, dismissive.

I wished I knew the geography of the garden better. Did the path continue past these shrubs, curving back into the main part of the garden? Or was this a quiet dead end, a carefully chosen spot for this angry encounter?

There was no way I could approach any closer without being seen. And I wanted very much to know who these combatants were. I carefully retraced my steps until I found a multi-trunked jacaranda. I slipped between trunks and settled down to wait.

It wasn't long. Hurried footsteps sounded. Keith Scanlon passed so close to me I could have reached out and touched him.

I wondered what Belle Ericcson would have thought had she seen her husband's face in the moonlight. There was no trace of the evening's genial host. He stared straight ahead, his face furrowed in a tight frown.

I stayed hidden. But no one else came around the curve. I waited a moment, but there was no sound, no telltale crunch of footsteps. I moved quickly. The path did indeed skirt the ti shrubs, leading back to the central part of the garden.

I reached the tiled walkway near the dining room. I saw

no one. I had no idea who had quarreled with Keith Scanlon. But I could be sure of one fact. It wasn't his wife.

Keith Scanlon had been a welcoming host, though somewhat ill at ease. I'd wondered why. Now I really wondered. I'd observed an impassioned encounter. What was the cause? And with whom did Keith Scanlon have such an intimate, angry relationship? What made it necessary for this clandestine meeting? Was the woman he met one of the family? That would be very interesting indeed.

Click. Click.

I stopped by the open archway to the game room.

There was no mistaking the huge figure of Stan Dugan bent over the pool table. He moved the cue with swift accuracy, caroming a ball into a side pocket.

I came up beside him.

He flicked me a cool glance. He chalked his cue, aimed, another ball rolled into a corner pocket. The unsparing light above the pool table revealed every aspect of his blunt-featured face: the deep-socketed eyes, the hawkish nose, the seamed skin, the determined mouth.

"All right. You've made it clear. You're a tough son of a bitch." I gave him a level look and tossed a question that I hoped might surprise him. "Is that why CeeCee fell in love with you?"

The last ball rolled silently into a pocket.

Dugan placed the cue in the rack, his face stern. I thought his reserve was going to hold, that I was up against a bedrock suspicion I couldn't disarm. Then a fleeting smile touched his lips. "I never asked her." He leaned against the pool table, folded his arms. "She never said."

"You loved her?" A bald question, but I asked because I had to know.

A hot, angry light flickered for a moment in his cold eyes,

then it was gone. "What the hell difference does it make to you, lady?"

I'd touched him on the raw. Maybe that told me what I needed to know. "Mr. Dugan, stop fighting me. We're on the same side. I want to know who killed CeeCee. So do you. That's why you came here, isn't it?"

His big hands balled into fists, then, slowly, he loosed them. "That's why *I* came, Mrs. Collins. But how about you? Are you here looking for a killer? Or looking for a way to make big bucks, write a book that will put you on easy street forever?"

"I'm looking for facts that will lead me to a killer. If I can get those facts by pretending to be writing a book, yes, I'll pretend." My voice was harsh. "I will do whatever I have to do, Mr. Dugan, but I am going to find out the truth. And I want you to help me."

We stared at each other.

I know what Dugan saw, an older woman with dark hair touched with silver and dark eyes that have seen much and remembered much in almost a half century of delving for facts.

I saw a big, powerful, arrogant, bereft young man.

Perhaps bereft.

But beneath my entreaty to him throbbed my own suspicions. I know how the face of love can be marred by jealousy, by unfaithfulness, by so many twisted emotions. I was seeking his help, but remembering all the while that so often the truth of murder can be found in the darkness of a lover's heart.

I would look at Stan Dugan just as closely as I would look at every inhabitant of this house. But now I smiled at him, held out my hand.

His huge hand briefly gripped mine. "All right. What do you want from me?"

"Tell me about the family." Yes, I'd begun to learn about them, but I needed to know more, so much more.

His gaze swung toward a gallery of photographs on the wall near the wet bar. He walked over to the bar, got down a couple of glasses. "Nightcap?"

I followed him. "Sure."

"Whiskey? Beer?"

"Club soda's fine."

He fixed himself a stiff Scotch with a dash of club soda, poured soda for me. As he handed me my glass, he looked again at the gallery.

"Mama Belle at the top," he observed. "Three Burkes to her right, three Gallaghers to her left. As for Keith, there's one of him in a bottom row of candid shots. But it's always the lead dog that sets the pace."

"And?" I prompted.

"Funny. Belle kind of likes me. So the rest of the clan treats me nicely even though they'd be horrified if they had to take me to lunch at the country club."

"You don't like them." The club soda was tart and refreshing.

Dugan rolled the whiskey in his mouth. "Not a matter of liking them. They don't matter."

His arrogance was chilling.

"Only Belle matters in this family. Quite a woman. Sure, she was born on third base, but she's a hell of a player. So was CeeCee. The rest of them? Also-rans."

"They don't matter?" The soda didn't wash away the odd taste in my mouth.

"Not to me. Anders worries more about animals than people. He agonizes over the plight of the lowland gorilla. Inner-city kids—so who gives a damn? Strange priorities. Joss worships at the throne of his almighty self, but CeeCee liked him."

"What about the Gallaghers?" They'd been young when

their father married Belle: Gretchen not quite ten, Megan eleven, Wheeler the oldest at seventeen.

"Ah, yes." His tone was sardonic. "The Gallaghers. Kind of like winning the sweeps when your old man marries a very rich woman. And one thing you have to say about Belle, she's generous. I'd say the Gallaghers lucked out. Even if it rubs Gretchen raw."

I looked up at a riot of red curls and freckled skin and bright hazel eyes. "Gretchen doesn't like money?"

"Oh, Gretchen loves money well enough." Dugan's grin was wry. "Actually, Mrs. Collins, I've not met too many people who don't like money. Last one might have been a nun. Nope, Gretchen keeps her greedy little paw extended for Belle's largesse. But she's never forgiven Belle for her dad's death. Belle was throwing a party that night, insisted he get the hell home for it. And the car went through the guardrails into the Potomac. CeeCee told me all about it. 'Course the fact that Gallagher was drunker than a Tammany politician on election night seems to go right over Gretchen's little red head. Small item of personal responsibility. But Gretchen welcomes those checks from home just the same. Now"—he leaned against the bar, sipped at his drink—"there's one Gallagher who's willing to go the distance by herself."

I nodded. "Megan."

"But something's bubbling behind that pretty face. Something not very pretty." The ice tinkled in his glass.

Megan had taken me by surprise at dinner. I wouldn't dismiss her again as simply a pretty face.

"How about Wheeler?"

Dugan's smile was derisive. "TFB, courtesy of Belle."

I looked at him inquiringly. "TFB?"

"Trust fund baby. The Burkes, of course, are both TFB and TGR."

"TGR?" I'm always willing to learn.

"Third generation rich. That, Mrs. Collins, says it all. But

TFB status is plenty good enough for Wheeler. He's high maintenance and he expects Belle to pick up the bills." Dugan downed the rest of his drink. "The only one worth a damn was CeeCee."

"Interesting," I said quietly.

Dugan's gaze was thoughtful. "Funny you should show up with the idea somebody in the family was behind the kidnapping. I've thought so for a long time."

I hadn't expected this. "For God's sake, what do you know?" I tried to keep calm. Did he have facts, something that would lead me to a specific person?

He gave me a bleak stare. "I'm not a criminal lawyer, Mrs. Collins. But I know some. And they have contacts nobody else can tap. Not the cops, not the feds. After CeeCee's body was found, I asked them to scrape around. Word gets out on the street. You know what they came up with?"

I waited, my eyes never leaving his blunt, aggressive face.

"Nothing." The word was light as silk. It floated between us like a strand from a spider's web. "Nothing." He kneaded his cheek with a huge fist. "I hired a private detective. Toby Karim. No great brains, but Toby can sniff around better than a hound after coons. Will it surprise you when I tell you that Toby found nothing?" Dugan leaned forward, his massive face predatory. "You know what that tells me?"

"No, Mr. Dugan. What does it tell you?"

"That there wasn't anything to find in the bars or coke houses or gambling joints. This wasn't a kidnapping planned by small-time—or big-time—crooks. This wasn't planned by an outsider."

He folded his arms tight. His cold, angry eyes challenged me.

I needed to remember that this man was a master of expression, that he knew when to frown and when to smile and when to soften—or harden—his voice as he leaned close to the jury box.

"Did the police explore this possibility?"

"Oh, yeah. They looked at everything. But somebody was clever, Mrs. Collins. Somebody was very, very clever."

He looked up at the gallery of photographs. The expression on his face was an interesting compound of suspicion, dislike, and ruthlessness.

Light has good connotations. It can spell warmth, safety, relief.

The light at the end of the tunnel.

Let your light so shine before men . . .

Light of my life.

But the light spilling out in a great golden swath from the open doorway to my suite scared the hell out of me.

I'd left a small lamp burning. Nothing more. Certainly not every light in the place.

I approached slowly on the walkway. Twenty yards away I stopped. I had no weapon unless the small flashlight in my pocket could be used as one. Moreover, whomever I might face—should there be someone in my rooms—would surely be much younger and much stronger than I.

I stared at the light.

I almost turned back to seek an escort from Stan Dugan. But I didn't want him to think his new confederate was cowardly. Or foolish.

Of course, it would be infinitely preferable to be embarrassed than to be dead.

Light . . .

Murderers move in darkness. Evil thrives in secret. It would take an odd turn of mind to wait in ambush in a flood of light.

Yet, I approached the doorway carefully, ready to whirl and run. And shout. And I grasped the flashlight to use as a truncheon.

Every light in the little living room was on. The overhead light glowed in the bedroom. The lights on the lanai blazed.

It was easy to see the larger rooms at a glance. No one awaited me. I checked the bathroom, the closet, the lanai. There was no trace of a visitor, other than the fact of the lights.

I was tired. I'd matched wits at dinner, confronted Lester Mackey, dueled with Stan Dugan. That could account for my visceral sense of danger.

But I couldn't deny the lights. And it would be absurd to attribute this flood of illumination to the result of a visit by a housemaid.

Not all the lights.

No. And though perhaps I could attribute the deep feeling of malignity to my fatigue, I was careful to close and lock the front panel and to shut and bolt the louvers. All the while I prepared for bed—but how could I sleep, even though I must sleep?—I continued to wonder what the visit signaled.

I was walking to the bed when I stopped and stared.

The spread was rumpled over the pillows.

Slowly, I reached down, yanked back the cover.

My throat closed tight. My chest ached.

There wasn't much blood. But then bats are small creatures. The little dead animal, its neck broken, looked pitiful rather than horrific.

But the act was ugly. The intention ugly.

And yes, I was frightened. I knew this was a warning, a clear announcement that I should leave, desist, withdraw.

And if I didn't?

Richard fell hideously. I didn't want to die. Not like that. Not at all. So the bat succeeded in its objective. Yes. I was frightened.

And yet, I could not leave.

I would not leave.

ten

I stood on the edge of my lanai. Mist obscured the tumbling falls, though I could hear their unceasing roar, rather like the muted rumble of a subway beneath city pavement. Closer at hand, a curious noise sounded. It took me back more than a half century to a Kansas plain and the squeak of the rusty hinge on the wooden door of the storm cellar. The sound came again, closer. I looked down and saw a brilliantly red bird with a salmon-colored hooked bill.

Squeak. Squeak.

"Good morning," I said in turn.

The bird launched in flight and for an instant was a spectacular streak of flame against the dense green of the canyon wall.

I couldn't see the valley floor because of the pools of thick mist, but the first tendrils of sunrise were curling over the top of the mountain, orange and red, mauve and apricot, gold and rose, colors more vivid than a shower of jewels.

CeeCee Burke found this rugged mountain ridge the loveliest place she'd ever been. I wished I could relinquish myself to beauty, shed cares and worries and grief. Perhaps that day would come. But not yet.

I draped a sweater over my shoulders. This morning I chose to go through the main garden. Although the cliff path ran well below the individual lanais, I didn't want to disturb those still sleeping.

Sunlight splashed in pools of gold in the huge living-dining area. I walked through to the lanai and the scattered tables around the reflecting pool. Only one small table was occupied. Keith Scanlon and Anders Burke looked up. Scanlon greeted me cheerfully. In his tennis whites he looked trim and muscular. Anders lowered his newspaper for an instant, murmured, "Morning," then resumed reading. He looked slight even in a bulky cotton sweater and baggy jeans.

Once again there was a bountiful buffet. I must confess to a great fondness for bacon and eggs. I added two pineapple fritters to my plate.

Scanlon and Anders stood as I neared the table.

"Please." I waved my hand.

They sat down, and I joined them.

Scanlon poured coffee all around. He and I made desultory conversation—the possibility of rain in the afternoon, the leader in the golf tournament underway on Maui, the best time of day to visit Waimea Canyon.

Anders was absorbed in the morning paper, though he rattled it hard once, peered at us, and announced in disgust, "Some fools still want to feed the dolphins." But he submerged himself in the newspaper again before either of us could answer.

Scanlon finished his coffee and pushed back his chair. "Will you come down for some tennis this morning?"

"Yes, yes, I'll definitely do that." I wanted to see him away from Ahiahi, talk to him on his own turf.

He sketched a quick map, while proudly describing his complex. "You can't miss it."

He moved away with a bounce in his step, a man obviously on his way to work he loved. Interesting. The easy assumption would be that he married Belle for her money. But equally obviously he didn't mind working, preferred to work. Certainly he didn't have to. So, did he marry Belle for love? Fascination? Excitement?

Anders put down his paper, piled jam on a croissant.

When the sound of Scanlon's footsteps had faded away, I turned to Anders. "What are you working on now, Anders?"

"Do you really want to know?" It was a challenge. He didn't believe in polite inquiries; he wasn't going to respond to one.

"Yes. Actually, I really do." I smiled at him.

"Why?" He cocked his head to one side, studied me as he might an unfamiliar life form.

"I always want to know all about everyone I meet." Yes, I did. I loved playing out the line and the thrill of discovery when someone answered me without pretense. Every human being has a story and every story is fascinating.

His eyes creased in puzzlement. "For God's sake, why?"

"Why do you care about animals?"

It was the right question and the wrong question. He unleashed such a flood of impassioned rhetoric that I had plenty of time to finish my breakfast and pour more coffee.

". . . don't appreciate how intelligent animals are, how much emotion they feel. All of them—elephants, wolves, bears, deer—all of them. You just don't realize!" His face was flushed.

"So what are you working on now?"

"Puppy mills. Do you know what they are?" His eyes flashed with anger.

"I know." I'd been with a sheriff once on a raid. It was the kind of memory that made you ashamed to be human.

"Doesn't it make you sick? Dogs crammed in little cages, not fed enough, not kept clean, not treated for disease and parasites, just kept alive long enough to breed and have puppies and then the puppies are taken—"

"I know." Unfortunately, mall pet shops get puppies as cheaply as possible and wherever a profit can be made; some will cut costs in any way they can.

"Don't you care?" It was an anguished demand.

"Yes." Yes, puppy mills are wrong, but the litany of wrongs—for me—has to begin with hungry children and the homeless. "So you're using the Ericcson Foundation to fight animal abuse."

It was interesting to see the anger seep out of his face and the sense of peace settle over him. The tight muscles in his face relaxed. He leaned back in his chair. "You bet I am."

"What would CeeCee have thought about the foundation going in that direction?"

He considered the question, then shrugged. "It's a winner-take-all world." The words were callous. But they had a tinge of the bravado used by small boys shouting unacceptable phrases.

I drank coffee, said nothing.

He wriggled uncomfortably and said quickly, "CeeCee never blinked at seeing things the way they really are."

I looked at him.

He folded his arms. "You surprise me, Mrs. Collins. No personal questions about my late sis? How she looked the last time I saw her? My favorite memory of her?"

I sipped the coffee, spectacularly good coffee. "You can tell me whatever you wish."

For an instant, he looked discomfited, then he said sharply, "If you write a book about her, don't be maudlin."

"I'm rarely maudlin, Anders. And I'm not writing a book about CeeCee."

"So you arrived coincidentally on the anniversary of her kidnapping?" He watched me carefully.

"No. Not coincidentally. It is also the anniversary of my husband's death." I looked away, toward the canyon. The sunrise spilled over the mountain, a golden cascade. "My husband died here. That's why I came."

He shaded his eyes from the sun. "So you're going down memory lane." He sighed. "Just like we are." His voice was resentful. "Carefully orchestrated, of course. Every year I wonder what would happen if we let it all come out. But it never happens."

"Come out?"

"The truth." His tone was defiant. "How we all felt about CeeCee. Belle acts like my dead sister was some kind of saint." Many adult children call their mothers by a first name. But I had the sense Anders was distancing himself from his mother. "Let me tell you, CeeCee was no saint. And being kidnapped didn't make her one. It just made her unlucky."

Anders wanted to talk about CeeCee. Maybe he still believed I was working on a true-crime book and was determined to get my attention. Maybe he simply wanted to talk, had wanted to talk for a long time.

I hoped to find out more about him. Perhaps this was as good a way as any. "Being kidnapped is more than bad luck. Someone planned it, Anders, someone picked her."

"Bad luck," he repeated stubbornly. "CeeCee was the first one to arrive at the lake. It could have been me. Or Joss. Any of us. I think somebody was waiting, somebody up at the lake."

"How do you explain the ransom note with CeeCee's name?"

"They grabbed CeeCee, then wrote the note and dropped it in the mail. Like I said, they could have kidnapped any of us." Anders rubbed the bridge of his nose. "There was a guy who worked for us, Johnnie somebody. I thought later he acted spooky as hell. I told the deputy, but he said Johnnie was okay. A little slow, but a good guy." Anders shrugged. "Maybe the deputy was in on it. It had to be somebody local. There're some tough dudes out in the country. I think it was somebody who lived around there, watched us, and that Friday night CeeCee came up by herself. Bad luck."

"So you think it had nothing to do with CeeCee personally?" I kept my voice casual, as if this were just a simple question, nothing terribly important.

"It had to do"—his tone was patronizing—"with money. M-O-N-E-Y. They didn't care who they snagged. What they wanted was Belle's money. And that's another reason I think it was locals. They didn't ask for enough money. Big-time crooks would know Belle's richer than shit. What's a couple of hundred thousand? They should've asked for a million."

"It would take a pretty big box."

"Small-time yokels." He took a bite of cinnamon roll. "Of course, I don't know if Belle would have paid up as quick for anyone else. They got her favorite. And now she's canonized CeeCee."

"What *was* CeeCee like?" The juice was so fresh the flavor burst on my tongue.

His chin jutted. "She was a first class bitch." Anders picked up his fork, speared a chunk of papaya. "So she was the oldest. Was that a mandate to rule the world?" He shoved the fruit in his mouth.

I sipped my coffee. "Was it?"

He chewed, swallowed. "*She* thought so. Always in charge, always sure that she had all the answers and the rest of us didn't have a clue. She was in rare form that last month. Had us all jumping through hoops. Joss and Gretchen and Wheeler and Megan and me. All of us. Stuck in Dallas working for *her*." He flung down the remainder of the roll. "The Ericcson Foundation. CeeCee's empire. Why didn't she do it and leave the rest of us alone? But no, that wouldn't do. We all had to work there. Joss made pitches to civic groups. Hell, I think he liked it. Give him a stage and he's happy. Wheeler handled the PR. Gretchen did the books. Megan was CeeCee's assistant."

"And you?"

"Was I lucky! I got to write all the promo stuff. As long as it suited CeeCee."

"But now you're in charge."

There was a flash of triumph in his eyes. "That's right."

"And the focus has changed," I said mildly.

"We fight for animals," he said proudly. "And for the environment. We make a difference."

"Is Belle pleased?"

His good humor fled. His face was suddenly bleak. "I don't know. She's never come there. Not since CeeCee died." He shoved back his chair, flinging down his napkin. He strode away, head down.

"Anders. Anders!" Peggy hurried across the lanai.

But Anders didn't stop.

Peggy stared after him, then marched determinedly to the table. "Anders loved CeeCee," she said breathlessly.

Maybe he did. Love has many faces.

She chose yogurt and a bagel from the buffet, then plopped into the chair opposite me, her earnest face intent. "Really, if you knew Anders better, you'd understand. Belle doesn't realize how hard it was for him, CeeCee always taking charge."

"Really," I murmured encouragingly.

Peggy pulled her chair closer. "Anders had his own ideas, but CeeCee always thought she knew best. And she was the oldest, you see."

I must have looked puzzled.

"I'm the oldest in my family," Peggy explained patiently. "I have five sisters. And, of course, you have to take charge. CeeCee meant well."

"I'm sure she did. Coffee?"

"Oh, yes, thank you, Mrs. Collins."

"Henrie O, please." I filled our cups.

She beamed at me and launched into a glowing tribute to CeeCee: ". . . so intense . . . very *serious* about life . . . felt the others were slackers and really that was so unfair . . ." laced with exculpatory justifications for Anders, ". . . really he and CeeCee were so much alike . . . CeeCee never saw how much his work for animals *mattered* to him . . . still grieving . . ."

It was like being swarmed by gnats. Finally I said, "I suppose coming here every year to mark the anniversary of her death must be very difficult."

Peggy stirred the fruit-laden yogurt. "It upsets Anders." She watched me carefully. "It really does. He was an adoring little brother."

I looked at her curiously. Egoists relate every situation, every comment to themselves. Peggy automatically linked every remark to Anders. Was it love? Or obsession?

"Now, Joss." Her tone was cool. "He's certainly gone right on with *his* life. And, of course, she was only a stepsister to Wheeler and Megan and Gretchen. Not that they weren't fond of CeeCee. But I don't think *they* make any pretense. Not like some people." She looked like a Persian cat smelling something disagreeable.

"Pretense?"

She looked swiftly around the lanai, peered into the dim interior, then leaned toward me. "Well, I told Anders I thought we should tell Belle. But he wouldn't let me." Malice flickered in her pale blue eyes.

Did she think I might make a good messenger? Whatever

it was, I was certain I would not tell Belle. But I kept a pleasant, inquiring look on my face.

"Stan Dugan ought to be ashamed of himself! He's never breathed a word to anybody about breaking up with CeeCee."

"He broke up with—"

"No. No. *She* broke the engagement. CeeCee called me that afternoon, that last afternoon, and told me she'd given his ring back. She said she'd tell me all about it when she saw me."

I fell in love with Keith Scanlon's tennis center. And I certainly understood why he enjoyed it. He might be a rich woman's husband, but he certainly knew how to run a tennis complex. Sixteen clay courts. And a clubhouse humming with activity.

Doubles on clay courts is heavenly. The clay slows the ball and is soft on your feet, pleasant attributes at my age. I swung my racket up and back-hand lobbed the ball over the net player into the far corner, one of my favorite shots. Her partner made a valiant effort, but the point was ours. Game, set, match. I thanked my new friends and joined them on the veranda for a drink. I stayed long enough to be courteous, then excused myself and set out in search of Scanlon. I found him behind some scaffolding at the exhibition court.

"How'd it go?" he asked cheerfully, shoving his tennis hat higher above a flushed face.

"Terrific. Great courts. And a beautiful clubhouse." I pulled off a terry-cloth headband and shook my damp hair loose. "How long have you been doing this?"

"Tennis? Oh, all my life. Played my college tennis in Austin. Then I did pretty well on the European circuit. A long time ago." His voice was wistful. There was just a trace of a flat Texas accent. He reached out, grabbed a railing on the temporary bleachers and gave it a hard yank. "Just checking.

We're going to have an exhibition match tomorrow. Want to be sure they put the bleachers together right." He looked at me earnestly. "There's a lot involved in running a tennis club. You have to keep on top of everything—stocking the pro shop, the food concession, hiring the pros, scheduling the classes, putting together weekend clinics, keeping the regulars happy."

The automatic sprinklers came on and the earthy smell of damp clay wafted toward us.

"That's how you met Belle, wasn't it?" I smiled encouragingly.

"Yeah. She came down from Dallas for one of our weekend clinics." He took off his hat to wave away a wasp that buzzed near the hibiscus. "Normally I teach the juniors." He paused, amended, "Taught the juniors. Anyway, I didn't usually do the women's clinics. But a couple of the pros got ptomaine, so I took over that weekend. It was supposed to be a clinic on lobs. Damn Belle won't lob." His expression was both bemused and wry. "She and I really got into it and that night I was trying to put a good face on it, so I invited her out to dinner." A sudden smile lighted his face and his considerable charm was evident.

So Belle refused to lob. I've known players like that. They see a lob as a confession of weakness. Me, I love lobs. But maybe that indicates I have a Byzantine mind. It certainly indicates I'll use whatever shot works. And if I ever played Belle, I'd lob her all day long. And enjoy it enormously.

"Did she persuade you lobs are for wimps?"

He laughed. "She was like a whirlwind. I've never spent an evening like that. Belle can outtalk anyone. And she was so much fun. We had a great time until—"

I don't suppose he would have continued. But I thought I knew. "Until the kidnapping?"

The happiness seeped out of his face. He looked suddenly

morose. "Nothing's been the same since. Of course, I know it can't be. But Belle's not the same."

I would have given a good deal to know his thoughts. I don't run a talk show, so I couldn't ask the man if he regretted his marriage. But I could make a stab at it. "Belle's a very remarkable woman."

He got a Dennis Thatcher look on his face, formally pleased and proud. "Oh, yes, she is remarkable."

"Do you miss Texas?" It was an idle question, the kind you throw into an interview to relax a subject. Nothing tough, nothing stressful. And sometimes—bingo!—you hit the jackpot.

Just for an instant, Keith Scanlon's broad face was unguarded, his eyes full of longing. "Oh, yeah. Yeah, I do. I had my own place. All mine. Took the money I'd earned on the tour and sank every penny into it. People came from all over. Oh, I wasn't as famous as Bollettieri, anybody like that. But I was getting a good name. And I had some kids who were good, really good."

"This isn't the same?" I gestured toward the compound of courts. There was the familiar *thwock* of balls, the occasional cries of success or frustration.

"No. This is—God, it's so temporary. People on a holiday. Just for a few days or weeks. Oh, we've got one kid—Tommy Yamamoto—God, he's good. But this is a small place. It isn't the same."

"Would you like to go back?"

"No chance." His voice was grim. "Belle doesn't—she can't—" He took a deep breath. "Well, anyway. Life changes, doesn't it?"

"Yes. Yes, it does."

His beeper sounded. He pulled it from his pocket, looked at the display. He gave me a quick, uneasy glance. "If you'll excuse me, Henrie O."

"Of course. Thanks for the tennis."

"Anytime. Please come again."

He walked swiftly around the path.

I waited for just an instant, then followed.

He walked around the clubhouse, heading toward the parking area. Huge hibiscus shrubs surrounded the lot. A path led between the shrubs and the first four courts. I plunged down the path, pausing every so often to peer through the thick tangle of greenery.

Scanlon reached his jeep, pulled out the mobile phone. He turned it on, punched in the numbers. His face was creased in a worried frown. "Why are you calling me?" He listened for only an instant, then said angrily, "Don't call me again. Somebody might hear you, for God's sake. Cool it for now." He punched off the phone.

I suppose the housekeeper kept an eye peeled to arrivals and departures. I was midway up the central path through the front garden when Amelia stepped out on the porch. "Good morning, Mrs. Collins."

"Good morning, Amelia."

A macaw hovered for a moment near the glossy leaves of a ti shrub at the main entrance. Placing a ti plant to the right of a home's front door is supposed to ward off evil spirits. In the midday sunlight, the colors were breathtaking—the bird's feathered stripes of crimson and jade, the glossy green of the huge shiny leaves. If sheer beauty could deter bad luck, success was ensured.

Everywhere I looked in the garden there was color—lavender of the jacaranda, orange of the African tulip tree, yellow of the golden shower tree, red of the royal poinciana. I was still new enough to Ahiahi that every view was startlingly lovely.

The quiet was broken only by the chirps and warbles of the birds, the distant rumble of the falls, the occasional hum of a vacuum cleaner, and the rustle of gardeners clipping and pruning. I didn't see any of the family in a quick survey of the main rooms.

The housekeeper waited until I reached her. "Ms. Ericcson asked me to wish you a good morning. She's gone to Princeville with Mr. Joss and Mr. Wheeler and Mr. Stan. They're playing golf and they'll be back late in the afternoon. She hopes you will have a nice day. If you need any assistance, please speak with Miss Ford."

"Thanks so much." Nice. Carte blanche to speak with Belle's secretary. Yes, indeed, I would take advantage of that. "I'll check with her after I change. And the rest of the family?"

"I believe Miss Gretchen is reading on the lanai near the library. Mr. Anders has gone out on the boat with Mr. Mackey. Miss Megan and Miss Peggy have gone to Hanapepe. There are some artists' shops there."

I wondered how Megan, elegant, thin, and aloof, felt about a day in the company of her stepbrother's garrulous wife. They would make an interesting combination.

"Rather an active group," I said pleasantly.

"Yes, ma'am. And, as always, there will be a buffet at lunchtime. That is the custom for all the mealtimes when there are guests."

"That's very sensible. I'm sure it will be excellent." I started to turn away, then paused. "Amelia, my husband—Richard Collins—died in a fall here."

She inclined her head gravely. "I know. I'm very sorry, ma'am."

"Were you working at Ahiahi when Richard fell?"

"Yes, ma'am." She looked at me solemnly.

"Do you remember the day he arrived?"

She brushed back a wisp of dark hair. "Yes, ma'am. It had been stormy. It rained heavily that afternoon. Later I wondered if he slipped from the trail."

"No one heard Richard call out?" A final, desperate shout, I could feel its vibration in my heart.

"No, ma'am. Not to my knowledge." Her face was smooth and impassive, but I glimpsed a sudden flicker in her eyes. A question? A thought?

So I kept after it. "Were you awake late that evening?"

"Yes, ma'am." She was polite, but the answer was grudging. She cleared her throat. "If you'll excuse me now, Mrs. Collins, I—"

"What kept you awake?"

For an instant I thought she wasn't going to answer. But courtesy was too firmly bred in her.

"Sometimes when it's stormy, my bones ache. I couldn't sleep. But I didn't hear Mr. Collins fall. Now, I must get back to work, Mrs. Collins." She turned away.

I stood and watched her go. She was walking quickly. Too quickly. All right, Amelia. For now.

I hurried up the walk leading to my suite. I felt a little chilled from the ever-present breeze here atop the ridge. I was in a hurry to get into my shower.

The room was already straightened, the bed made, everything in order.

A folded sheet of notepaper lay in the center of the bed. I picked it up. The message was printed and unsigned:

SPOUTING HORN, NOON TOMORROW.
IN RE DISCUSSION OF SUBJECT WHO FELL FROM DOCK.

I folded the note into a small square. Lester Mackey was a liar. But maybe he was ready now to tell the truth. I didn't understand his role in CeeCee's kidnapping, but he knew more than he'd ever told the police. I was sure of that, or Johnnie Rodriguez would still be alive.

Lester Mackey, soft spoken, devoted to Belle. Yes, I thought I could count on that. Whatever had happened to him in Vietnam, Belle had been his rescuer. I was sure of it. So his loyalties, always, would be to Belle. How did that figure into CeeCee's kidnapping?

I needed to know more about Lester Mackey. I knew he drank. Did he gamble? But even needing money in the worst way, I couldn't believe he'd betray Belle.

Something didn't jibe here. I tucked the note into my purse. But I'd no more than clicked the purse shut when I opened it, retrieved the paper. I tore it into tiny strips, flushed it away. Someone—witness the disappearance of my notes on the family, the dead bat on my pillow—was keeping a close eye on me. And women house guests do not carry their purses to dinner.

I wouldn't forget this appointment. And before I arrived at Spouting Horn, I'd know more about Lester Mackey. Stan Dugan had hired a private detective to scour Dallas after the kidnapping. That detective would surely have nosed about everyone who'd been at Lake Texoma that weekend. Yes, I'd talk again with Stan Dugan before I drove to Spouting Horn tomorrow.

eleven

I slipped quickly and quietly into Belle's office. I didn't turn on any lights. It took me only a few minutes at the computer to print out a sheet with a single line repeated several times. All caps for emphasis:

TONIGHT. SAME TIME. SAME PLACE.
WE HAVE TO TALK. I'M SORRY.

I found scissors in Elise's desk, cut the sentences apart, four of them. Then, strolling casually, I wandered by the guest bedrooms. It wasn't hard to figure out the occupants: a new book on the vanishing rain forest in Anders and Peggy's room; elegant matching luggage with the initials MMG in Megan's room; half-opened drawers, a sea-green negligee flung across a chair, a travel guide to Bali on the coffee table in Gretchen's room.

I left the notice tucked in Peggy's bath powder. I took a

leaf from Lester Mackey's book and put the notices to Megan and Gretchen squarely in the center of their beds. I did the same in Elise's quarters when I found them, two doors down from Lester Mackey.

It was certainly a variation on the old familiar ALL IS DISCOVERED, FLY AT ONCE. But it never hurts to try.

Satisfied, I strolled to the dining room. A petite maid smiled at me. "Please." Her voice was soft. "Everything is ready. Guests are welcome to eat whenever they wish."

Gretchen hurried in from the lanai, a book in her hand. "Hi, Henrie O. Good tennis?"

"Super. Have you had a nice morning?"

She waggled a hand, "Comme ci, comme ça. Getting a little restless. I loathe golf, and I can't abide funky shopping. When I shop, I want stores that glitter and glow. I've seen enough shell necklaces to last me a lifetime. But I love to show off tourist highlights. How about a trip to the Nurses' Beach?"

"Sure." On our long-ago trip to Kauai, Richard and I had walked hand in hand on the beach made famous in the 1958 *South Pacific* movie. The wind ruffled his hair and he'd smiled when I pointed toward dancing dolphins. The children built sand castles. Bobby was six, Emily eight, perfect ages for a beach holiday. I'd written Emily a letter, casually said I was going to be in Hawaii this week. She'd probably receive it today. I hadn't wanted to call her. She reads my voice too well. Yes, I'd like to see that lovely beach again. It had golden memories for me.

In just a few minutes, a picnic basket in hand, we were on our way in a little two-seater sports car. Gretchen was indeed a good tour guide. We drove down to Hanapepe and turned left onto Kaumualii Highway. Gretchen kept up a running commentary. ". . . if you look up that way"—withered gray trees, splintered and broken—"you can see where the hurricane barreled down the mountain. The amount of destruction depended upon the geography. Fortunately for Belle, it missed Ahiahi . . ."As we reached Kalaheo—". . . that's the best pizza place on the island . . . there are some rocks with Hawaiian petroglyphs down that way but you have to get permission to see them. They're on private property . . ." We swept past the outskirts of Lihue and turned north on Kuhio Highway. ". . . there's Mount Kalepa. It's the closest high point to Oahu. A long time ago, they used to raise flags there to indicate to canoes from other islands that they could come to trade . . . the Wailua Falls are up that way, but actually I don't think they are any prettier than ours . . . Look to your right, those sand dunes are an ancient burial ground . . ." All the way up the coast, she talked a mile a minute, her eyes bright, her face pink from the sun. The commentary spewed from her, too strong a stream for me to divert. I smiled and occasionally responded.

We'd just passed Princeville, the expensive north-shore resort, when I said cheerfully, "Have you considered a job with the Kauai Chamber of Commerce?"

She laughed. "Sorry if I've overwhelmed you." Her good humor fled and her face was thin and tense. "I'm just so damn glad to get away."

"From Ahiahi?"

Her hands tightened on the steering wheel. "I feel trapped up there. That grave is so damn macabre." She shivered.

I looked at her curiously. CeeCee's grave had a serene beauty and repose. But perhaps Gretchen was too young to see that.

She leaned forward in anticipation, her eyes intent. We came around a bend and below us spread a huge, magnificent valley.

Gretchen brightened. "Hanalei Valley. Isn't it wonderful?"

Far below, a narrow bridge crossed a river. Taro patches

covered the valley floor. To our right was a spectacular view of the bay.

"Wait until you see Hanalei Beach." She hummed a snatch from "Puff, the Magic Dragon." "We'll do the Nurses' Beach—Kahalahala—after lunch. Tourists call it Lumahai, but it's really Kahalahala."

When we reached Hanalei Beach and spread the blanket for our picnic, I remembered looking for Puff the Magic Dragon in a rocky cave along this shore. Just for an instant, I pictured two beloved faces, Bobby and Emily, like cameos in my heart. Yes, Hanalei Beach was indeed a magical place, a two-mile crescent of golden sand, the incredible sweep of the headland, and, always, the surging cobalt blue water. Today the surf thundered. There were no swimmers, not even surfers. It was beautiful, but deadly. As is so often true in Hawaii, beauty masks terrible danger. Every year tourists drown, despite the efforts to warn visitors.

As we carried our blanket and basket to a spread of immaculate sand, a group of young men playing volleyball paused long enough to notice Gretchen. She flashed a quick, lively smile with a hint of enticement, then flounced ahead of me. They looked after her regretfully. I'm sure if I had not been there, she would soon have had a bevy of admiring companions. I suspected this was a game she often played, and played superbly. But she ignored their looks of inquiry as we settled on the sand. She handed me a plate with smoked salmon and chicken salad, papaya and mango and a mound of macadamia nuts. We had a choice of beer, wine or mixed juices. I took the juice and found it a fascinating blend of pineapple, guava, and orange.

As we ate, I studied my companion. Her unruly red hair was pulled back into a ponytail. She wore a gingham shirt with the tail tied at the midriff, khaki shorts and espadrilles. She had all the attributes of an ordinary vacationer, but there was a shadow in her eyes, and her mouth was too often folded into a thin line. This was not a happy young woman.

She looked up, caught my glance. Her eyes glittered with equal parts anger and sheer unhappiness. She tried to smile, but couldn't quite manage.

I understood. It takes a serene heart to enjoy beautiful surroundings. A serene heart was no longer mine. How could I immerse myself in beauty? And obviously, Gretchen wasn't soothed by the magnificent vista.

Gretchen stared out at the water, her face hard. "I thought if we got away for a while, I'd feel better. But I don't! I wish I were a million miles from here." The skin stretched tight across her narrow face. "Even if it weren't for that grave, and God, it's so lonely up there, at the end of nowhere, just CeeCee and silence. But even if she was buried in Dallas, I'd hate it here. Nothing ever happens on this island. It's so . . ."

I said nothing, but I thought how wrong she was. This island had all of life that mattered, births and deaths and love. And, unfortunately, hatred and sadness and despair. But it was all here.

". . . damn bucolic. Not like D.C. I can't wait to get home." She stared out at the pounding waves as if she wished she could fight her way through them.

"That's where you grew up, isn't it?" I savored a handful of macadamia nuts.

The taut muscles relaxed. A look of almost unbearable sadness glistened in her eyes. "Oh, yes. We lived in Georgetown in an old Colonial house. An alley ran behind it. In the spring we had these gorgeous azaleas and a magnolia tree. I've never forgotten the way magnolia smells. And the way the leaves rattle in a breeze, like dominoes clicking on a wooden table. We had so much fun. Megan and I pretended we were highwaymen robbing the coach on its way to Alexandria." She laughed, but there was a tremor in her laughter. "Bloodthirsty little creatures. There'd been an inn next door and we'd heard all the old stories about travelers and what happened to some of them. So we played highwaymen and soldiers and come-find-me-if-you-can. It was perfect when we were little. I wish it could have stayed that way."

I understood. Don't we all look back in longing, those of us who had happy childhoods? Because the greatest loss we ever know is not the loss of family or place or money, it is the loss of innocence. There is forever a hollow place in our hearts once we realize that darkness rings the campfire.

Gretchen picked up a handful of golden sand, let it trickle through her fingers. "There was always laughter in our house. Giggles and belly laughs, snickers and whoops. That's what I remember—noise, excitement, like the quiver on a rail when the train's coming. And Dad—the world seemed brighter when he was around. He was a loud, swaggering, crazy Irishman, and we adored him. But he was really a lamb underneath that bluster. Everything was wonderful—until Mother got sick. It all went wrong then. Mother was so sick and Dad started drinking way too much. After she died, he was drunk most of the time. Then he met Belle." Gretchen looked out into the bay at the huge crashing waves, her face once again drawn and tight.

I shaded my eyes. "Did it make you unhappy when he married Belle?"

She reached for a sliver of driftwood. With swift strokes, she made neat Xes in the smooth golden sand, her face carefully blank. "I was almost ten. Pigtails and braces and knobby knees. And here came Belle, gorgeous and . . . and overpowering. It was all pretty exciting. I mean, Belle's a big deal, you know. Famous and rich and beautiful." Her voice sounded faintly puzzled, perhaps recalling the child trying to fit an unknown quantity into her life.

"How long were they married?"

"Two years." She scraped the stick across the sand, making it smooth again. She drew a gravestone.

"I understand you blame Belle for your father's death."

Her hazel eyes flicked toward me. "And who suggested that to you?"

Normally I avoid creating trouble. But now I welcomed it. Raw emotion often reveals truth.

"Stan Dugan." A huge wave crashed, flinging a massive tree limb shoreward.

"Dear old Stan. Always has a kind word for everybody." She managed a tight smile, but her eyes were agate-hard. "It's too bad CeeCee didn't live long enough to marry him. He's such an arrogant asshole, I'd have loved to see what happened when she started screwing around on him."

I looked at her in surprise. "Why would she do that?"

Gretchen laughed. It wasn't an attractive sound. She rolled onto her knees and began to gather up the remnants of our picnic. "Because my departed stepsister was a high-class slut. Or maybe that's uncharitable. Let's just say she had a high-level sexual appetite which she indulged with a variety of young men. And not so young men." She turned to look at me, her eyes mocking. "Will you put that in your book?"

I lifted the blanket and shook it. "I'm not writing a book." I didn't say it with passion. I began to see the object of our afternoon trip. Yes, Gretchen probably wanted to get away from Ahiahi, but more than that, she wanted to give me her version of CeeCee Burke. So it was okay with me if she continued to think a true-crime book was my raison d'être.

Gretchen picked up the basket. I followed her across the sand. She unlocked the car, stowed the basket. I tossed in the blanket.

As we drove off, Gretchen said briskly, "Right, Henrie O. You're not writing a book. Of course not. And Belle's having us here because she loves us. Yeah. And it snows here every July."

"Why do you come if you hate it so much?"

We turned north again and left Hanalei, the road twisting and turning. We came around a sharp curve and Gretchen pulled up beside a stone wall. As we got out of the car, she said bitterly, "Have you ever tried to withstand Belle? It would be easier to push back the tide. Oh, no, I have to come. And it isn't remembering CeeCee that bothers me."

She walked ahead, leading the way to a muddy, rutted trail that wound down through clumps of pandanus trees, the onshore breeze rustling their drooping fronds. "It's rough here. Watch your step."

Suddenly the beach lay clear and perfect below us.

"Nurses' Beach," Gretchen announced proudly.

No lovelier beach exists: sparkling white sand, jagged black lava rock, tumultuous, pounding waves, and midnight-blue water stretching out forever. Some say life's a beach. If so, it should be this beach.

"It's too rough to go down to the beach today," Gretchen warned. "People get swept out to sea very easily here when the surf's up." She gave a tiny sigh. "But it's so beautiful."

Beautiful and dangerous, nature's favorite combination.

"So there's something you like in Kauai."

She grinned. "If I could be a tourist, I'd like it a lot." Then the bleak and lonely look returned. "But to come here and be stuck up on that mountain with a ghost—I hate it!"

She whirled around and climbed swiftly back up the trail. I followed more slowly.

In the car, I braced as she made a sharp U-turn. "Now we have to go back," she said glumly. "And tonight will be worst of all. We'll sit around and talk about CeeCee. It's so damn spooky." Abruptly, she gave a peal of laughter.

At my look of surprise, she laughed again, a little wildly. "I'm sorry. But CeeCee would have hooted at the whole idea, this come-and-let's-talk-about-our-dear-dead-sister bit. Nobody was more down-to-earth than CeeCee. She'd have wanted us to get out and have fun." The road ran straight and the car picked up speed. "Although I have to hand it to Belle. She does her best to make it a holiday. But it's all wrong!"

I waited until we were past Hanalei, then said gently, "Perhaps it will help you if you look at it from Belle's point of view. She wants to talk about CeeCee as if she were in the next room and might suddenly walk in and smile at everyone."

We were climbing now. The taro patches in the valley floor glistened like jade in the afternoon sun. A herd of buffalo milled around the far end of the valley, incongruous but charming.

"But CeeCee never will. She never, never, never will." The car picked up speed, swerved dangerously fast around a curve.

I wondered at the rasp in Gretchen's voice. Was it anger at the kidnappers? Or at Belle?

"Do you miss CeeCee?"

"Me?" It was a spurt of surprise. She glanced at me, an odd look on her face. "Look, Henrie O, she was my stepsister. I thought she was ancient when Belle and Dad got married. Why, she was almost as old as Wheeler." A smile slid across her face. "Funny, how little kids think a big teenager's so old. But they seemed old to me. Then they went off to college while I was growing up. Oh, yeah, I knew CeeCee. But we were never close."

"CeeCee was Belle's favorite." We were already passing the old lava rock church, Saint Sylvester's. It never takes as long to return as to go.

"You got that right." But the ache I had detected in Anders's voice was absent in hers. After all, Belle was her stepmother, not her mother. Gretchen drove a little over the speed limit, pushing the car in front of us. "But Belle's pretty high on all of us. She always loved the way we teased each other." As we drove down the coast, she regaled me with some of the more entertaining episodes. "Funny, Belle's private as hell about some things, but she liked the way the press touted us as the Hi-Jink Kids. That's all over. Ever since CeeCee died."

"No more jokes? Not even from Joss?" I welcomed the soft current of air through the open window. Hawaii definitely has a sports car climate.

Gretchen grinned and her face was pretty when it lighted up. "Joss always came up with the wildest scenarios." She slowed for a traffic light by the Kukui Grove shopping center. "But now that he gets to display his talent in Hollywood, he doesn't have to find a private stage."

She drove fast through the outskirts of Lihue.

"Tell me about Lester."

That caught her by surprise. She gave me a startled look. "What about Lester?"

"How does he fit in?"

She turned north out of Hanapepe. "Oh, Lester's wonderful." Perhaps for the first time that afternoon, I heard genuine softness in her voice. "Lester—hell, he loves all of us, even the late-come Gallaghers. Equal-opportunity foster pop, that's Lester."

I remembered the shine of tears on his stubbled cheeks the night before. "He loved CeeCee?"

"Oh, yes. Maybe it was harder on him than anyone. After CeeCee disappeared, God, he looked awful."

We reached the end of the cane road and she punched the intercom to signal we were coming up the mountain.

"And now you're all scattered."

"Yes. But that's better. You can't stay home forever. Even Belle has to realize that. Though I don't know if we would ever have gotten free except—" She broke off.

"How often do you see each other?"

"Twice a year. Christmas and now."

"Does anyone seem especially changed? Different?"

The sports car sped up the narrow road. "Of course, we've all changed." Her voice was disdainful. "Nothing's been the same since the lake."

The car jolted to a stop, and the bronze gate began to open.

As we walked into the fairyland garden, she gave me a scathing look. "What else would you expect? Why do you ask?"

"I wondered if it were someone here who's making you uncomfortable. Perhaps it isn't remembering CeeCee that upsets you." Was Gretchen one of those people—they used to call them sensitives—who subconsciously react to the psychic emanations of those around them? Was Gretchen's irritability a reflection of a killer's hidden anger?

I felt the danger here at Ahiahi, the emanations of menace and hostility. Perhaps I had a stripe of the sensitive, too. But I had hard knowledge, the poster and Richard's daybook, my missing briefcase, and, last night, the hoary bat with a broken neck and a splash of bright red blood.

The shade from a coral tree dissected Gretchen's face, but couldn't hide the hard angle of her jaw. "I'm not upset," she said sharply. She whirled away, pausing only long enough to slip out of her shoes. She grabbed them up and ran barefoot down the garden walkway.

Ahiahi drowsed in the afternoon sun. Black clouds bulked to the north. Only the click of the gardeners' shears and the drone of a blower sounded against the distant roar of the falls.

When I reached my room, I entered warily. I looked in the bath, the closet. Yes, I checked the bedspread, but it lay smooth and tight over the pillows. I stepped out on the lanai. The silvery ribbons of the falls splashed down the cliff face, sending up lacy sprays from the pools below. A gentle breeze rustled the monkeypod and kukui trees. The susurration of leaves and the trill of birds and the rumble of plummeting water created a lulling song of enchantment.

But I could not afford to be enchanted.

"Richard."

I said his name softly, more a plea than an evocation.

A memory flashed in my mind, as bright and crisply delineated as a glossy black-and-white photo. We stood in the shadow of the Cathedral in the Zócalo Plaza in Mexico City, waiting for a minor government official who'd promised to bring proof of the president's involvement in the assassination attempt on the opposition party's candidate. I'd met our informant at a cocktail party the week before and set up this clandestine appointment. Richard was intrigued, but skeptical. "We'll listen, Henrie O. But then we'll dig. It always comes down to this: Who wins? Who loses? Who's afraid? Who's angry? Who's lying? And why?"

The memory was so sharp and distinct I could smell coal from a vendor's brazier and hear the bray of a donkey carrying firewood. And almost reach out and clasp Richard's warm and living hand.

Then the memory was gone. But the words glittered in my mind like polished crystals: Who's lying? And why?

The huge living-dining area was shadowy. I found a panel of light switches beside a bamboo-framed mirror. I flicked them on one by one. Pools of light dispelled the gloom, but the immense room remained daunting. This huge expanse needed people, talking, laughing, moving about. Quiet and untenanted, it had the lonely air of a deserted stage set.

A stage for Belle, of course. I'd not even glimpsed her today. Was she providing me time and space to seek out Richard? Was she simply absorbed in her family? Or was she avoiding me?

I would see her at dinner. But this was the evening devoted to memories of CeeCee, not an appropriate time for me to talk at length with my hostess. I could not suspect her of engineering the gathering to evade me. This evening had been scheduled long before I ever knew I would be at Ahiahi. If I were simply a guest, I'd have dinner in my room, afford this troubled family the privacy to recall CeeCee. But I was not simply a guest.

I would join them in this room tonight as they gathered, amid the cool and soothing Japanese screens, overseen by a blue terra-cotta laughing Chinese judge and an elegant cast bronze sea lion, to bring up the spirit of the dead.

Was that why this huge and eclectically decorated room was making me so uncomfortable? I felt edgy and nervous, as if danger lurked near. Was this an atavistic response, like that of a suddenly tense tiger poised to step upon seemingly innocent brush masking a hunter's pit?

It was quiet, so quiet. To me, a foreboding, forbidding quiet. With the sudden change that can mark a mountaintop, a thick cloud abruptly settled over the canyon. I could no longer see the falls, but I could hear their constant roar, a menacing sound in a world hidden by gray mist. The milky fog wreathed ever closer until I could see only a few feet across the lanai, not even distinguishing the Chinese vases on their pedestals.

And—I jerked around. Then smiled in relief. A small green lizard flickered up the wall near me. But my smile faded. I still found the atmosphere oppressive. As if I were observed by unfriendly eyes.

I moved swiftly, eager to complete my task and leave this room behind. My thongs slapped against the planked floor.

When Stan Dugan and I had talked, he looked at the gallery of photographs above the wet bar and said that somebody'd been very, very clever.

I wanted to look again at the photographs. Faces do tell tales. Even formal studio photographs reveal much of the subject. But this gallery included a mélange of informal photos. It was these I particularly wanted to see. The candid shots, a hundred or more, were mounted within a six-foot-long frame that was, in effect, a time line of Belle's married life. They began when CeeCee, Anders, and Joss were little schoolchildren. They wore uniforms and stood stiffly in front of a low building with a humpy, treeless brown mountain in the background. CeeCee looked inquisitive, her fine-featured face alert. Joss smiled, his rosy cheeks plump and appealing. Anders had turned away, one shoulder higher than the other, his narrow face drawn in a frown.

There were so many photos: of a radiant Belle and a remote Oliver Burke hand in hand in a Japanese garden; of Belle in fatigues hurrying down a plane ramp; of Belle and the children each holding a wriggling Dalmatian puppy; of CeeCee on a pony; of Belle and Oliver in evening dress; of Joss and Anders fencing; of a teenaged CeeCee at Trevi Fountain; of Belle and her children on the steps of the Capitol; of Belle in the exuberant embrace of a red-faced and ebullient Quentin Gallagher at their wedding.

Now the gallery included shots of the Gallagher children: Gretchen—as she'd said—with pigtails and knobby knees and a lost look; of Megan graceful and poised at a birthday party; of Wheeler kicking a soccer ball, and of all the children—growing up now—at dances and hay rides, deb parties and barbecues. And at the lake, Keith Scanlon gunning a speedboat, Wheeler lazing in a hammock, CeeCee and Joss elegant in all white as they played croquet.

It was like overhearing soft voices tell intimate secrets as I studied the faces, captured in unguarded moments.

Belle rarely revealed her inner self, usually maintaining a reserve, presenting a public face even in private moments. It is the response developed by most politicians: a quick smile and a pleasant mien so often exhibited they become automatic. But occasionally the photographer captured her in an open moment, her intelligent face quizzical or amused or affectionate.

CeeCee's expressive, open face revealed that she came at life head-on, like a swimmer breasting a wave, welcoming the foam and the sparkle of sunlight and the struggle.

Anders was always at a little distance—half-turned or looking away or frowning—never quite in sync with the others. But there was one picture of Anders hand in hand with Peggy, and there was a private, special warmth in his smile.

Joss performed. Always. Only once had the camera pictured him without an FDR-bright smile. The shot was a little out of focus. He stood at the end of a pier, looking out across a choppy expanse of water, his face a study in isolation.

Gretchen was alternately vivacious and sullen, sometimes delirious with excitement, sometimes drooping with despair.

Wheeler's heavy-lidded eyes and slow smile exuded sexuality, no matter the occasion. It was no surprise that he was often pictured with eager girls standing close.

Megan was always perfectly dressed with a perfect smile. Every picture was suitable for a magazine.

Keith Scanlon usually managed a smile, but he never looked quite comfortable, more like a visitor than a family member.

There were no photographs of Belle's secretary, Elise. Elise had been with Belle for a number of years now. At the lake, it was Elise who had handed Belle the fateful envelope with its terrible message.

But, of course, this was a family record.

These were superior photographs, sharp and distinct, artfully composed and cropped, and, more importantly, filmed with care and thought and love. An excellent photographer's work is distinctive. I would have wagered my plane ticket back to the mainland that most of these photographs had been made by the same person. And I felt confident I knew who had held the camera, watched these lives unfold, catching ephemeral moments forever with eyes of love. What was it Gretchen called Lester Mackey? Equal opportunity foster pop. That was nice. Very nice.

But what did he know of the evening that CeeCee Burke was kidnapped?

I turned off the lights. The room once again shrank into obscurity, the photographs becoming dim blotches.

I stopped occasionally to listen. I still had a sense of another presence, watchful and wary, just as I had while I surveyed the photos. Then I shrugged. I stepped out onto the walkway. The entrance to Belle's study glowed through the fog. I hesitated, then headed that way. I didn't deliberately walk quietly. But thongs make little noise. Elise sat at Belle's desk, her face bleak and hard, staring out toward the foggy lanai, her thoughts clearly unpleasant. Obviously, she had no idea anyone was near.

Ordinarily, I would have slipped away, left her alone. But these were not ordinary times, not for me. Richard came here to die, and this young woman had been with Belle for years. Something was troubling her. It might be entirely personal, but it might reflect something of this family, and whatever I could learn about any of them could be helpful to me. I stepped into the office.

Her head jerked toward me. A cold and icy anger glittered in her eyes.

"I'm sorry to bother you." Then I looked past her, toward the railing that guarded against the long, long fall to oblivion, and cared not at all that I was intruding into her personal, troubled world.

She struggled to regain her composure, dissemble, bury the anger I'd glimpsed for an instant. "Mrs. Collins. What can I do for you?"

An abacus was propped against a jade bowl on the red-lacquered table. I picked up the abacus, twirled the beads. "You knew my husband Richard." My voice was crisp.

"Yes. Of course. He was an old friend of Belle's."

"Did you see him when he came to Ahiahi? The last time?" The beads were smooth and fast; they spun without meaning.

"I was here when he arrived." She looked at me curiously.

"You talked to him?"

"Briefly. He came in mid-afternoon and asked for Belle. I knew who he was. I'd seen him several times. He came to the lake when CeeCee was kidnapped. He wasn't expected here at Ahiahi. But he and Belle were old friends. I didn't know—" She broke off.

I've finished a lot of sentences in my time. I had no trouble with this one. "You didn't know he was married," I said pleasantly. "Richard and I often had assignments that kept us apart." I wasn't going to ask this girl about Belle and Richard. If ever I asked, I would ask Belle. And I knew now—now that I was here at Ahiahi—that I would ask Belle. But there were other questions to be answered first.

"The housekeeper left him in the game room—"

"Where the photographs are?"

She looked surprised. "Yes. That's where he was standing when I came in."

Why had Richard moved to them?

"Was he looking at the photographs?" The abacus beads were still as I waited for her answer.

"Yes. Then he turned toward me." She paused, an odd expression on her face.

I knew she was recalling that moment and Richard, my tall and handsome Richard, looking at the photographs, turning toward her. Elise was remembering something in particular, a finite moment in time, the small parcel of time left to Richard.

"He glanced at the pictures and he said, 'Is—' And then

he hesitated for an instant before he said, 'Is Belle here?' I think he was going to ask for someone else." Surprise lifted her voice. "And then he didn't. I'm sure of it." She gave an embarrassed laugh. "It's odd how you remember things, isn't it? I'm sure he started to say another name. But it doesn't matter, does it?"

"I don't suppose it does. But thank you, Elise, for taking time to talk with me." Boorish, determined, desperate me. "Is there anything I can do to help you?"

Pride stiffened her shoulders. "Oh, no. No, I'm fine. I just . . . sometimes I feel so far from home."

When our hearts ache, we remember home, even if it hasn't existed for years.

"Where is home?" I asked gently.

She shook her head. Suddenly tears welled.

"Whatever it is," I said softly, "I'm sorry," and I turned away. By the time I reached the garden walkway and looked back, she was disappearing onto the fog-ridden lanai.

I was held for a moment, wondering what was wrong in her young life, a seemingly idyllic life.

But were there any idyllic lives in this lovely home? Wasn't I confusing, as the world so often does, the proximity to ease and wealth and luxurious background with happiness? And happiness is like a capricious maiden, bestowing her favors without regard to rank or riches.

I looked out at the foggy garden. It was odd to know that only a few steps away, unseen now, bloomed plants in brightest red or gold, softest lavender, coolest blue. I heard the faraway slam of car doors, the sound of voices muffled by the fog. So some of the others had returned. I didn't envy them their tortoise-slow ascent through the fog. But it encouraged me to move as quickly as I could on the path toward Lester Mackey's quarters. My quest would not take long.

Ahiahi's lack of doors suited my purpose well. Lester

Mackey's living room lay open to my arrival. Even without sunlight the room was warm, the oak walls shiny as honey, the koa floors vivid as sun-drenched amber. The Japanese-style furniture was spare, ascetic. No books, no pictures. Not even a scrap of paper marred the smooth surface of a koa table. A room such as this demanded introspection. Lester Mackey, whatever and whoever he was, was surely a man with an examined life.

Every step was an intrusion into this bone-spare room. The slap of my thongs sounded loud. This room invited silence.

One wall was made up of oak cabinets. No handles broke their smooth surface. The cabinets were cunningly designed, an open square affording fingers an edge to pull.

I opened the first cabinet and felt a surge of satisfaction when I saw two shelves filled with cameras. In pride of place was a state of the art Nikon—

"What the hell are you up to?"

I jerked around.

Wheeler Gallagher, his sloe eyes glittering with anger, moved menacingly toward me. My purse was in my room. And so, of course, was the Mace canister I always carried with me. There was nothing to serve as a weapon in this cell-like room. I'd glimpsed a sheathed tripod in the bottom of the cabinet, but Wheeler was almost upon me.

There was no trace of last evening's bonhomie in his taut face. His broad mouth twisted in a scowl. He came close to me, too close, close enough that I could see the irises of his eyes, smell a mixture of sweat and talcum, hear his short, quick breaths, and feel his anger.

"I've been watching you. I was in the living room when you came in. I saw you check to see if there was anybody around. You decided you had the place to yourself. But it's your bad luck I blew off the golf. I've had a bellyfull of Stan Dugan. I decided to see what you were up to. You headed straight for the pictures. I thought maybe you were going to steal some of them. Then you badgered Elise. But when you started this way, I knew you were up to something." Contempt curdled his voice. "You've come here, wormed your way in. The poor widow woman. That's your pitch. But you aren't out there looking over the cliff where he died—"

Oh, Richard, Richard.

"—oh, no, you went to the beach today with Gretchen. Did you ask her a lot of questions about CeeCee? And Belle? And all of us? And last night I heard you talking to Stan—"

I stood silent as he berated me. It is hard to respond when clearly in the wrong. There was no acceptable reason why I should be opening a cabinet in Lester Mackey's living room.

"—and who's Stan to dump on us? And why are you sneaking around in Lester's rooms?"

I made an effort to deflect him. "Do you spend all of your time eavesdropping?"

He was young, but not young enough to be cowed by irrelevancy. "Not as much time as you spend snooping. What are you looking for?"

Oddly, I decided the truth, or at least a portion of it, would best serve, as it often does.

I spoke quietly, thoughtfully. "I wanted to know if Lester Mackey took the photographs above the wet bar." I waved my hand toward the open cabinet.

"Oh, sure." Wheeler folded his arms tight across his chest. "The pictures. That's what you want, isn't it? For your damn book. Well, I can tell you that you'll never get them, not a one, not a bloody one. Not from Lester."

"For money?" I inquired softly.

"Not for a million dollars, lady." His eyes blazed with assurance.

"You can speak for him?" I sounded deliberately skeptical.

"Yeah, yeah, I can." Like a dog's hackles subsiding, the tension was seeping out of the room. Wheeler was no longer focusing on me. His eyes moved past me to the open cabinet and the cameras. "Yeah, I can tell you about Lester. He's a quiet guy. Always in the background. But he's a rock, lady. A guy who's been like an uncle or a big brother to a bunch of kids who needed him. He wouldn't sell us out. Ever."

I gently closed the cabinet door. "I believe you, Wheeler." Then I slipped past him and walked briskly across the room, through the open doorway.

I didn't wait to see if he was coming. I wasn't worried about it. I'd learned what I needed to know. And more besides.

I was feeling pleased with myself when I reached my quarters. That sense of satisfaction lasted until I walked into the little living room.

Belle was waiting for me.

twelve

Belle rose. It was difficult from the low couch. She levered herself up with her cane. That made her suddenly seem vulnerable. And her lovely face, though smooth and welcoming, looked fragile and uncertain.

"Amelia said you were here. I hope you don't mind my waiting?" She smiled, that cool, meaningless smile, but her deep blue eyes looked at me warily. "I wanted a chance to visit with you."

"I'm delighted." And uneasy. And unsure how to proceed, how to respond, what to say.

"I had Amelia bring us tea." She spread her hand at the service on the bamboo table.

"That's wonderful."

We settled on the couch and she poured tea and offered me biscuits and little sandwiches.

"And how is your daughter and her family?" Belle asked.

How many times over the years had both of us held fine

china cups, spoken cheerfully with beautifully dressed, socially poised women? It was such a familiar ritual. Yet this time dark emotion underlay the graceful moment, the shark's fin beneath placid water.

"Having fun," I said brightly. Oh, Emily, how I wish Richard could see you now, take pleasure in your life now. "She and Warren recently relocated to a small town in east Texas. They bought the newspaper there. Warren's the publisher, Emily's the managing editor, the best kind of mom and pop newspaper." Not so common anymore across the country, with so many small-town newspapers gobbled up by one of the big newspaper chains.

Belle seemed genuinely interested and she had the good reporter's knack of drawing out details—

Yes, Emily's children were fine. Diana was playing lots of tennis and Neal never met a crawling insect he didn't like.

This was a second marriage for Emily. Yes, I liked my new son-in-law quite well. It was a good match. I hoped to visit them soon.

"Are you pleased with your visit here?" Another social question but her gaze was intense.

I sipped Earl Grey tea and managed to smile. "I have found it very interesting." And that was certainly true.

Tea and inconsequential conversation and searching blue eyes.

Belle replenished my cup. "I know coming to Ahiahi," she spoke slowly, "has been hard for you. Have you found what you came for?"

Now was my opportunity to speak out, to tell this lovely, vulnerable woman what compelled me to travel so far.

I was tempted. I wanted terribly to share this burden, to have help, to come out in the open, flood secret places with light, wrench the truth from its hiding place.

I opened my mouth. Fog wreathed on the lanai. I glanced toward the bedroom and remembered so vividly the sight of the little dead bat. I felt a chill and the nearness of danger. Fear was always near me now, touching me with spectral fingers. Was someone close in the fog, listening to us?

What if I told Belle everything?

I couldn't take that chance. I knew I was in danger. I couldn't put Belle in danger, too. I had nothing to substantiate my claim, no hard, solid facts. Not yet. I needed to know more.

"I'm finding out a great deal." I spoke loudly for listening ears. I was angry, and I was scared. I knew someone listened. "I'm learning more and more about Richard's last day."

"And about my children?" Belle's face was grim.

I understood then why she had come. I picked my words carefully. "I am not writing a book about CeeCee." An announcement for Belle. A revelation for a listener?

Our eyes met and held.

Slowly, she smiled, and now it was genuine and friendly. She reached out, clasped my hand.

When she left, I waited until the sound of her cane was gone. Then I slipped quietly out onto the lanai. I looked down the steps. I could see just a foot or so. I heard a rattle as a stone fell. But I'd not catch our killer now. The fog was too thick, the escape too easy.

Some moments are forever etched in memory. Sometimes you are aware that a particular time or event or happening will remain clear and sharp in your mind no matter how many years pass. Such was this moment as we gathered to remember CeeCee Burke.

I looked about the lanai. The guests blended well with their tropical aerie, the women in bright Gauguin colors, the men in white jackets. There was a general flurry of movement as we settled into the chairs, carrying after-dinner coffee. The soft-cushioned wicker chairs and couches were arranged in an inner and outer half-circle facing the canyon. Chairs scraped. Spoons clinked against china cups.

Belle stood with her back to the railing, silhouetted against the velvety purple of the tropical night sky. A quick flurry of rain just before dinner had dissipated the fog and now stars spangled the dark expanse of sky like sequins glittering on a witch's hat. The pulsing sound of the falls was constant—exhilarating or ominous, depending upon mood. A choppy breeze whipped the flames in the corner torches and rustled the ti leaves and the palm fronds. The moist, soft air flowed over us and should have been as warm and soothing as the stroke of a masseuse's hand.

But there was no ease on this lanai.

I was at one end of the outer half-circle. Deliberately, of course. I could see each person, though the faces were fitfully illumined by the undulating flames of the torches.

Each and every person had a special relationship to CeeCee Burke.

CeeCee's fiancé—Stan Dugan hulked in his chair, a big brooding presence, his blunt-angled face stern and watchful, his massive hands braced on his legs.

CeeCee's brother and his wife—Anders Burke shrugged away his wife's hand as she tried to take his drink. No coffee for Anders. He tilted the glass, emptied it, waved toward a maid. Peggy made little bleating noises, like bird wings brushing against plate glass.

CeeCee's youngest brother—Joss Burke stared into the distance at the moonlit falls. His handsome profile was as sharply etched as an engraving, his mobile mouth compressed, his jaw set. His arms were tightly folded across his chest. He could not remove himself physically, so he had removed his attention.

CeeCee's mother's secretary—Elise Ford completed the inner half-circle. Her makeup was thick, but it didn't hide the tight, hard angle of her jaw. The fingers of her right hand drummed nervously on the chair arm.

CeeCee's mother's husband—Keith Scanlon was in the first chair of the outer half-circle. He moved uncomfortably, as if his muscles were tired. The flame in the near torch surged, touching him with a ruddy glow, illuminating his stony gaze. But he wasn't looking at Belle. His face was turned toward the front row. Who was he watching? My glance slid over Stan, Peggy, Anders, Joss, and Elise. Which one? And why?

CeeCee's stepsister—Gretchen Gallagher bounced to her feet. "Don't worry, Anders, time hasn't been called yet. I'll get you a stiff one. And me, too." She moved, a little unsteadily, toward the wet bar.

CeeCee's stepbrother—Wheeler Gallagher reached out, but Gretchen eluded his grasp. Wheeler frowned in exasperation. His eyes flicked toward me, then toward Lester Mackey.

CeeCee's other stepsister—Megan Gallagher was, as always, breathtakingly lovely and as elegant and remote as a faraway eagle glimpsed high in the sky. She stirred her coffee, and the clink of her spoon was startlingly sharp as silence fell on the lanai. But not as loud as the rattle of ice cubes when Gretchen handed a tumbler to Anders, then made a half-curtsey toward Belle. "Excuse me." The proper words, but her tone was brittle. Wheeler grabbed his sister's arm and pulled her roughly down to her chair. "Shut up." It was a command. Her eyes blazed, but she settled in the chair, her mouth folding in resentment.

CeeCee's mother's faithful retainer—Lester Mackey once again had removed himself from the group. He'd left the chair next to me vacant. He stood in the shadow of a huge carved black wooden swan, a dim figure dimly seen, his slight figure made smaller by the immense sculpture. Lester Mackey, the observer. Lester Mackey, superior photographer.

Lester Mackey, who Wheeler had said "would never sell us out."

"This is, as every year, a very special night for me." Belle's voice was soft, reflective, eager. She gripped her cane tightly. Moonlight added a silver glow to her smooth hair and fine-boned face and a luminescent sheen to her sky-blue sheath dress.

I felt such a rush of sorrow for her that I was shaken. I know what it is to grieve for a dead child as well as a dead husband. I know what it is to face the abyss of separation, colder than an arctic plain, wider than any sea, deeper than a pit in hell.

And yes, memory is the only bridge that can span the abyss, the memory of laughter and tears, joy and anger, whatever memory comes. For that instant, a face and voice and touch live again in the mind, as real as a photograph that holds a finite instant of the universe in its exact molecular structure.

Abruptly, passionately, I wanted this evening to answer Belle's demand, to satisfy that endless hunger within her for the daughter taken from her.

Belle smiled, her lips curving into delight.

There was no hint that she sensed the turmoil around her. She appeared to be oblivious to the tempest of emotions swirling beneath this carefully ordered social scene.

I scanned the watching faces quickly. I saw suspicion, fear, jealousy, dismissal, concern, rejection, avidness, misery, and appraisal.

Lester's face I could not see.

Was Belle blind? Still she stood, a sheen of tears in her eyes, a tremulous smile curving her lips. Abruptly, I realized a terrible truth about Belle Ericcson. Belle saw—perhaps had always seen—what she wished to see: the world according to Belle Ericcson. She was the central figure: a beautiful woman, a superb reporter, a good wife, a loving mother. What would she put first?

That wasn't a fair question. Not for Belle, not for any woman. Life has many compartments and only the innermost soul can ever know what came first, who came first, and judge the power of the claimants.

However she'd ordered her life, Belle lived with great passion. It was passion that lifted her beyond the ordinary, made her a remarkable woman. But how much did she see or understand of the lives around her?

"CeeCee loved old movies. The Westerns." Belle lifted her cane, sighted as if along a rifle, cocked a finger around an imaginary trigger. "She collected them. She'd find them in out-of-the-way shops, at rummage sales." Belle lowered the cane, leaned it against the wall. "Her favorite actor was Randolph Scott. I doubt if any of you"—she glanced toward me—"if anyone besides Henrie O and me remember him. Very tall, of course, with a steady, far-seeing gaze. Lean. Serious. Lantern-jawed. And honest. Always honest." Belle clasped her hands together. "That was what captured CeeCee's heart. Honesty. It mattered more to her than friends or success or power or any of the goals most of us set. So now I like to watch the old movies—John Wayne and Gregory Peck and James Stewart. It makes me feel close to her. If CeeCee were here tonight, she'd say, 'It's great, Mom. The posse comes over the hill and the bad guys go down. You can't beat that.' So that's what I wish for all of us, now and in the future—the thunder of hoofbeats and the posse coming over the hill."

The rumble of the falls seemed suddenly louder, nearer. It was the odd effect of the profound silence on the lanai.

Anders gave a grunt, half snort, half laugh. "But what the hell, it depends on whose ox is being gored, I think maybe." He spoke slowly. He was just drunk enough to enunciate carefully.

Peggy said shrilly, "I have a favorite memory of CeeCee, a very favorite—"

Stan Dugan spoke at the same moment. His deep, resonant, determined voice boomed over the lanai, making the sound of the falls as soft and distant as the rumble of summer thunder. "Belle, we all have memories." Dugan surged to his feet. The swan statue seemed to shrink, receding into the background, no match for Dugan's heft and bulk. Lester Mackey looked even slighter and less substantial.

Light and shadow flickered across Dugan's massive face as the flame wavered in the torch, creating the effect of a ridged bronze mask, elemental as the night. "But if memories aren't shared, they don't exist. So I'd like to ask a special favor of everyone here." He took two steps and stood beside Belle, towering over her.

He reached out, took one slender hand in a tight grip.

Everyone waited. There was a sense of portent, of actions to come that would forever alter these lives.

Dugan bent forward. His voice was low and soft. "We may never come this way again. Who knows what a year may hold? And every year that passes puts us farther from CeeCee and her last words to us. That's what I want to know!" It was an urgent demand. He looked at each and every face, his eyes blazing. "That's what I want us to share, each of us. What were CeeCee's last words to you?" He pointed at Keith Scanlon. "What did she say to you, Keith?" He thrust his hand toward Joss. "And to you, Joss? I want to go back to CeeCee's last day. Monday will be CeeCee's birthday. That's the day we can share favorite memories. But tonight, tonight let's walk beside CeeCee as the hours ran out."

I could have kissed Stan Dugan, shouted huzzah, beat cymbals. Was it our talk that had galvanized him? Whatever the reason, he was seizing this moment as it might never be possible to seize it again. They were here, all of them, the ones who came to the lake that weekend. They were here and captive for this moment.

I sat quietly, scarcely daring to breathe, doing nothing to draw attention to myself and away from his flamboyant, overpowering presence. The moment belonged to the big trial lawyer. This man held juries in thrall and he was going to have his way this night even though fear and uneasiness crackled on the lanai like the tongue of a rogue fire racing up a draw.

I felt their resistance, those who had been at the lake that last weekend. These memories they didn't want to share. One of them most particularly must damp down the neurons of recall in the darkness of the night or had by now suppressed deep within the last encounter with CeeCee.

Or did I impose my own response upon a murderer? Did this killer recall with glee? Evade any memory? Endlessly justify? Callously dismiss? Ache with regret?

But the communal sense of discomfort was palpable.

Anders lurched to his feet. "Last words! So you can put them in a scrapbook?" These words were not quite so distinct, but Anders's suspicion and anger were clear. "Oh, no, wait a minute. You're the shill, aren't you? This is just a clever-ass way of beating the bushes for her." Anders waved his arm toward me.

Hostile faces swung toward me.

But Stan Dugan was a man who dealt with bloodied and battered bodies and spirits. Stan Dugan matched wits with stone-cold-sober lawyers who could joust with the devil and cling to a mount. Anders wasn't in Stan's league.

Dugan let Belle's hand drop. He took one long step, two, deliberately, provocatively, aggressively moving into Anders's personal space, looming over the smaller man, huge, powerful, intimidating. "Is there some reason why you don't want to remember CeeCee's last words, Anders?"

Anders ineffectually shoved at Stan. Breathing heavily, he

made inarticulate sounds of rage deep in his throat. Peggy's pathetic whimpers were a frantic counterpoint. Elise pressed a hand to her mouth. Joss jumped up and moved toward the big man and his brother. Megan leaned forward, her chiseled face intent. Gretchen clapped her hands and gave a shrill whistle. Wheeler grabbed her shoulder, shook it. Keith was on his feet. "That's enough, boys."

I was trying hard to pick up words and phrases from Anders. ". . . sorry . . . bitch . . . make me . . ."

Belle's clear, crisp voice cut through the melee, much to my disappointment. Visceral emotion reveals the truth of the heart.

"Stan, Anders, please." Her clear voice was compelling.

Even Stan Dugan gave way to Belle.

In an instant, with a touch of Belle's hand, Stan was back by the railing and Anders was subsiding into his chair. Peggy's fluttering hands quieted. Joss returned to his seat.

The flames from the torches flickered scarlet against the inky sky, their faintly sulfurous glow making Stan Dugan loom even larger against the darkness. Was I the only one who saw him as an avenger?

Belle gently patted Stan's arm, then she stepped to Anders, bent, and lightly kissed his tousled hair. She stopped midway between the two men, both hands outstretched. "What Stan is asking is hard for all of us. But we have to help each other find solace. Let's go back to that last day." Her voice was cool and even. It brooked no disagreement. "We will do this for Stan."

Stan stepped forward, once again the focal figure. Stan would always be first chair. "Friday morning." Stan's deep voice intoned the words. "CeeCee's last Friday morning." His massive head turned slowly toward Belle.

Everyone looked at her. She stepped forward into a pool of moonlight that clothed her in a serene radiance. "I was walking in the garden, very early. CeeCee joined me. I thought—still think—that CeeCee had something special to tell me. Perhaps I think that because the moment matters so much to me now. Our last talk. Ever. CeeCee was so lovely that morning, as lovely as the crocuses that were starting to bloom. Her blouse was a crisp white with black buttons. The neck and sleeves were rimmed in black. Her skirt was long and black with a design of little purple flowerpots with yellow blooms. When she walked, the skirt swirled and it looked like the flowerpots were dancing." Belle's gaze moved to Stan. "I don't know . . ." There was an unaccustomed hesitancy in her voice.

"Whatever CeeCee said." Dugan was insistent.

It was as if Belle and Stan were alone, speaking only to each other.

"We were almost back to the terrace and CeeCee took my hand and said, 'Mother, what would you do if someone you love was unfaithful?' She held my hand very tight."

Did I hear the faintest of sighs, the catching of a breath quickly suppressed?

"Just another episode on—" Gretchen's sotto-voce comment broke off. Wheeler had clapped his hand over her mouth.

But Belle was looking gravely at Stan.

He rocked back on his heels, his face impassive. "What did you tell her?"

Belle spoke with a quiet dignity. "Love must always be honored. Or it is not love."

Just for an instant, his composure wavered. He bent forward, his fists doubled, then slowly rose to his full height. "What did CeeCee say?"

"Nothing. She gave me a hug and her lips brushed my cheek. I'll always remember that touch, swift and delicate. And the scent. I'd given it to her for her birthday a few days early. The Enchantment of the Moment, that was its name. The Enchantment of the Moment."

It was as if this, too, were an enchanted moment. No one moved or spoke. The poignant silence was broken unexpectedly by Elise Ford. "It was a lovely perfume. I complimented CeeCee on it. I saw her in the hallway. She was looking for Belle and I told her to go to the garden."

Dugan looked at Elise inquiringly.

"That's all. I'm sorry. I know it isn't important. That was all we said to each other. That—and she smiled and said it was a beautiful day."

As the words faded away, Dugan once again faced his audience. His eyes moved slowly from face to face. Or were these witnesses to be called? Dugan pointed at Keith Scanlon, a commanding, peremptory gesture. "CeeCee was waiting for you at the garage that morning."

Scanlon's head jerked up. "Waiting for me? I don't know why you put it like that. I happened to see her there."

Dugan pounced. "I put it like that because that's how it was. A gardener was trimming the crape myrtle. One Pedro Martinez, age nineteen at the time. He saw CeeCee step out from behind a weeping willow when you came around the path. She walked up to you. You tried to shake her off, step past her, but she wouldn't budge. She talked fast and hard. You and CeeCee were both angry. You kept shaking your head, then you pushed past and hurried to your car. What did CeeCee say to you, Keith?"

No courtroom was ever quieter, waiting for a defendant's response. But this quiet pulsed with different, far different, emotions than when the evening began.

I understood why. These people had gathered to remember CeeCee Burke and now they faced a man with steel in his voice, but more than that, an aggressive man bristling with concrete, specific facts of CeeCee's final day.

And they didn't know how Dugan knew these facts. Or why. Or what facts he intended to reveal.

But they knew now that this was not simply an exercise

in recall. Anyone who'd spoken with CeeCee that day, if there was anything odd or discreditable or unpleasant, that person had to wonder and worry now if Dugan knew. The wonder and the worry were reflected in their faces, wary, alert, careful faces.

Anders's eyes squeezed to narrow slits. The brother who put animals before people, the brother who became director of the Ericcson Foundation.

Peggy held a plump hand to her throat. Yes, she was CeeCee's friend, but all that really mattered to her in the world was Anders.

Joss stared in surprise. He loved to act and now he was in Hollywood. Would he be there if CeeCee were alive?

Elise stared at Scanlon. She touched her temple as if it throbbed.

Gretchen clasped her hands tightly together, her face still and white. Why was she afraid?

Wheeler hunched his shoulders. He shot a look of pure hatred at Stan Dugan.

Megan smoothed back her perfect hair. Her glance darted from face to face, seeking, searching.

Lester remained in the shadows. If I'd had a spotlight, I would have beamed it on him. Lester Mackey was just a little too retiring for my taste. What was he hiding?

Keith Scanlon darted an uncertain look at his wife. Belle's eyes were locked on Stan. Keith blustered, "I don't know what the hell's wrong with you, Stan. What's the point—"

"Answer the question, Keith." Dugan's eyes bored into Scanlon's. "What did CeeCee say to you?"

Belle stood quite still, her face smooth as porcelain, her head bent attentively.

Keith flung out his hands. "Hell, it was nothing. Just CeeCee on a hobbyhorse. It wasn't enough that the Ericcson Foundation was going all out to elect a woman who's pro-choice. No, CeeCee wanted me to set up a tennis tournament to raise money, and I told her hell, no. A lot of women play tennis who are anti-abortion and I didn't want to get in the middle of that damn fight. Life's too short."

"Life's too short. Is that what you told her?" Stan snapped.

Keith ignored him. He spoke to Belle. "I'm sorry. Christ, I'm sorry. And I never told you. I didn't want you to know that's how it ended between us. Belle, I wouldn't have fought with her if I'd known. But none of us knew. How could we know?"

Belle's shoulders relaxed. "We didn't know, Keith."

But someone here, one of those who had spoken or who would speak, that person decided on that long-ago Friday that CeeCee Burke was living her last day.

"A walk in the garden with Belle. A quarrel at the garage with Keith. Then we come to CeeCee's office at the foundation." Dugan's gaze moved from Anders to Joss to Gretchen to Wheeler to Megan. "Which one of you wants to go first?"

The silence quivered with tension.

"No takers?" Dugan's mouth twisted. "Fine. Let's start with Anders."

"Why don't you just read your friggin' private detective's report, Stan? Have you got it with you? Is it your special nighttime reading, a little old report on all of us?" Anders lounged back in his chair. He was drunk, but he wasn't stupid.

Peggy blurted, "I don't understand what's going on here. Have you been spying on us? Is that what's happened?"

Joss's voice was grim. "Yes, Stan. You owe us an explanation."

"Hear, hear," Gretchen called out. But her voice was thin and angry.

"Anders is right. I've got a report from a private detective. A very capable private detective. I didn't need to bring it with me," Dugan said quietly. "I know every word in it by heart." He stared combatively at Anders. "Somebody killed your sister—and we don't know who. So, yes, when the cops didn't find anything, I hired a private detective. I know where CeeCee went that last day. I know who she saw. But there's a lot I don't know, a lot I want to know. Take you, Anders. You slammed out of CeeCee's office at the foundation that morning. The secretary remembered it clearly. You yelled at CeeCee. Why?"

I think all of us expected a tirade from Anders. Peggy gripped her husband's arm tightly.

But Anders slumped down in his chair. He didn't look at Stan. "That dress she had on." The words were slurred. "Stupid little flowerpots. Same color as one she gave me when we were kids. Mine broke, so CeeCee gave me hers." Tears spilled down his cheeks. "I stood in the door of her office and yelled at her. I told her she was an officious butthead and somebody was going to bump her off someday because she was such a butthead. That's the last time I saw her and she—she was looking at me so damn puzzled. She didn't know why I was mad. God, she didn't understand."

"Why *were* you mad, Anders?" Dugan's voice was gentle.

Anders used his sleeve to wipe his face. He shook his head back and forth. "Nobody cares. You look around—kittens dumped in a parking lot and it's a hundred and five degrees, dogs kicked and starving. Goddammit"—he jolted forward in his chair, his voice rose in anguish—"nobody cares! That's what I told CeeCee. She could use the foundation's money. We could open a refuge for deserted animals. We could—" He broke off, slumped back down in the chair. "But she wouldn't listen. Nobody ever listens. Nobody cares."

Peggy grabbed her husband's hand, held it tightly. "Yes, we do care. We do," she cried. "And now we have a wonderful refuge. And it's all because of you, Anders. You made it possible."

I had a question from some of the reading material I'd picked up when I visited the foundation. Maybe it was out of place. But this was not a night for niceties. "The foundation's just opened a new animal refuge near Plano, hasn't it, Peggy?"

She nodded eagerly. "Yes. Oh, it's beautiful, beautiful."

"With money from the foundation?"

The elation left Peggy's face so suddenly, she looked stricken. Her mouth formed an O.

Anders began to laugh, a hiccupping, high laugh. "Watch out, the old witch'll get you!" He pulled free from Peggy, pointed at me. "The witch," he crowed, "the witch'll get you every time."

"You don't understand." Peggy jumped to her feet. She stumbled in her eagerness to get to me. "Listen, I talked to CeeCee that afternoon. Friday afternoon. She said she'd been thinking about what Anders said, and he was right. And we talked all about how wonderful it would be, The Ericcson Animal Refuge. We planned it on the phone. That afternoon." Her eyes bulged with sincerity.

And what of her story to me earlier that CeeCee had returned her engagement ring to Stan? Had that been sheer invention?

"That's right." Joss's smooth actor's voice rang with conviction. "I can confirm that."

Nice. Their stories were interwoven like reeds in a basket. I studied Joss and was reminded of Tyrone Power in *Witness for the Prosecution*. Smooth, handsome, such a good actor. Who wouldn't believe him?

Me, for starters.

Joss's face was earnest, serious. "I was in CeeCee's office when she talked to Peggy. I overheard her conversation with Peggy. At least, I heard CeeCee's end. And I was pleased. I thought it was a great idea. I thought it would be a grand way for me to end up my time with the foundation."

"End up your time?" Dugan asked in surprise.

"Right." Joss was casual. "I told CeeCee I'd be leaving in a couple of weeks. I'd decided to go out to California."

"You told CeeCee you were leaving the foundation?" Dugan stared at Joss, clearly in disbelief.

A sudden frown marred Belle's face.

"That's right." Joss smiled at his mother. "I didn't mention it later, Mom. There didn't seem to be any reason to get into it."

"Because the foundation changed direction when CeeCee died?" Dugan glanced toward Anders.

Joss's glance was steady, his voice even. "Of course it changed. Different people have different aims."

"So you don't miss CeeCee?"

"Miss her?" Joss's face was somber. "Without her . . ."

"You were free to go to Hollywood." Dugan put it on the table without apology.

"Without her . . ." Joss repeated softly ". . . without her, I was a little brother with no big sister." Then he looked past the inner half-circle with a sweet smile, "But with two lovely stepsisters."

"Aha, the Gallagher clan." Anders twisted in his seat. "Fully integrated into the Ericcson Foundation. No sibling discrimination permitted."

Peggy was tugging on his arm.

Ignoring his wife, Anders gave a foolish grin. "No discrimination at all. CeeCee told each and every one of us exactly what to do and when to do it. And it always pissed Gretchen off. Look, you can see the fire in that redhead's eyes even if it is dark. As for Wheeler, man, he'd do anything for CeeCee. Climb a mountain, walk the plank. Yeah, everything but welcome old Stan. Wheeler was not a Stan fan." Anders giggled. "I like that. Not a Stan fan. Not a"—He lurched to his feet "—Stan fan. Come on now, all together, follow the bouncing—"

Lester Mackey moved fast. "Let's get a nightcap, Anders. Come on, let's walk out this way and—" Lester had an arm around Anders and was gently maneuvering him toward the end of the lanai. Peggy clattered behind them, once again making those plaintive, worried whimpers.

"And I thought the Gallaghers had to worry about Demon Rum," Gretchen said wryly. "But I can finish out this little inquisition with a smile. Sort of. It was a hairy day at the foundation. The blow up with Anders put a sharp edge on CeeCee's morning. I went in next and she was a bitch." Gretchen gave Belle a rueful smile."She really was and you know how CeeCee could be—I'd cut the budget on a picnic fund-raiser for her pet candidate. So I slammed out of her office in a snit. But she was in a better humor later. I heard her and Wheeler laughing like crazy and I wondered if they were planning a joke on somebody. Then she went off to lunch with Stan and stayed forever and I had to handle a bunch of calls I didn't know what to do with. She finally came back about two. She looked grim again and said she was going to work on the budget for next year. She sent Megan to ask me for the latest figures."

"Which I did." Megan was reflective. "Actually, CeeCee wasn't focused. She kept looking out of the window and losing track of our discussion. She looked depressed. Finally, I told her maybe we should leave it until next week. She said that would be fine." Megan smoothed back a lock of hair. "I stopped in the doorway. And I don't know why this happened. I'm not a mother hen, but I said, 'CeeCee, be careful.' I don't know why I said it, but I had a feeling that something was going to happen and the words came out without my even thinking."

So Megan was the sensitive in this household. It was Megan who absorbed nuances, filtered emotions, sensed distress.

"How did CeeCee respond?" Stan asked sharply.

"CeeCee said . . ." Megan's voice was very precise. " 'Being careful is just another way of copping out. I won't do it. Not anymore.' "

"Does anyone know what CeeCee was talking about?" Stan gazed around the lanai.

No one spoke.

Then he swung toward Wheeler. "What was so funny?"

Wheeler stared at him.

"That morning. Between you and CeeCee. What was so funny?"

Wheeler was absolutely blank for an instant. "Funny." He was marking time. "Yeah. I remember. It was just a joke we were going to play on Belle. We were going to put pink flamingos all over the lake house. One in Belle's chair in her office and one on the hood of her car and a couple in the speedboat. Everywhere we could think of. She loved it when we covered the lawn for her 54th birthday."

Just another lighthearted moment for the Burke and Gallagher clans.

Once again, I chanced a question. I hadn't been booted out yet. "Where were the flamingos?"

Wheeler blinked at me.

"That weekend. Where were they?" I repeated.

"Oh. Well, I hadn't got them yet. We were just talking about it. We didn't have the flamingos yet."

Nor would they ever have. Whatever led CeeCee and Wheeler to laugh that last day, it wasn't now something he wanted to reveal.

Joss stood. "So that wraps it up, doesn't it? Are you satisfied, Stan? Learned what you wanted to know?"

"Actually," Gretchen said, and her voice was light and pleasant but with an undertone of malice, "we haven't all told what we know, have we? How about you, Stan? You had lunch with CeeCee." Gretchen's eyes slid toward him. "I just happened to notice—when CeeCee got back from lunch—she wasn't wearing her engagement ring."

Dugan was a pro. He'd been slugged in the gut in a lot of courtrooms. He gave an easy shrug. "I suppose she'd taken it off for a moment. Probably because she was going to the lake and might go fishing."

I wished Peggy were there. I glanced back into the huge dim room, but it was quiet. Peggy and Lester had successfully removed Anders. And themselves. Did Lester want to protect Anders? Or did he want to evade Stan's questions?

"You weren't at the lake, Stan." Gretchen's voice was sharp, challenging.

"No, I was coming down on Sunday."

I slid the question in like palming an ace. "And what were CeeCee's last words to you, Stan?"

He jammed his hands into his trouser pockets, hunched his shoulders. His harsh face softened. " 'I love you, Stan.' Those were her last words to me, 'I love you, Stan.' "

Peggy told me CeeCee had returned the engagement ring to Stan. But when asked about her last conversation with CeeCee, Peggy claimed they talked about creating the animal refuge Anders so desperately wanted. Joss provided a backup for Peggy's claim.

Wheeler trotted out those useful flamingos.

Keith pitched an old political fight as the reason he and CeeCee quarreled.

Belle remembered a question of fidelity.

Stan insisted CeeCee told him she loved him.

So many different stories.

I remembered Richard's wry admonition yet once again. Who was lying? And why?

thirteen

I stepped carefully along the cliff path. I'd waited half an hour after the gathering on the lanai broke up. The good nights were brief and constrained. No one had lingered. I'd returned to my suite and made notes, then changed to my navy blouse and slacks.

It would be shocking if I encountered anyone else on the path. And quite likely dangerous. Who is abroad in the night, except for nefarious purposes? And—I smiled wryly—those seeking hidden facts. There was so much I needed to know to plumb the hearts of those at Ahiahi.

In my right hand, I carried my rental car keys, the keys poked between my fingers. It was the next best thing to brass knuckles, an eye-gouging defense against an attacker, sharp as hell. A small Mace canister was tucked in my pocket. But I was wary, pausing every so often to listen. An occasional call of an owl added a mournful solemnity to the ever-present roar of the falls. *Whoo-ooo. Whoo-ooo.* Who, indeed, companion of the night?

I reached the steps leading up to the lanai where we had re-created CeeCee Burke's last day. Or part of it. And had any of those moments had a bearing upon her murder?

The scarlet flames in the torches wavered above me. I climbed swiftly up the steps and moved across the lanai and through the huge darkened room to the garden. Now I must simply take my chance that I was unobserved. I darted from shadow to shadow until I was deep in the garden, my goal the cluster of ti shrubs where Keith Scanlon and a woman had quarreled bitterly the night before.

I found the shrubs. Moonlight silvered the huge waxy leaves. A nearby bougainvillea provided an inky shadow. I wormed my way well off the path but with a clear view. I dropped the keys into my pocket. I would wait a half hour to see if the bait had been taken: TONIGHT. SAME TIME. SAME PLACE. WE HAVE TO TALK. I'M SORRY.

I'd had only a glimpse of the angry figures the night before, but it seemed to me that I was overseeing—if not a lovers' quarrel—certainly an encounter between a man and woman who knew each other well. And the woman was not Scanlon's wife. There were only four young women at Ahiahi. I didn't think it was a stretch to believe Scanlon would be involved with a young woman. Men with much older wives rarely have affairs with older women.

I ran over in my mind the possibilities for Keith's clandestine companion.

Megan. Did she come to mind because she was strikingly beautiful, the kind of beauty no man could ignore? I could recall no hint of connection between Megan and Keith. Their interchanges were casual, friendly, unremarkable. But that would be the drill, wouldn't it?

Gretchen. I can't judge another woman as a man would,

but today when Gretchen and I were at the beach, the vigorous young men near us had certainly noticed her. And Gretchen had a hard-edged, restless quality some men might find very appealing.

Peggy. Surely not. Anders found her attractive. But Anders sought reassurance, devotion, stability, direction. Keith Scanlon was a man who enjoyed women physically and wouldn't waste an instant figuring their psyches. Or expecting them to figure his.

Elise Ford. Belle's capable, competent, exceedingly attractive secretary. That was the old saw, a man and his secretary. It would be just a slight variation: a man and his wife's secretary. This afternoon Elise had been distraught. Angry. Even a dream job in paradise doesn't guarantee happiness.

Of course, it was possible Keith might take advantage of an employee. There were several maids. One was old and limped. Two were young, one plump and pretty, the other thin and plain with skinned-back hair and a turned-down mouth. But I was almost certain none of them stayed the night at Ahiahi, other than the housekeeper. My immediate response was, no, not Amelia. She seemed a woman of grave dignity. But I had no sense of the maids. For all I knew, the thin maid might have a light foot for dancing and a lust for passion. Neither requires a smile.

Was Keith the kind of man to exploit an employee? This morning when I was playing tennis, Keith had patted the arm of the pretty little pro with the bouncy ponytail. A more careful man would never touch an employee, male or female.

I simply didn't know.

If no one came, it could be that I was wrong and it was a maid who—

Footsteps crunched on the crushed oyster shells. Elise Ford hurried around the curve in the path. She jolted to a stop, walked slowly to the ti bush, began to pace. She waited fifteen minutes. Then, her voice bitter, she said, "Damn you, Keith," and whirled to leave.

I stared after her. Perhaps my note was a dirty trick. But I doubted either she or Keith deserved better.

CeeCee had spoken to her mother about an unfaithful lover.

Was Keith the lover she meant?

Click. Click.

A soft glow of light spilled down onto the pool table. Stan Dugan sighted along the cue.

I stepped through the archway. Just as last night. Except Dugan's hair was damp, and his uneven face looked even more like a gritty block of broken-up cement.

He glanced toward me, held up his hand, then bent back to make the shot. As the ball rolled into the pocket, he nodded in satisfaction. He replaced the cue.

I joined him.

"I took a swim. Had the pool to myself. Then I stopped by your room." His voice was casual. "There's not a whole lot shaking around here tonight. Everybody scuttled off to their burrows after our session on the lanai. Except you." He leaned against the table, pushed his thick-lensed glasses high on his nose. "Still sniffing around?"

I remembered Elise Ford hurrying to a nonexistent rendezvous. "I took a walk in the garden."

"Solo?"

"Yes." That was true.

The huge lens magnified his eyes, cold, probing eyes. "I expect you to ante up, Mrs. Collins. I'm hunting for a killer. Don't hold out on me." He folded his arms across his big chest.

"If I discover anything that will help you, I'll tell you." So far as I knew, an affair—an ending affair?—between Elise Ford and Keith Scanlon had no bearing on CeeCee's kidnapping and murder. But if it was an affair, I had to wonder how long it had been going on. I felt a little pang of disappointment. Had Elise, who seemed to be an appealing young woman, been slipping around corners to meet Belle's husband for years? I would not have thought it of her. I needed to know a good deal more about Keith and other women.

I didn't dance around the question. "Your private investigator—did he find any extramarital flings by Keith?"

"Funny you should ask." He looked at me curiously. "You carry around a mental fidelity monitor, slide it over people like a metal detector?"

I waited.

Stan turned toward the table, took the rack, and placed the balls in it. "Keith's been married twice before. No kids. Each time the gal divorced him for screwing around. Always had a chick on the side. But Toby went over everybody's life like an old maid checking the locks. With what he'd picked up on Keith, he expected to find a present-day chick. But Toby said Keith was being a very careful man if he was involved with anyone. Toby didn't find a trace of a shady lady. Of course, when a man marries big bucks it encourages a little care. Who knows? It might even encourage fidelity."

Ah, but it apparently hadn't. At least not in recent times.

"It might," I said mildly. "But let's assume the leopard still had his spots. What would CeeCee do if she found out Keith was cheating on Belle?"

"Handle it. CeeCee wouldn't have ignored it. Oh, yeah." He nodded swiftly. "Maybe that's what she was leading up to with Belle that morning."

That had occurred to me, too. But there were other possibilities.

"CeeCee asked her mother's advice about infidelity." I stared up into cold, magnified eyes. "Had you been unfaithful to CeeCee?" There was no question I wasn't willing to ask.

The silence between us was odd and dark. Dugan's gaze

moved away from me, focused on the photographs on the wall above the wet bar. "That would have made it simple. But sometimes things aren't so damn simple, Mrs. Collins."

He moved slowly to the gallery, stopped to look up at CeeCee, smiling, carefree, happy. He reached up, gently touched the frame. "She was so goddamn alive. Being with her was like skiing down a black-diamond trail, quick and fast, in air that made you gasp." His hand fell. "But I told her, I'm a one-woman man—and I had to have a one-man woman. She had to choose. Me. Or Wheeler. I asked her to give me back my ring. And not to come back unless she dumped Wheeler for good."

"Wheeler?" But even as I asked, the pieces slotted into place. Wheeler with his hungry eyes and sexual magnetism.

Dugan leaned against the bar. His big head sank on his chest. He didn't look at me. Or at anything. "For a long time before we met. Wheeler. Then another guy. Then Wheeler. Then we came together. But she spent the weekend before she died in New York with Wheeler."

"He was her stepbrother." The pieces fit, but the shape was ugly.

"Yeah. He was, wasn't he?" Dugan's voice was harsh.

I left him standing by the gallery of photographs.

I walked slowly up the garden walkway, wondering about Stan Dugan and CeeCee Burke and Wheeler Gallagher. About Elise Ford and Keith Scanlon. Love and desire, despair and betrayal. Whose heart was broken, whose passion unfulfilled? I was even with the rooms where Dugan was staying when I saw that the lights were out on the next segment of the walk.

Burned out?

Turned off?

I'm not a fool. I had no intention of walking into the spider's parlor. I shook my head, turned and moved swiftly through Dugan's open rooms to his lanai and the steps leading down to the cliff path. The lights along the trail illuminated the path. I hurried, eager to gain my own lanai.

When I looked up, I looked up into darkness except for the flicker of the torches and the star-spangled sky. I reached the steps to the empty quarters, the rooms I'd declined in favor of the last suite, where Richard had stayed.

I don't know what warned me. A rush of sound. Perhaps stockinged feet slapping on the tiles. Or perhaps it was more basic than that, the atavistic instinct of terrible danger. But I knew, knew even before I saw the black mass hurtling down at me, knew and jumped forward and caught hold of the waist-high rope along the trail, caught and held and pressed myself against the cliff, felt the crumbly ridges of dirt against my cheek, smelled the sharp, green scent of a plant springing from a crevice.

The plummeting mass—and it was big, big enough to gouge a chunk from the path behind me—didn't make much noise. Not enough to rouse anyone, bring anyone. I clung to the rope for a long time, while my heart thudded in my chest.

I clung and listened and waited.

It was a long time—five minutes, ten?—before I crept forward. When I reached the steps to my lanai, once again I waited. I had my keys spread through my fingers and the Mace canister clutched tight in the other hand as I eased up the steps.

But my lanai held no dangers. It took me only a moment to search the suite, make certain it was empty. My opponent wanted an accident. Only an accident would do.

Thank God for that small advantage.

But when my door was closed and locked and the louvered shutters drawn with the bolt slid shut, I sank into a chair and began to shake.

I must be getting close. So close.

* * *

The next morning I walked along the lanai by the empty suite. Sharp marks, perhaps made by a chisel, left angry scratches on the pedestal where a huge Chinese vase had sat. I looked over the railing, shaded my eyes, and saw the torn patches where the vase had bounded down the canyon.

I carried that image with me to breakfast. I drank coffee. I wasn't hungry. The fear curdled in my stomach, cold and hard and indigestible. I glanced around the beautiful, empty room. The buffet was in place. But the bright fruits, the silver serving pans with their quiet elegance and hospitality did nothing to lift the feeling of menace. I was frightened. I supposed I would move in fear every moment I spent at Ahiahi. No one else arrived. Last night Stan Dugan said everyone had scattered to their burrows. Apparently, they intended to stay there.

I set out in search of company. The tennis courts were empty. I didn't take the path to CeeCee's grave. I planned to avoid canyon trails. No one splashed in the pool. But I saw a graceful hand trailing over a chaise longue. Not a vestige of sun reached the pale white limbs beneath the huge orange-and-purple-striped beach umbrella. The ever-present breeze ruffled the canvas, stirred Megan's long blond hair as it would be rustling the leaves of the ohia tree by CeeCee's grave.

Such a thin body. The scarlet bikini—two strips of flame-colored cloth—revealed Megan's malnutrition. Without the latest Paris creations to clothe her gauntness, she looked ill, as indeed she was, her body deprived of sustenance, all in the pursuit of chic. The too-thin face turned toward me, oversized sunglasses hiding her eyes.

"Good morning, Megan. Have you been in the pool yet?" I dropped into a cane chair beside her.

A faint—very faint—smile. "Chlorine's verboten. Can't hit the runway with green hair."

I scooted my chair into the circle of shade. "No sacrifice too great?" I said it lightly.

A languid hand—the scarlet nails glossy and perfect—lifted the sunglasses. Huge cobalt blue eyes looked at me without pretense. I saw a flicker of anger overlain by pride and defiance and sorrow.

"What price freedom, Henrie O?" She studied me, as if I were a column of sums to be added. "I suspect you've counted some costs. Haven't you?"

Honesty compels honesty. Sometimes. "Yes." Oh, yes, I'd counted costs. More than I would admit, more than I wanted to recall, more than I was willing to tot up until the final accounting came.

She slid the sunglasses down, pushed back a silver-blond curl with no taint of green. "I will not be dependent on Belle." Her unaccented voice was as clear and unequivocal as the crack of a rifle shot.

"Why you?" A jacaranda blossom drifted past me, touched my arm with feathery lightness. "Of all the children, why you?"

Megan smiled at that, a cool, amused smile. "I'd like to say it's because I have more character. It may just be that I'm luckier. What if I didn't make pots of money? Would I be so damned independent then? Or would I be like Gretchen?"

The breeze freshened and a flurry of blossoms swirled around us. Megan reached out and caught one, cradled it in her hand.

"Gretchen strikes me as pretty independent." Certainly she'd minced no words on our picnic yesterday.

Megan's lips curved into a sly smile. "Does she? Well, I can tell you that Gretchen's dancing to Belle's tune these days. She doesn't have any choice. Why, she may even have to slink out here to live if she can't get another job." She tossed the lavender bloom away.

"I thought she worked for a wire service. In D.C."

"Downsized." She said it matter-of-factly. "A couple of weeks ago. Belle wants her to stay here."

"I doubt if Gretchen's eager to do that." This could account for Gretchen's irritability. "Wouldn't Belle like Joss to stay, too?"

Megan nodded. "Oh, yes. Mom's golden boy. Yes, she'd like that. She's starting to come out of her shock and grief. And she misses us. But no one wants to move here. Especially not Joss. But he's no dummy. Hollywood pays like crazy when you're working. He lives carefully between gigs."

"And Gretchen hasn't been so careful?" Gretchen was the one who skipped shopping in Hanapepe. She preferred glitz over funk. Glitz costs a good deal more.

"Gretchen can spend money faster than the mint can print it. And even Belle's largesse has limits. Generous, yes. Indulgent, no." A dry smile. "And I don't loan money to relatives. Sink or swim."

Megan pulled herself erect, reached for a towel and began to pat her cheeks. I didn't see even a faint erosion of her makeup, but I suspected her sense of beauty was too well-honed ever to let perspiration go unchecked.

"So you don't accept any money. But you come when Belle calls?"

Megan patted the back of her neck with the towel. "I almost didn't come this year." Her face turned toward me. "After last night I'm not sure I'm glad I did. Is Stan crazy?"

"He seems very rational to me."

"Because"—her tone was puzzled—"if you think about it, why should it matter what we all said to CeeCee that last day? What matters . . ."

I worked a loose piece of rattan back into the arm of the chair. "Yes? What matters?"

But she didn't continue. Her face looked wan and pinched. Megan was nobody's fool.

"Henrie O . . ."

I wished I could see past the opaque lenses of her sunglasses. I felt that her gaze was intent upon me. But why? What did she need of me? Or want of me? I waited, alert and hopeful. I had a feeling that this moment mattered, that Megan was balancing options.

". . . is it true that you and Belle had never met before?"

Her question surprised me. And disappointed me. Was I grasping at meaning in every encounter simply because I knew there was so much that was hidden beneath the glamorous surface of Ahiahi?

Megan's face was as still as a deep lake on a windless day. The sunglasses hid her eyes, but once again I felt certain she was watching me, trying to read my face, divine my thoughts.

I picked my words carefully, the way a cat delicately tiptoes through dew-damp grass. "Belle and my husband were great friends." And more? "But she and I hadn't met until now."

"Then why did Belle ask you to come here? Why now?" Her voice was sharp.

A dozen answers slid through my mind, like goldfish glimmering in a murky pool. I sorted through them in a flash, hoping this wasn't—from Megan's point of view—the wrong answer. "I don't know," I said bluntly. "Do you?"

Megan took off the opaque glasses and looked at me with anxious, somber eyes. "I wondered if it had to do with her accident last year."

Belle's accident last year.

Belle walking with a cane.

Belle's accident!

And the message that brought me here, ensured my presence here.

"What happened to Belle? When?" I've asked questions in a shout at news conferences, run alongside moving trains and called out, flung words at the backs of striding politicians. I've cajoled and pled and demanded. But I don't think ever in my life I'd asked in a voice that absolutely brooked no evasion, no refusal, no denial.

Megan shook back that shining hair. Something moved in that mournful gaze, an acceptance, a realization. Megan, the sensitive, who felt emotions, calibrated them, absorbed them. She gave one small, reluctant sigh. "Last year when we were here, the brakes went out in her car. Going down the mountain."

Going down the mountain, down that twisting road with no guardrails and a drop to eternity.

Megan folded her sunglasses, slipped them into her woven carry-on. "You didn't know about it?" Her voice was thoughtful.

"No. How in God's name did Belle survive that drop?"

"She slid across the seat, opened the passenger door and flung herself out. Her right hip shattered when she landed on the road. She's had three operations. But to think that quickly . . ." Amazement and admiration lifted Megan's voice.

"The car?"

"It bounced down the mountain and exploded. All that's left is a burned-out hulk. You can still see some of the scars it left on the way down. But now ferns have covered it. Like it never happened." Megan pulled on a cerise cover-up without disturbing a single strand of hair. "But it made me wonder about Ahiahi. Your husband fell off the cliff. Belle's brakes went out. That's why I came. I wanted to see if anything was going to happen this year." Her eyes locked with mine. "Then you arrive. I thought Belle asked you to come. I know who you are. You've been involved in big stories. Crime. I thought maybe she asked you to come and find out about the brakes." She looked at me levelly. "Oh, I know the car's rusted out. There's nothing to be found there. But I can tell you one thing. Those brakes were all right the day before Belle's accident. I drove her car down the mountain. The brakes were fine. But the very next day, Belle steps on the brake pedal and nothing's there."

Megan's face was somber. She clasped her hands tightly together. "The car exploded. We heard it and hurried down the road and found her. We got an ambulance. They rushed her right into surgery. We didn't get home from the hospital until real late. But the next morning I went out early, before anyone was up. Belle always parked in the same place. There was a spot or two of oil, but no pool of brake fluid. Full of fluid one day, gone the next without a trace? I don't think so."

"You believe someone sabotaged the brakes?"

"What do you think?" Her tone was sharp.

The Socratic method. Work it out yourself. Add up the numbers. Tally the column.

Megan gathered up her bag, slipped into her thongs, stood gracefully.

I rose and faced her.

She hesitated, then said, "I don't know why you're here. But if you can help us, I hope you will. Before something else happens."

I watched her walk away, graceful, lovely, and worried. What else could happen? I knew the answer to that question.

Belle could die.

I'd traveled halfway across the world to try and discover what had happened to my husband. I'd come resenting the claim Belle Ericcson had on Richard's life.

I'd met Belle, a fascinating, vulnerable, grieving woman. I liked her. I admired her. And why should that surprise me? Richard had cared for her. I knew she'd cared deeply for Richard, the Richard I had loved so long and so unreservedly.

Now it was clear to me that my task was twofold. I would

avenge Richard. And protect Belle. And I felt, despite fear and stress and daunting challenge, a curious sense of peace.

I'd left the rental car unlocked. I glanced over it. When the motor was running, I eased around and went a few feet, then jammed on the brakes. Call me spooked, if you will. Certainly call me careful.

I slowed at the first curve. Now that I was looking for it, it was easy to see where Belle's car had crashed over the side. Last year, when everyone gathered to remember CeeCee.

The timing mattered, of course. So many things mattered.

CeeCee's character. Johnnie Rodriguez's call to Richard. Richard's arrival at Ahiahi. Belle's accident. The challenge bringing me here.

Megan urged me to figure it out. That's just what I intended to do. I had some sums in mind as I drove cautiously down the twisting, curving road. But the equation still needed to be proved. Was someone trying to kill Belle? Was I decoyed here to protect her? To serve as a scapegoat? Was I right that someone in the family circle had arranged for CeeCee to be kidnapped?

I wondered if Lester Mackey would show up at Spouting Horn. No matter. I would find him there or at Ahiahi. I did not intend to be deflected. Not now. Because the strands were coming together.

Tourists wandered about, sunburned and cheerful, pausing to look over the stalls of the flea market. Coral and shell necklaces, koa and monkeypod bowls, silk leis and ukuleles, something for every taste. I hurried past the booths, up the sloping sidewalk.

Lester Mackey leaned on the bright green chain-link fence, looking out at the huge spume of water as it exploded forcefully from the lava tube, making an unearthly sound like an asthmatic giant's wheeze. From a distance he looked boyish, once again in a checkered shirt and faded jeans. But when I came closer I saw the flecks of gray in his faded-blond hair. The bright, midday sun showed the deep lines on his face as clear and distinct as the crevices in the lava shelf that harbored Spouting Horn. He continued to stare out over the slippery, wet black lava, taking no notice as I gripped the fence beside him.

"You love the children," I said softly.

A lacy column of seawater rose, white as Grecian marble. He waited until the moan of the expelled air subsided. "They're my kids," he said simply in his light, whispery voice. "I helped raise CeeCee and Anders and Joss. I helped them with their schoolwork. I took them to their lessons—swimming, dancing, horseback riding. I packed up their stuff for camp. And I did my best for Wheeler and his sisters when Belle married Quentin. Wheeler went off to college the next year, but he was still a kid, he still needed somebody to care about him, especially after his dad died."

"Wheeler says you've always been there for them."

He squinted against the bright sun. "I covered for them when they came in drunk. I loaned them money. I cheered when they won."

"And encouraged them when they lost." I understood. I've been there.

He reached back, pulled out his wallet. Pictures of each of the Burkes when they were little: CeeCee playing jacks, Anders cradling a puppy, Joss kicking a soccer ball; and of the Gallaghers as teenagers: Wheeler playing drums, Megan pouring tea, Gretchen climbing a tree.

He smoothed a finger gently over the picture of CeeCee. "I went to work for Belle when CeeCee was five years old. She had a lisp. She couldn't say Lester. She called me Wethter. The last time—" He broke off, bent his head forward, squeezed his eyes shut.

His pain pulsed between us.

"CeeCee called you Wethter, didn't she? That Friday. At the lake." I spoke gently. No matter how many wrong choices this man had made, he'd made them because of love.

Slowly his eyes opened. He looked at me and I saw emptiness and torment and terrible sorrow.

"Oh, Jesus God, I thought it was a joke! The next day, when the ransom demand came, I couldn't believe it! I didn't know what to do. I went to the cabin. It was empty. No CeeCee. Not a trace of her. I got sick in the woods. But it didn't help. I was shaking and my insides felt like I'd eaten acid. I ran back to the house, but Belle wouldn't see anybody. She sent for your husband. I tried once to talk to her, but she sent me away, said not then, later. And what did I have to tell? I was ashamed, I didn't want to tell her what I'd done. And I didn't understand what had happened, how anything like this could have happened. I thought it would all come out and Belle would know it wasn't my fault. When they found CeeCee in the lake, it was too late. And then I was scared. I decided it was some clever crooks. They could have found out about the jokes the kids played from the newspapers." He looked at me in plaintive appeal. "They could have, couldn't they?"

"It was all in the newspapers," I agreed. And it had been, the pink flamingos and the computer tricks and the scavenger hunts. "You got a letter or a note—"

"I found the note in my car Friday afternoon. Down at the lake."

"Telling you to 'kidnap' CeeCee as part of a joke to celebrate her birthday?"

He'd lived with the memory of that cloudy spring afternoon for a long time. He nodded wearily. "Just a joke. Toy guns. But CeeCee was always a sport. She laughed when Johnnie and I held her up, told her she had to come with us. She let us blindfold her. All part of the joke. The letter had a map in it, to a shabby little rental cabin about a mile away, up a narrow dirt road. We took CeeCee inside—the front door was unlocked and there was a chair with handcuffs fastened to one arm. We were supposed to handcuff her to the chair, but she said no. She promised she'd stay there and then she grinned and pointed to a picnic basket. She said, 'Must have been planned by Joss. He never misses a meal. And a bottle of Dom Perignon. Okay, Wethter, I'll play the game. But the picnic better be *damn* good.' "

"Why did you involve Johnnie?"

"To make it more fun. We wore handkerchief masks like bad guys in the old cowboy movies. CeeCee got a kick out of that."

"Later, did you and Johnnie ever talk about what happened?"

"Just once. I told him it must have been planned by some crooks who knew all about the kids. We decided we couldn't go to the police. We didn't think anybody would believe us. And we hadn't done anything wrong. We didn't know anything that would have made a difference to the police."

And Belle would have been furious.

"You had the letter, setting it up," I said sharply. "That could have helped—"

He was shaking his head. "The last part told me to put the letter and the toy guns in the rowboat by the boathouse." He kneaded his temple with his fist. "Somebody stole the rowboat that night. The police found it drifting near a public boat ramp."

As Dugan said, somebody had been clever, very, very clever.

Lester Mackey's faded blue eyes pled with me. "It could have been anybody, anybody at all."

But he and I knew that wasn't true. Maybe he couldn't have known it then, but he knew it now.

"Richard."

Mackey's eyes slid away from me. "I thought he fell."

"Richard talked to you when he came to Ahiahi." I tried to keep a dangerous edge out of my voice. I needed this man's help.

Slowly, Lester nodded. "Just for a minute. Late that afternoon. He said he'd seen Johnnie and Johnnie'd told him how we staged the kidnapping. He asked me if Johnnie'd ever talked to me about later that night, the night CeeCee disappeared."

The night that Johnnie went for a walk in the woods. Back to the cabin where CeeCee waited for the joke to continue.

I waited for Lester's answer as Richard must have waited. Richard was looking for confirmation. I was looking for a name.

I knew the answer before it came, knew and raged within.

Lester massaged one temple. "But I told him I'd only talked to Johnnie once and he hadn't said a word about that night. Not a word."

So only Richard knew whom Johnnie saw with CeeCee.

Richard was dead.

Johnnie was dead.

I was suffused with despair. I'd come so far, certain I would know the truth of Richard's death when I discovered who had sent me the poster.

Now, I knew.

But I didn't know enough. And this man couldn't really help me. I stared out at the tower of water wavering in the limpid air.

Lester gripped the green knob of the fence post. "Ever since CeeCee was killed, I wake up in the night scared to death. Something's wrong, dreadfully wrong. At first I don't know what it is, and then I remember, I remember." Spouting Horn gave its mournful moan. "But I couldn't believe it was one of the kids. I couldn't believe it."

Wouldn't believe it.

He put his hands together, cracked the knuckles. "Your

husband could have fallen. Anybody can fall. But Belle's accident last year—I kept thinking about it. At first I was just so glad she was alive. But I kept thinking about the brakes going out. And then I thought about your husband and the fact that everyone was coming now. And I was scared."

"So you sent that poster to me." Lester with his artistic talents and his reluctance ever to be noticed.

Defiantly, Lester met my eyes. "I thought if you came, maybe you could prove it one way or the other. I thought maybe I was crazy, making it all up, because everything's been so weird since the lake. But when you said Johnnie drowned, just a couple of weeks after your husband came here, then I knew. Johnnie never stumbled off his pier. I don't care how drunk he was. Somebody killed Johnnie. That means somebody here killed your husband, and that means . . ."

Someone in the family killed CeeCee at the lake. And tried to kill Belle here.

Add up the column. Tally the figures.

"Lester," my voice was insistent, "the letter you found in your car, the letter setting up the joke. Who signed it?"

He licked his lips. "It had to be forged."

"Lester, who signed it? Who did Johnnie Rodriguez see at the cabin?"

"It's all so tangled. It doesn't fit together. And why the hell didn't Johnnie tell me if he saw anyone at the cabin? I'm the one he should have told." His voice was sullen.

"What would you have done?" I asked bitterly.

"I'd have done something. And now, now I don't know what to do."

"You've got to tell Belle everything. We have to warn her."

He stepped back, glared at me. "We can't tell her. Listen, let me see what I can find out."

"What do you know?" By God, he knew something!

"I don't *know* anything. I can't blame somebody if I don't know." His anguish was clear. He turned away, hurried down the sidewalk, his head lowered.

I ran after him. "Lester, tell me who signed that letter."

He shook his head. "That's not the answer. I know it's not." He walked faster.

"Lester, damn you," and I shouted it, "tell me!"

He broke into a run, loped to his car. I followed as fast as I could. I didn't care that curious faces turned toward me. But the car peeled out of the lot, leaving me standing in its dust.

fourteen

I had to talk to Belle. It was no longer solely a matter of discovering what happened to Richard. It was, imperatively, urgently, a matter of Belle's safety. Yes, I could remain silent about what I knew when it was a question of vengeance. I could not remain silent now.

Last year someone in a very small, intimate circle—her husband, one of her children or stepchildren, her son's wife, her secretary—one of them tampered with the brakes on her car.

The first face that flashed in my mind was that of her husband. I couldn't be certain, but there seemed no plausible reason why Elise Ford and Keith Scanlon should quarrel—bitterly, clandestinely—unless they were involved in an affair. Did Scanlon want to break off the affair? It figured. He'd had a pattern through his life of inconstancy. But no matter whether he enjoyed running a tennis center, he obviously enjoyed being married to a very wealthy woman. But perhaps he was tired not only of his lover but of his wife. He could go home to Texas much more comfortably as a fabulously wealthy widower.

Anders Burke was obsessed with protecting animals. Was there a limit to Belle's largesse to the foundation, a limit that would ease with her death and his inheritance? Anders was still jealous of his dead sister. Had he resented Belle's tenderness for CeeCee enough to plan the kidnapping and murder?

Joss Burke wanted to stay in Hollywood. Had he killed his sister to win the freedom to go there? Would he kill his mother to win the wealth to stay there?

Wheeler Gallagher was high maintenance. Belle was a generous stepmother. No doubt he would have access to even more money if she died. Had CeeCee finally told Wheeler they were finished, that she was going to leave him behind forever for Stan Dugan?

Megan Gallagher starved herself to be free. But models have a very short life of fame and riches. Would she shorten Belle's life to have the money to be free always? "What price freedom?" she'd asked me. Perhaps she knew the answer. But it was she who told me about the brakes in Belle's car.

Gretchen Gallagher needed money. Gretchen resented her father's marriage to Belle. And Gretchen, too, won freedom when CeeCee died.

Elise Ford was involved with Keith Scanlon. To what length would she go to have him to herself? To be chatelaine of Ahiahi? Or could it be even darker? Had Keith spurned her to return to his wife and was Elise consumed with jealousy?

Or, in the swirl of conflicting desires and emotions at Ahiahi, the attempt on Belle's life could be independent of CeeCee's murder. I went back and forth, uncertain, sure only that Belle, unaware, was stalked by deadly peril.

I was determined to face Belle that day. I returned to Ahiahi with that one goal in mind.

Belle was gone.

Elise was apologetic. "Belle was so sorry you weren't here. She especially wanted you to come. There's a wonderful coffeehouse in Kalaheo. But they should be back by mid-afternoon." Belle had left just before noon with Gretchen and Megan.

"And the others?"

"Oh," she said carelessly, "some are here and some aren't." Elise's voice was pleasant, but there were dark shadows under her eyes. "It's all very casual, Mrs. Collins."

Casual. And frightening. But Belle should be safe with Megan and Gretchen. It was tonight that concerned me and the remainder of the nights while this gathering lasted. This was the dangerous period, while all the family was here.

I didn't know what I would say to Belle, what I *should* say to Belle. Should I reveal all of it, including my suspicions about Keith and Elise? Or should I focus on CeeCee and Richard's trip here in search of CeeCee's killer? I didn't know.

I was too restless simply to await Belle's return. I wandered about Ahiahi.

I found Amelia in the kitchen, conferring with the cook. I waited until she walked out to the garden.

"Amelia?"

She turned, looked at me gravely. I think she knew why I wanted to see her.

"Ma'am." She waited attentively, but her dark eyes were troubled.

"The night my husband died and you were awake quite late, whom did you see?" I kept my voice even, quiet, unemotional, as if this were a simple piece of information, nothing to remark.

She was reluctant. Yet, why should she be? Unless she too thought Richard's fall was no accident. But the questioning look in her eyes surprised me. Shocked me a little. I realized she was suspicious of me, of my motives. Why had I come? And what mischief did I intend?

It's odd to realize you've been misinterpreted entirely. It made me wonder what discussions might have ensued among the staff.

"Mrs. Collins." She was still polite, but for the first time she spoke to me as an individual, not as Belle's employee. "Anyone can be awake late at night. Especially as you get older. Yes, I saw someone. I'd gone to the kitchen to fix myself a cup of camomile tea. Mr. Mackey was on the lanai by the reflecting pool."

"Did he see you?"

"I don't believe so. I had my tea and was carrying it back to my rooms." Her voice was firm.

But Lester Mackey had no reason late at night to be on that lanai. Was he going to go to Richard? Or had Lester seen someone else abroad at that very late hour and followed to see what was happening? Did Lester see someone go to Richard's suite?

Lester saw someone or something. But not enough to make him suspect murder when Richard died. Especially since Lester did not want to make that linkage. He'd resisted until Belle's "accident." That frightened him, caused him to entice me here.

"If that is all, Mrs. Collins . . ."

I looked at Amelia. I suppose my face was grim. "Yes. That's all, Amelia."

She gave me a sharp, thoughtful look, then moved quietly away.

The hard *thwock* of tennis balls led me to the clay courts. Stan and Joss, their faces dangerously red, their sweaty clothes clinging to them, played tennis as if the future of the world depended upon the outcome. I walked on and found Peggy sunning by the pool.

Peggy looked at me like an African villager sighting a marauding leopard. "What do you want?" She pulled the lime-green beach towel up to her chin. The childlike gesture almost touched me until I balanced it with her swiftness to lie when she thought Anders was threatened and her creativity, claiming that CeeCee had approved the plan for the animal refuge that last Friday afternoon.

"A little more truth and a little less lies." I pushed a chair into the shade of the umbrella, its canvas rippling in the breeze. Jacaranda blossoms floated in the pool. Pretty, but a hazard for the filters.

The sweet, summery scent of coconut oil wafted toward me as she struggled to sit up. The towel slipped down. Her skin had a bright, greasy sheen, and her hair clung to her head in damp, limp ringlets. "It *is* the truth. CeeCee decided the refuge was absolutely a wonderful idea."

I looked at her dispassionately. It was almost too easy. The old when-you-hear-this-word-what's-the-first-thing-that-comes-to-mind game. Yes, Peggy was quite willing to lie, but she had yet to learn how to dissemble. If I'd had any doubts about her creative recall, this settled them. That made Joss's ingenuous support quite interesting.

But maybe I could pan a little truth from Peggy's lies. "At breakfast yesterday—"

It might be a mundane beginning, but it certainly had Peggy's full attention.

"—you said CeeCee told you that she'd given her engagement ring back to Stan."

"That was *after* we'd talked about the refuge." Peggy's eyes glistened with cunning.

Oh, Peggy. Would a woman who'd just broken her engagement start a conversation with a discussion of charitable plans?

"Did CeeCee call you?"

"Yes. About two-thirty." Peggy was comfortable here.

Sifting the truth wasn't going to be hard. CeeCee had returned from the lunch where she—or Stan—had ended their engagement and she called her best friend.

"Was CeeCee upset?"

Peggy nodded emphatically. "Oh, yes. Or she wouldn't have called me." Peggy'd forgotten for a moment about the refuge. "Of course CeeCee kept her cool. She just said she and Stan were through and she'd tell me all about it at the lake." She smoothed the towel over her lap. "But her voice was shaking."

"What about Wheeler?"

Peggy's prim face shifted and there was a sudden sexual light in her eyes. "Oh." She looked at me with respect. "How did you know about that?"

"I suppose it wasn't common knowledge."

"No." Peggy picked up a corner of the towel, pleated it in her fingers. "They had a thing for each other." There was a tiny edge of envy in her voice. "But CeeCee simply couldn't face Belle. Not about Wheeler. Because Belle always made so much fuss about the great, wonderful family. I told CeeCee over and over that Wheeler wasn't her brother. I mean, that's silly. They were teenagers when they met. And that's what happened, of course. Right from the first . . ." Again, that little surge of envy. "Of course, they had to keep it hidden then. You know how adults are about sex!" For a moment it was as though she were a teenager again in a secret world. "And they kept it a secret for so many years and acted like brother and sister and that made it, well, like it was wrong. CeeCee kept trying to fall in love, one guy after another. But she always came back to Wheeler. I thought it was going to be okay when she met Stan." She looked at me earnestly. "CeeCee really fell for him. I don't know what happened."

I did. If Stan's story was true.

But it could have happened just a little differently. Instead of Stan asking for the ring, maybe CeeCee returned it because she'd decided, after all was said and done, that she loved Wheeler and that she would have him no matter what.

And how might Stan Dugan have reacted to that?

But why would Stan have hired a private detective? And why last night would he have pummeled the "witnesses" about CeeCee's last day?

There was always the possibility of a twist within a twist within a twist.

Stan Dugan could have hired a private detective because it was the kind of action a flamboyant, bereaved trial lawyer might be expected to take when the crime wasn't solved.

And last night Stan could have been playing to me, the retired reporter reputed to be an expert on crime. If Stan took the dossiers from my room, he would certainly be likely to think I was after more than material for a book. And his performance last night could be a charade of innocence. But Stan wasn't here last year when the brakes went out in Belle's car. Still, it was always possible that the attempt on Belle's life had nothing to do with CeeCee's kidnapping.

Peggy watched me warily.

I wasn't finished with her. "Did CeeCee say anything about Wheeler to you?"

"Not a word. Just that she would tell me everything at the lake."

That seemed to be that. I stood. Then, as an afterthought, I asked, "Did she mention Belle?"

"Not then."

Reporters are persistent. It's not a habit you lose. "When?"

"The night before. There was a dinner in Belle's honor at the Adolphus. Some donation she'd made. And when Belle walked up to receive the plaque, CeeCee had a strange look on her face—half sad and half mad. She said, 'I won't see Mother taken advantage of. It's just rotten. I won't!' Then Belle began to speak. After dinner, CeeCee left with Stan. So

I didn't have a chance to ask her what she meant. But that was the night before."

The next morning, CeeCee asked her mother what she would do if someone she loved was unfaithful. That evening CeeCee drove up to the lake. Belle would be coming. There would be ample opportunity for CeeCee to speak with her mother. And tell her that her husband was an adulterer?

Rotten. Yes, that put it very well indeed.

Joss sprawled on a chaise deep in the shadow of an arbor covered with bougainvillea. I stepped into the dusky enclosure. I looked around.

He opened his eyes, regarded me without enthusiasm. "If you're looking for Stan, he's gone."

"You lost?"

"The bastard's serve jumps around like a clown on a pogo stick." He mopped his face with a towel.

"Really? I'd have thought he'd go for power."

"Oh, he does," Joss said sourly. "Just about the time you've got the damn corkscrew serve figured out, he barrels one right down the center line."

"Stan found out about CeeCee and Wheeler. Just before she went to the lake."

Joss pushed up, swung his feet to the flagstones, scrubbed his wet hair with the towel. Then he stood, grabbing his racquet. "Should be a pretty choice part of your book. Sex sells every time." His parting glance was derisive.

As he walked past, I said, "So maybe you didn't have to lie for Anders."

He shook his head and kept on walking.

I listened as the sound of his footsteps faded.

Did Joss confirm Peggy's story that CeeCee agreed to the animal refuge because he was afraid for Anders, afraid for the driven brother who cared more about animals than people?

Or did Joss lie because he knew very well that Anders was innocent? If Joss killed CeeCee to gain his freedom to go to Hollywood, he knew better than anyone in the world that Anders was innocent.

Had Joss really told CeeCee he was leaving the foundation? No one else knew of it. And it was becoming clear to me that this close-knit group of siblings and stepsiblings knew a very great deal about one another.

If only I could pull from one, then another, enough scraps of knowledge to piece together what happened to CeeCee as she waited for the joke to unfold that chilly spring evening at the lake.

We stood on the lanai outside Belle's office. On the day I arrived at Ahiahi, she had pointed to the grove of kukui trees where Richard's body had been found. I glanced down at the light-colored leaves, then faced Belle.

She was turned a little to one side and I couldn't see her cane. She looked quite young in a cerise tunic and slacks. A sprig of silver hair had escaped from her chignon. She brushed it back, looked at me with a smile. The smile slowly faded. Her fine-boned face was abruptly alert. "Yes?"

We looked fully at each other and there was uncertainty in both our gazes. She sensed this was no social approach, and I still struggled with what I should say.

I hadn't known how I would begin. I'd left it to my heart. I heard my words without surprise, with a sense of completion.

"Richard was murdered, Belle." My hands curled into fists. "Pushed off the cliff trail. Because he knew who kidnapped and killed CeeCee."

The muscles in her face tightened until the cheekbones and chin were sharp and pointed like a vixen's muzzle. Her eyes glittered with shock. Whatever she had expected, it was not this, never this.

I've never talked faster, harder. I began with the poster that yanked me from my carefully rebuilt life, took me to Dallas and the lake, and brought me ultimately to Ahiahi. I told her about Lester Mackey and the letter he received and the joke he and Johnnie Rodriguez had played on CeeCee and how they left her in a shabby little rental cabin with the picnic basket. I told her about Johnnie and how he liked to wander along the country lanes in the dark. I told her about Richard's trip to the lake to talk to Johnnie. "Then Richard came here and—"

Belle held up her hand. "Wait." She walked into her study, punched an intercom. "Lester. Come to my office. Now." Simple words, spoken with terrible restraint and a deadly intensity. She walked back to the lanai, her face as still and cold as a frozen landscape.

"Belle, I'm almost sure that Lester has an idea—"

Once again she held up her hand, the flesh so thin it was almost translucent. Her wedding ring, a double row of diamonds, flashed in the afternoon sun.

Belle Ericcson was accustomed to command. Had I continued to speak, she would not have listened. Could I have battered past her resistance? Should I have kept on talking, told her of the jealousies and passions among the children she loved, the unfaithfulness of her husband, the treachery of her employee, the faintheartedness of the loyal subordinate who'd been there—sometimes unwisely—for the children as they grew up?

But I stood silent. She would only listen when she had proof. And Lester Mackey would be her proof. Her heart refused to listen to me. This was a woman who had suffered terribly and I was now bringing her more suffering with the brutal accusation that someone she loved and trusted had robbed her of her first child, taken a vivid life and snuffed it out behind the facade of laughter. I was insisting that there was a false face among the family gathered about her, that behind a familiar countenance burned a murderous passion that was not yet satisfied.

Was it any wonder she would not listen?

Rubber slippers slapped softly on the garden walkway. Lester walked into the study.

Belle lifted her cane imperiously.

Lester saw me. His gaze checked for an instant, moved on to Belle. "Yes, Belle. Do you need me?" His faded eyes squinted against the sun spilling in from the lanai.

"I want the truth, Lester. Through all the years, I've known I could count on you. Always." Her eyes implored him. "What happened to CeeCee?" She held the knob of her cane with both hands, leaned on it.

His look of startled surprise was perfect. "But—" He was a study in bewilderment. "Belle, why are you asking me?" His whispery voice was calm, unworried.

Belle drew a deep breath. "Do you swear to me, Lester, do you swear on the night we met outside the bar in Saigon, do you swear to me that you don't know what happened to CeeCee?"

Their eyes met and held.

"Belle, I swear to you, I don't know what happened."

I heard the faintest, telltale emphasis on the third from last word.

"Lester—" The cry was wrung from me.

They both turned toward me.

I knew even as I reached out toward him that this moment was exacting a dreadful toll from Lester Mackey. His face was white and rigid.

"Lester, you know Belle's in danger. Please, we—"

"That's enough." Belle's voice was as sharp and thin as the crack of a whip.

I took a step toward her. "Belle, every word I've—"

"—said is a lie." She looked at me with cold, remote, reproving eyes. "It's time for you to go. You came with a lie, that's how you're leaving. For Richard's sake, I will try to believe that you are sincere, that you believe this demented tale. But I will not have you in my home. Please, leave now."

She turned away, her cane clicking on the hardwood floor.

And I heard the whisper of thongs—

I whirled around. "Lester, Lester . . ."

But he was gone, my desperate cry to no avail. And Belle had ordered me to leave.

I was to be banished. And Belle was still at risk.

All the way down the mountain, red dust flying from beneath the jeep's wheels, I struggled with indecision. What to do first, where to go, what possible recourse I had.

First things first. I must do what I could to keep Belle safe for the coming night. I drove directly to Keith Scanlon's tennis center. He was teaching on a near court. I waited near a fragrant, glossy-leaved plumeria. The sweet smell, always recalling welcoming leis and happier days, caught at my heart. Once Richard and I had arrived in this lovely land and walked hand in hand and smelled this special, particular scent. We'd come to paradise, though we knew that paradise existed within ourselves, waiting to be found. And now—

Keith's suntanned face was wreathed in a satisfied smile. He clicked off the ball machine. "Good work, Tim. I'll see you after school on Monday."

The lithe teenager flashed a grin. "Okay, Keith."

Keith Scanlon was married to one of the world's richest women. But on Saturday afternoon he was ending up a lesson at his tennis complex.

I wasn't surprised. A man who's cheating on his wife always finds reason not to be home.

Keith wound up the cord, covered the ball machine with a tarp. He was whistling as he came through the gate.

I stepped into the path.

"Hi, Henrie O. Looking for a game?" A smile wreathed his face.

For a moment, his welcome shocked me. Then I realized he had no idea I was an outcast and absolutely no idea I knew about him and Elise.

I didn't smile in return, however. Bonhomie wasn't my goal.

"Keith, as you will discover when you return to Ahiahi, I am no longer a guest. But I want to make absolutely clear to you—without any possibility of your mistaking me—that if anything happens to Belle, now or in the future, any kind of clever accident like the brakes going out in her car, I will immediately contact the Kauai police and tell them all about you and Elise."

I whirled and walked swiftly away.

I didn't have to look behind me to know he was staring after me as if I'd sprouted horns.

I didn't give a damn.

I checked into the Poipu Beach Hyatt Regency, glad to find a vacancy. I ate an early dinner in my room, picking at a salad I didn't want, forcing myself finally to choke down one of the high energy bars I always carry with me when I travel. My mind churned with possibilities. I knew that only a confession from Lester would convince Belle. I had to persuade Lester Mackey to tell the truth. Somehow I had to reach Lester, force him to admit the truth: There was a killer at Ahiahi. And I had to convince Lester now. Tonight.

The lobby of the Hyatt Regency is as lush as any tropical jungle. The screech of the clipped-wing parrots on their bars pierced the squeal of running children and the animated chatter from the various bars. I wasn't interested in a drink. I wanted to be as alert as I've ever been this night. I wandered restlessly around the meandering lagoon until night fell.

Finally, it was time to go.

I left all traffic behind me when I turned on the cane road. I drove past the barred entrance. I nosed into a narrow gap in the cane not far from the gate. I left the jeep well-hidden.

I walked back to the gate and slipped past it, easy to do on foot. It was dark, but there was enough moonlight for me to walk up the road without using my flash. I wore my navy blouse and slacks and jogging shoes.

It was a long, steep ascent and it took me almost an hour to reach the parking area outside Ahiahi. There was plenty of light there, of course, light that I avoided. I slipped around the edge of the parking area, my objective the stucco wall that marked the perimeter of the grounds.

I wasn't surprised to find a freshly mown grassy border on the outside of the wall. It wasn't necessary. But it was nice. The very rich always enjoy the best of manicured surroundings. Nor did it surprise me finally, in an inconspicuous corner at the far end of the tennis courts, to find a toolshed and an entryway from the outside to the sports area. There was room for gardeners to maneuver lawn mowers easily in and out.

I heard again the solid *thump* of well-hit tennis balls. The lights shone down on the first court. I stepped softly, avoiding the shell path, and moved closer, keeping behind a line of ten-foot hibiscus. Enough light slanted through the leaves for me to realize I was walking along the edge of a croquet lawn. Between the lawn and the shrubs were several bricked areas with benches. I wormed my way between two shrubs until I could see the court and hear Gretchen and Wheeler as they talked in short bursts between points.

"... think we can do anything about it?"

Gretchen served and the ball went wide. Her second serve was a soft shot that Wheeler returned to the backhand court, far out of her reach.

"No. But it isn't the book that bothers me." She served

and they rallied until she curved a lob behind him to the baseline. "Right now Belle's furious. But first there was Stan and his crazy stuff about CeeCee's last hours, then this Collins woman claiming one of us planned CeeCee's kidnapping, then killed her husband, for God's sake. Of course, Lester showed her up for a liar. But what if Belle starts thinking there's something to it?"

Wheeler scrambled back. He got his racket on the ball, but it spun lazily over the backstop. "Oh, she won't. It's crazy. Don't worry about it."

Gretchen pulled a ball from beneath her tennis skirt. She served and Wheeler hit into the net. She took the last two points, slamming one overhead, making an ace. "Thanks, Wheeler, that was fun. God, it's nice to have fun sometimes."

At the bench, as they slid their rackets into covers, Wheeler said abruptly, "I heard Belle and Mrs. Collins this afternoon." His hand tightened around the handle of his racket. His face was suddenly heavy and somber, all traces of pleasure gone. "I remember one time—" He broke off, stared down at the ground.

"What, Wheeler?" There was an odd note in his sister's voice.

"Lester. One time when I was back from college. I was drunk and I had a wreck. Nobody was hurt, thank God, but I would've lost my license. I drove away, made it home. The next morning, Lester told Belle he'd run the car into that big oak tree at the foot of the drive." Wheeler lifted his eyes to his sister, eyes full of misery and pain.

"Lester wouldn't—" Gretchen's hair shimmered as she shook her head violently. "Lester wouldn't!"

"Lester's lied for all of us." His voice was deep and harsh. "But this time, oh, Jesus, this time—if one of us killed CeeCee, I swear I'll rip the world apart to find out. I will." His face was savage. He lifted the racket, brought it down with all his might against the wooden bench, then whirled toward the gate.

"Wheeler. Wheeler!" But he was gone.

Gretchen had to know about Wheeler and CeeCee They all knew, everyone but Belle. But perhaps Gretchen hadn't realized how inconsolable was his grief. She stood alone on the beautiful red clay court, her shoulders slumped, staring forlornly after her brother.

"Oh, Wheeler, dammit, she wasn't worth it! Wheeler, she wasn't!" There was a sob in Gretchen's voice.

I could hear its echo long after she walked out of the tennis enclosure.

I waited a good half hour before I slipped through the gate. I didn't encounter any other residents of Ahiahi. I went directly to the suite where I'd stayed. I took off my running shoes and walked in my socks across the room. The bottoms of the shoes would be stained by red dirt from my climb up the mountain road. I didn't want to leave any trace, anywhere.

I was confident I could remain in my former suite undisturbed and undetected. This was a week for family only at Ahiahi. Except for Stan Dugan, I had been the only intruder. The suite would have been cleaned after my departure and there was no reason for anyone to come to it.

I settled on a very comfortable chaise longue on the lanai. And now I must wait until quiet reigned, until no one was abroad. I knew Stan Dugan was likely to wander to the pool table when it was late. But I could slip past unseen on the cliff path.

As I waited, I looked out across the night-shrouded valley, the shadows so deep and dark that the hillsides looked like piles of coal. Above, the stars seemed close enough to touch, as coldly lovely as pearls. The falls glistened in the moonlight like strands of silver Christmas foil. Their roar pulsed against me.

"Richard."

There was no one there to hear my call. I knew that. I don't believe in conjuring up the dead.

I do believe in memory.

A memory came, as sudden and inexplicable as the burst of joy that can lift your soul when touched by beauty. We all can remember such moments: the drone of cicadas and the smell of wet earth on an August afternoon; an unexpected smile and the touch of your mother's hand; coming around a bend in the road to see a farmhouse at once so familiar and so strange your heart almost stops . . . we all remember moments like these, when the world is touched by magic.

I had a sudden picture of Richard lifting Emily high in the air. She was two and we were picnicking by a placid pond and as he whirled around with her, I could see their moving reflection in the water.

That was all. The moment was gone. I don't remember now where that picnic was or what we ate that day or why Richard swung his daughter so high.

As long as I have memory, I can live.

Memories. Perhaps that's how I would approach Lester Mackey. I had to reach him, to touch his heart. What happened the night he and Belle met? That was a special memory for her. I knew it would be a special memory for him.

Somehow, tonight, I would reach—

It was only a whisper of sound, but it wasn't the falls, wasn't the rustle of the ever bending foliage.

I slipped to my feet, moved quietly to the railing.

My lanai was dark. But, as always, the rim of lights along the cliff path lighted the way. The moving figure was still dark, indistinguishable. But I knew who was passing. Only Stan Dugan was that tall, walked with that long a stride.

He rounded the bluff.

This path reached a fork. One way led to the tennis courts and the pool, the other to CeeCee's grave.

I thought I knew his destination.

It was almost an hour later that I heard him returning, an hour I'd spent thinking and planning, though I knew there wasn't much I could plan now.

At midnight, I went to the bottom of the steps, put on my jogging shoes. I had a flashlight in my pocket. I didn't think I would need it. I walked quietly along the cliff path, pausing occasionally to listen, but there were only the sounds of the night, the rumble of the falls and the sighing of the trees. I was utterly attuned to this moment, moving with care and caution, looking into every shadow, listening with the intensity of a fugitive.

I breathed more easily when I was past the public rooms of the house and reached the steps to the narrow passageway by the kitchen.

I stopped once again, took off my shoes, tied the laces together and hung them around my neck. I moved up the steps in my stocking feet.

Dim lights burned. Ahiahi was not a house that would ever drowse in total darkness. But there was no movement, no sound of voices, no hint that anyone else was awake.

Still, I was careful. Anyone else abroad would also treat this as a sleeping house, refrain from making any noise.

But I felt quite easy when I reached the garden. I was almost there. Almost there, almost there, the phrase danced in my mind. Once again, I slipped into my shoes.

A lamp burned dimly at the edge of Lester's lanai. A golden swath of light flared through his open archway. So Lester was still awake.

I damn well hoped he was having trouble sleeping, that he was wrestling with the enormity of his lie, that he was beginning to worry and wonder how he could protect Belle.

He had to have a plan, of course. He loved Belle. He'd used his sensitive artist's skill to create the dark message that brought me here. I knew he cared. Surely he would realize that Belle's life was more important—if it came to that—than his cherished place in the family.

Of course, he knew Belle much better than I. Perhaps he was certain she would never forgive him.

I didn't know if she was a forgiving woman.

But I would do my best to persuade Lester that she was.

I reached the open doorway. I took off my shoes, carried them in one hand.

The high-backed chair almost obscured him where he sat at the desk. It was so quiet. I wondered if he had fallen asleep.

My stocking feet made very little sound on the bare wooden floor. Certainly not enough to wake a sleeper. But I knew before I circled around the desk that Lester Mackey was not asleep.

Lester Mackey was dead.

fifteen

This was a room designed for tranquillity: the wide expanse of honey-bright wooden floor, the gleaming oak walls, the geometrically shaped furniture in matte soft blues and grays. A room where space served an equal function with decor.

Not a room for violent death.

Never a room for self-inflicted death.

I stood across the desk and looked at Lester's body, at the scorched small hole in his right temple, at the bright red blood that had oozed down his cheek, at the .22-caliber pistol cupped in his lax fingers.

And at the note in the center of the shining, otherwise bare, oak desk. I came around the desk, leaned forward to read.

DEAR BELLE,
PLEASE FORGIVE ME.

That was all. There was no signature. I am not an expert in handwriting analysis, but the writing appeared smooth and uniform. I had no doubt it had been written by Lester. Otherwise it wouldn't be here.

Suicide.

Lester Mackey, the man who'd spent his life loving Belle and her children, the man who'd been an unwitting accomplice in the kidnapping of CeeCee Burke. Lester Mackey, accomplished photographer, trusted servitor, reclusive aesthete.

Lester Mackey, suicide.

In a pig's eye.

"You damn fool." Yes, I said it aloud as I stared at the lifeless husk of a gallant, irresolute, caring man, said it with a catch in my voice.

I'd been wrong about Lester Mackey. I thought he lied to Belle because he was afraid of losing her love. It was worse than that. He lied because he would not—could not—accept the reality that someone in the family had engineered CeeCee's death. And yet, flickering within him was a terrible knowledge. He had an idea who might be guilty. Once he realized that Richard had been murdered, the pieces came together. He saw someone that night, glimpsed a familiar figure on the cliff path. He would not reveal it, yet he was afraid enough for Belle that he made an effort to talk to that person.

Tonight. Here. Tonight the circle finally closed. Yes, it was one of them:

Strident Anders who cared more for animals than people.

Obsessive Peggy who would do anything for Anders.

Clever Joss who could so perfectly mimic a killer's glower.

Sensual Wheeler who had never forgotten the girl he loved.

Moody Gretchen who remembered Georgetown when her family was whole.

Clear-eyed and coldly beautiful Megan who valued freedom above all.

Tough Stan Dugan who would always have his way.

Charming Keith Scanlon who married money but hadn't lost his roving eye.

Pretty Elise Ford who turned out not to be the perfect secretary.

One of them.

Belle?

The name whispered in my mind. Surely it was not Belle whom Lester protected. But Belle, too, was on this mountaintop tonight.

No. Some proofs you don't need. I didn't need proof of her innocence. Her grief for CeeCee was genuine. And whether her injury came from an accident or a dark design, I knew she sought the truth from Lester Mackey.

Not Belle. The circle was complete without her.

I felt an emptiness in the pit of my stomach. Some of it was sorrow. Lester Mackey deserved better. He was a damn fool, but he deserved better. And part of it was dismay.

Would the police accept this as suicide?

I paced slowly around the desk. Such a clever killer. There was nothing out of place or untoward anywhere, nothing to suggest this was staged, nothing to indicate anyone else had been in this room except Lester.

The gun was positioned correctly. He could have held it. I felt an instant of hope, then shook my head. There must have been a second shot, when the killer held the gun in Lester's hand. I was sure Lester's skin would show traces of gunshot residue. But what had absorbed that second bullet? A cushion, a pillow?

I took a moment, walked into Lester's bedroom. It was as spare and cell-like as the living area, its emptiness a celebration of simplicity. One bed, one pillow, a smooth, white bedspread.

But this killer would have come prepared, bringing a spare pillow from a bedroom. And, of course, carrying it away afterward. That pillow could be anywhere, stuffed in a dark plastic bag, weighted and flung far, far down into the overgrown, densely vegetated valley.

If I told the police everything that had happened, would they listen, would they look at this scene with more questioning eyes?

And how would I be described to the police by Belle Ericcson, the rich and famous and renowned Belle Ericcson?

I would have no credibility.

If I could convince the police to look in the valley, hunt for the pillow or cushion— But the chance of finding anything flung over the edge of the cliff was so remote.

I walked back into the living room. The killer had staged it perfectly.

The idea came to me suddenly, brilliant in its simplicity, staggering in its implications.

I am a law-abiding person. I do not run red lights, not even at midnight when the streets are empty. I've never knowingly defrauded or cheated anyone. I follow the rules because there are reasons for rules, and we flout them at our peril.

But now I stood and looked at the gun in Lester's hand and had the same breathless feeling as a skier poised to jump.

It was up to me.

I hurried into Lester's bedroom, stepped into his bath, used a tissue to open a cupboard. I tucked the tissue in my pocket and grabbed a washcloth, shoving the cupboard shut with my elbow.

Back in the living room, I spread the washcloth over the "suicide" note and crumpled it into a tight ball, then poked the wad of paper into my pocket.

I looked down at the shiny gun. I hesitated. And then I thought of Richard, my handsome, wonderful, loving Richard, plummeting through beauty to nothingness. If I walked away, refused to gamble, my hope of discovering what happened to Richard would be ended. I was barred from this house. I was a pariah to this family. If ever I was to find the truth, I had to be willing to break taboos, discard a lifetime of obeisance to established authority.

My husband's murderer was within a stone's throw of me.

I walked to the open archway, looked out into the garden. No movement. Only the sounds of Ahiahi, the crackle of palm fronds, the rustle of the shrubs, and always, always the steady drone of the falls.

I hurried to the desk. I wanted to be out of there, my task done as quickly as possible. I placed the cloth over the barrel of the gun, picked it up. As I did, the edge of my palm touched Lester's wrist, warm flesh against cool. The minute I felt the barrel hard and solid within the cloth, I bent low and darted across the room to the lighted doorway. Swiftly, I slipped into my running shoes, then plunged into the garden.

My heart thudded. If anyone found me now . . . The sound of my shoes on the oyster shells shocked me. I slowed to a tiptoe. I sought a familiar way. I reached the ti shrubs and poked the gun deep within the branches.

Now I could breathe again. I swung toward the house, my goal the exterior lanai and the steps down to the cliff path. I moved cautiously through the huge living area. I reached the lanai.

So close now, so close.

I ran to the railing and threw the washcloth into the valley. I took two steps toward the stairs and the overhead lights blazed. I whirled to face the house.

Anders Burke carried a book in his hand. He stared at me in disbelief. "What the hell are you doing here?"

Sometimes a strong offense is the only recourse that remains.

I hurried toward him, my hands outstretched. "Anders, I have to talk to Lester Mackey."

Anders was focused on my unexpected arrival. "Where'd you come from?" He looked past me toward the valley.

"The cliff path," I said quickly. "I walked up the road and came through the tennis enclosure, then down to the cliff path." I hoped this careful listing of my purported route would fix clearly in his mind that I had just arrived on the lanai. "All I want is a chance to talk to Lester."

His narrow face hardened. "Mother threw you out. She said you were making things up, that you lied about Lester—"

"It's Lester who lied." I didn't try to keep my voice down. I didn't care if we woke the world. "Anders, listen to me. Last year the brakes in your mother's car went out. She could have died. Somebody drained out the brake fluid. It all goes back to CeeCee's kidnapping."

"What are you talking about?" But there was worry as well as anger in his voice.

I told him. And it was a story I'd better tell well and smoothly, for soon I would have to face questioners who would wonder indeed when and why I had arrived tonight at Ahiahi.

"Anders, if you want to protect your mother, you'll let me talk to Lester. Come with me. Give me a chance to save your mother."

"Mother—" He looked at me with fear in his eyes.

I met his gaze. "Who drained the brake fluid out of your mother's car? Think about it, Anders."

"It was an accident." But his voice was uncertain.

"Megan drove the car the day before. The brakes were

fine. If there's another accident, Belle may not survive. Come with me. Let's make Lester tell the truth. You know how he's lied for all of you. Like the time Wheeler was drunk and had a wreck and Lester said he'd smashed the car into a tree himself. Lester's covered up for all of you, not letting Belle know things that might upset her. And he doesn't want to believe that one of you actually tried to kill her. But he knows, Anders, he knows."

Anders gripped the book tightly in his hands. "Lester's always known everything." His eyes bored into mine. "I don't like you. I don't trust you. Why should you want to help Mother?"

"I want to catch a killer."

He didn't want to believe me. Who would? But his sister was dead. Belle almost died. Richard had died. He tossed the book on the counter of the wet bar. "Come on." He turned and headed toward the garden.

I caught up with him.

The sweet scent of plumeria graced the night.

As before, light flared out from Lester's living room.

"He's still up." Anders walked faster. "He'll tell me the truth."

We reached the archway.

I called out. "Lester? Lester, we want to talk to you." I hurried across the shining floor, came even with the desk, turned to face it. "Oh, God." I pressed the back of my hand against my lips.

But it didn't matter whether I was as adept at playing roles as Joss. Anders had no eyes for me.

He stopped. His face went slack. He reached out a shaking hand. "Lester. Lester!" Anders turned toward me, his face flaccid with shock. "He's been shot."

I spoke gently. "We're too late, Anders. I'm sorry. But not surprised. We've got to call the police." I walked toward the desk, my hand outstretched.

He grabbed my arm. "No. We have to get Mother. We have to tell her first."

"But the police—"

His grip tightened. "A few minutes won't make any difference." Fighting tears, he looked again at Lester. "I have to get Mother."

I didn't resist. I had no standing. But, as I followed Anders, plunging through the garden toward his mother's quarters, I realized anew Belle's power.

I broke into a run, trying to keep up with Anders. We reached the lanai and curved around a rim of the canyon to Belle's rooms. Kyoto dragons stood sentinel at either end of her veranda, their shadows monstrous in the moonlight.

Anders shouted. "Mother, Mother."

He didn't have to say something was wrong.

No mother could hear the timbre of that call without knowing there was trouble.

Lights flashed on in two rooms. Belle appeared in the first doorway, her silver hair streaming onto her shoulders, her pale blue negligee soft against her body. Keith bounded out of an archway ten feet away. He wore boxer shorts, nothing else. His arms and chest were muscular, his legs powerful.

So Belle and Keith didn't share a bedroom.

That was important. Now I knew how Keith could slip to a rendezvous in the garden with Elise. And to Lester Mackey's room?

"Mother." Anders's voice broke. "Somebody's killed Lester. Somebody shot him."

I was watching Keith Scanlon, had eyes for no one but him. It was important that he had his own bedroom, but the expression on his face as Anders blurted out his news was much more important. It was fleeting, but for an instant there was a look of sheer surprise. "Somebody shot him?" Keith's voice rose.

I made up my mind. I'd found the killer. I didn't know

yet the ins and outs of everything Keith had done, but now I felt certain it was Keith who planned CeeCee's kidnapping. It was Keith who pushed Richard to his death, got rid of Johnnie Rodriguez, tampered with Belle's brakes. It was Keith who shot Lester Mackey.

Why else that look of utter surprise? He'd expected news of Lester's suicide, not his murder.

"Lester . . ." Belle's voice was stricken. She stood for a moment in her son's embrace. They clung to each other, the dark head bent protectively over the light.

Then Belle stepped back. Her face was gaunt and harsh in the moonlight. As always, she was in command. And, as always, she was cognizant of her surroundings, no matter the force of emotion within her. She looked at me.

I stepped forward. "I came back. I had to talk to Lester. I was too late."

She limped past me to the railing and stared out over the dark valley, toward the tinsel ribbons of the falls glittering in the moonlight. "Lester lied." Her words fell into the silence of the night.

I came up beside her. Far below, the silvery kukui trees glistened. "Yes. He lied. He was so afraid you would hate him. He thought the kidnapping was a prank, one of the jokes the children loved to play. Later, he was afraid to tell anyone what had happened."

Belle faced me. "Did Richard come here to talk to Lester?"

Here was the hardest truth. "And to someone in the family. Johnnie Rodriguez must have seen someone at the cabin with CeeCee. That's what he had to tell Richard. And that's why Richard came here. Lester knew a part of it. But someone else knew it all." I reached out, took a thin, cold hand in mine.

"Someone in the family." Her voice was cool and remote.

"Yes." The faces flashed in my mind, as I knew they flashed in Belle's.

"So that's why Richard came." Belle's hand gripped mine. We stood, linked by loss.

I wanted to help her. But there was nothing I could do or say to ease her pain. Or mine. "Yes, he came." My voice was weary. "He talked with Lester—and with someone else."

Belle dropped my hand, stepped back to look at the house.

The rooms lay dark along the rim of the canyon.

"Someone here." Belle's voice was cold and harsh and unforgiving. "Someone here killed CeeCee and Richard—and now Lester."

And pushed Johnnie Rodriguez into the lake.

"That's crazy!" Keith exploded. "If anybody killed Lester, it's her," and he pointed at me. "She's the one who's come here causing trouble."

Belle ignored her husband. She limped across the lanai into her room and returned in a moment in an ivory robe and slippers. She walked past us.

Keith started after her. "Where are you going?"

"To Lester." Her cane clicked on the tiles.

We all followed through the garden. Once again I stood in Lester's shining room. This time, I looked not only on death but on sorrow. Belle bowed her head, struggled for composure. Anders clasped his mother's hand.

"Someone here," she said faintly. Slowly she lifted her head. She stepped away from Anders. She studied the position of Lester's body. She noted the wound. Her eyes moved to Lester's hand resting empty on the bare expanse of desk.

"God, this is awful," Keith said huskily.

"No weapon," Belle announced.

I nodded. I didn't feel any thrill of triumph. I had done what I felt I had to do, exchanged one set scene for another.

She reached out, almost touched that sandy graying hair, then let her hand fall. "Call the police, Keith."

Only a few words, but they marked Belle's passage from heartbreak to vengeance.

Once again we followed, this time to Belle's study.

Belle sat at her desk. Her face was composed, but her eyes were dark with pain and anger.

Keith made the call. When it was done and he had placed the phone in its cradle, there was a moment of silence. I don't know what Belle or Keith or Anders envisioned in that moment, but I had a sense of inexorable progression: the unleashing of the force and majesty of the law. An investigation once begun is never ended until there is completion, whether now or years from now. A murder file once opened is ongoing until the crime is solved.

I was focused on the present moment, the tidal wave of examination that would soon wash over us. I should have realized that Lester's murder and the reason for it would sweep Belle back to the crime that began it all.

She leaned forward, clicked a button on her intercom. "Attention, please." She pressed another button. A shrill whistle sounded. "Attention, please." Her voice was cold and commanding. "Everyone is to gather in the living room. Immediately." She clicked off the intercom and stood.

That grim announcement sounded in every room in this luxurious house. It was a shocking end to sleep for those in innocent slumber. But one listener was not innocent. To that person, the summons had to engender a moment of terror.

"Belle, what are you doing?" Keith asked. His eyes were bewildered. And worried.

There was a burning determination in her eyes. "I have to hurry." She moved quickly across the room, her cane flicking against the wooden floor.

"Mother, wait. You're upset—"

She shrugged away from Anders's outstretched hand.

We followed, of course.

Belle reached the huge living area first. She went to the panel of light switches, punched them all, until every light in the room glowed. She took her place at the edge of the lanai, facing the room.

I watched faces.

I don't usually second-guess an intuitive flash.

But as the roused household gathered in the immense living room, I wondered if I'd properly gauged Keith's look of surprise when Anders announced that Lester had been murdered.

Why should Lester Mackey protect Keith Scanlon?

He wouldn't have done so when CeeCee was kidnapped.

But what if his suspicion of Keith was late-blooming? And uncertain at best. What if Lester became suspicious only after Belle's accident?

That timing made sense. What if Lester put pieces together over the years and suspected Keith but had no proof? What if Lester's goal was to protect Belle and he felt the best way was to warn Keith and urge him to leave?

That was possible. Foolish, but possible.

And I knew Lester was foolish, a man who tried in every way to ignore the reality of murder within this family he loved.

Good motives. Ignoble motives. Lester lied to keep Belle from learning of his unwitting complicity in CeeCee's kidnapping. Had Lester decided that Belle, just now coming back to some sense of joy in life, was too fragile to learn that the man she'd married, the man she'd trusted, the man who knew her as only a lover could, was the man who had killed her daughter?

Lester tried for years to evade thought about the kidnapping. Lester had protected the children of this family from many consequences. He wouldn't connive to protect

CeeCee's killer, but he might well be willing to give the person he suspected a chance to explain, to convince Lester of innocence.

Lester wanted them all to be innocent.

But one of them was guilty.

So I looked carefully at faces as they hurried into the room in response to Belle's call.

Peggy, her eyes wide and frantic, gave a scream of relief when she saw Anders. She darted to him and burrowed her face in his shoulder. She wore white cotton shorty pajamas with pink bows on each shoulder.

Joss thudded to a stop, his eyes moving swiftly around the room. He'd pulled on a faded pair of jeans but no shirt. "What the hell's going on?" His uncombed hair and stubbled face were at such a variance from his usual well-groomed appearance.

Wheeler came into the room like a prowling animal, his gaze alert and suspicious. He wore a T-shirt and boxer shorts.

Gretchen blinked sleepily. "What's wrong?" Her voice was high and scared. "Something's happened! What's wrong?" One hand clutched at the neck of her pink nightgown.

For once Megan's hair was ruffled. Without makeup, she looked like a ghostly replica of her daytime self.

Stan Dugan, too, was shirtless and in jeans. He saw me and his eyes glowed with interest.

Elise Ford had taken long enough to slip into a tailored navy robe. She stared uneasily at Belle, carefully did not look toward Keith.

The housekeeper wore a muumuu. She stopped in the entryway, looking questioningly toward Belle.

There was a babel of voices.

"Quiet." Belle stared at them. This was her family, her staff. And she looked at them icily.

One by one, they fell silent, staring at Belle, at her bleak and stony face, her burning eyes. She stood straight and still and looked at each one in turn. "The police are on their way. One of you shot Lester tonight."

I scanned their faces. I saw shock and horror and dismay. But one face was well schooled, one face was accustomed to feigning emotion.

"I have only a few minutes before the police will arrive. But that is long enough." Belle's voice was fierce.

Joss took a step toward her. "Mother, what—"

Belle held up her hand. "I want to know," and every word dropped like a pellet of ice, "where each of you was the night CeeCee was kidnapped."

Once again, a low murmur rose. Once again Belle's hand moved, and there was a painful quiet. They stood unmoving, staring at her. Presumably only CeeCee and Lester were at the lake on Friday night.

Belle pointed at her husband. Keith looked at her in hurt surprise. She waited.

His face slowly hardened. "I went to a rodeo. In Mesquite. You didn't want to go."

"I didn't hear you come in." She looked at him as though he were a stranger.

Keith didn't say a word, but the muscles in his neck bunched.

Peggy blundered forward. "Anders and I were together. We'd gone to dinner at Casa Rosa and then he came over to my apartment. He spent the night."

Anders reached out and grabbed her arm. "Goddamn it, Peggy, I don't need an alibi. I didn't kill my sister."

"Where were you, Anders?" His mother looked at him intently.

He threw back his head. He opened his mouth, then took a deep breath. "No place, Mom. I just drove around."

"Why?" I asked.

He looked at me blankly.

"Why? Were you driving off a quarrel, Anders?" I looked deep into his dark eyes.

His glance slid away from me. "It doesn't matter now." His voice was very tired. "It doesn't matter."

Far away, a siren sounded.

"Quickly," Belle instructed. "Quickly. Joss?"

"Slow night in Dallas. Went to a movie. By myself." His voice was relaxed but his eyes kept turning toward Anders.

Gretchen shrugged. "I was bar-hopping." She held up both hands. "I know. Nice girls shouldn't. But sometimes I do."

"I worked late." Stan's voice was grim. Was he thinking that if he hadn't asked CeeCee to return his ring that he would have been with her at the lake and she would be alive now?

The siren rose and fell, nearer and nearer.

"Wheeler?"

"I was in my room, Belle. Reading a book." And thinking about the girl he loved who was perhaps still planning to marry another man?

"A night class," Megan said quietly. "But they didn't take roll."

"I was in my room, too," Elise said dully.

The siren shrilled, then stopped abruptly. The police had arrived.

sixteen

A thirtyish patrolman with shiny black hair and a flat, calm face watched us. He stood at ease, hands behind his back, his dark eyes moving constantly around the room.

The garden blazed with lights. We could hear the occasional slam of a car door, the murmur of voices. Right now the homicide unit was performing its duties, but eventually the detective in charge would be ready to talk to us.

We sat in tired, tense silence. The patrolman had instructed us not to talk. "Lieutenant Kanoa will speak with each of you soon."

Keith Scanlon stared somberly at the floor. Occasionally he glanced at Belle, then looked away from her icy face.

Elise huddled in an overstuffed chair, her arms wrapped around her knees.

Joss, his curly hair tousled, slumped back in his chair, his face bereft, a study in grief. If it was acting, it was superb.

Wheeler paced back and forth, back and forth, across the lanai, his sensuous face twisted in a scowl.

Gretchen stood by the wet bar, looking up at Lester's gallery of photographs, her eyes shiny with tears. All of her kinetic energy seemed to have drained away.

Megan reached out to smooth her sister's tumbling red hair. Megan's lovely face drooped in sorrow.

Anders stared balefully toward the brightly lit garden. He looked resentful as well as anguished. Occasionally he shot a puzzled, worried look at his mother.

Peggy sat close to her husband, one hand clutching his arm. Peggy's glance caught mine. Outright hostility flashed in her eyes. It is always tempting to blame the stranger.

Stan Dugan straddled a chair, his massive arms folded on the top. He looked curiously from Peggy to me. "Watch your back, Mrs. Collins." Although he spoke in—for him—a normal tone, his booming voice jerked every face toward him.

"Thanks," I said coolly.

The patrolman held up a warning hand, as if stopping traffic. "Quiet, please."

Anders pulled away from Peggy, jumped to his feet. "What the hell does that mean, Stan?"

Our guard swung toward Anders.

There was a melee of sound:

". . . looking for trouble, that's . . ."

". . . what's she doing here?"

". . . who's in charge . . ."

"Enough." Belle's crisp voice cut through. Again the silence was sudden and absolute. Everyone looked toward her.

I don't know if it was the anger in her eyes or the merciless line of her lips, but the silence took on an uncomfortable, threatened quality.

Slowly, Belle rose to her feet. She stood very straight, both hands clasping the knob of her cane. "I will know the truth. Before this night is out." She looked at each one in turn.

"Ma'am." A young policeman stood in the archway. He inclined his head politely to Belle. "Lieutenant Kanoa will see you now."

Five minutes passed. Ten. The policeman returned. "Anders Burke."

Peggy popped to her feet.

"One at a time, ma'am," the officer instructed.

"Anders." It was a frightened wail. And I didn't think Peggy was afraid for herself.

"It's all right," Anders said impatiently. "I found Lester, Peggy. They need to talk to me. I'll be back in a few minutes."

But Peggy simply stood there, staring after him.

Stan Dugan's big mouth curved in a malicious grin. "He's a big boy, Peggy. I'll bet he can even zip his own trousers."

Her face flamed. "You think you're so important." Her voice trembled. "Well, I know CeeCee dumped you. She told you that last Friday, didn't she?" She looked wildly around the room. "CeeCee dumped him. Did you know that? It's true. So why is he here? What right does he have?"

"Ma'am, ma'am." The patrolman moved close enough that Peggy backed away, sank down on the couch. But she glowered at Stan.

The big lawyer sprawled back in the overstuffed chair, his hands behind his head, his face expressionless.

The patrolman returned every few minutes, ushering out in order Peggy, Keith, Elise, Joss, Wheeler, Gretchen, Megan, Amelia, and, finally, Stan.

No one returned. I assumed they were told to go to their rooms when the interviews ended.

It didn't take me long to wonder why I wasn't being called early on. All the possible reasons came up hard and sour like pinball lemons:

I was the intruder.

My jeep was hidden in a side lane near the road to Ahiahi.

I'd quarreled publicly with Lester at Spouting Horn. The police would trace his last day, learn about that encounter.

Amelia would report that she'd told me this afternoon that Lester had been near the cliff trail late the night Richard died.

When Stan and I had been the only ones left, I read the same judgment in his craggy face.

"If you're looking for a lawyer—"

"Quiet, please," the patrolman had said.

Then Stan was gone.

I stood and walked across the room.

"Ma'am," the patrolman said quickly.

"The ladies' room," I said firmly.

He hesitated, then nodded.

He took up his post right next to the door.

I shut the door. Quickly I pulled the crumpled note from my pocket and tore it into tiny pieces. I flushed the toilet and some of the tension eased out of my shoulders. I splashed water on my face, washed my hands.

When I opened the door, two of them waited. The younger man said, "Lieutenant Kanoa will see you now."

I'd gotten rid of the note just in time.

As I followed my escort, I moved slowly. I was so tired that every step was an effort. But I needed to be alert. I needed to remember so much in this upcoming interview. I must be careful, but I must answer easily, without hesitation. I must appear confident and unworried. And I must do these things while groggy from exhaustion. It was a quarter past three in the morning. My mind felt clogged, like a silt-laden pond. My body ached with fatigue.

The patrolman stood aside for me to enter Belle's office. "Mrs. Collins, sir."

I blinked my eyes, took a deep breath. One more time, I had to perform, think, grapple, combat, respond, defend, attack. I reached deep inside for a surge of alertness.

My first glimpse of Lieutenant Kanoa roused me, like a shock of cold water, like the crash of a thunderous wave. He dwarfed Belle's desk. He had to weigh at least two hundred and fifty pounds. A moon face and a neck like a concrete piling rested on a tree-trunk thick torso. His aloha shirt pulled across his massive chest. His arms bulged with muscles. Hamhock-sized hands made the notebook and pencil in front of him look like a child's toys.

"Come in, please." His voice was so deep it sounded as if he spoke from a cavern.

He was so immense, it took a moment to look beyond his size at sleepy eyes in a bland face.

A danger signal flashed in my mind. I knew an affectation when I saw one. Sleepy eyes, yes, but I had glimpsed, just for an instant, a quick, keen intelligence.

Lieutenant Kanoa had now talked to everyone but me. He had a great deal of information—and misinformation—about the stranger within the gates, the suspect stranger.

I walked up to Belle's desk.

"Sit down." A command.

For an instant, I almost opted to stand. What the hell could he do about it? But I was tired, tired to the bone. I couldn't afford to waste any energy, not an atom of it. I sat down in the straight chair. And shaded my eyes. The gooseneck lamp on the desk was twisted to spotlight the chair. Old hat, I felt like saying. But I saved that tendril of energy and squinted against the glare and waited.

He reached out a meaty hand and flicked the switch on a small black tape recorder. "With your permission, Mrs. Collins?"

"Of course." The bright light hurt my eyes. I leaned forward and pushed the lamp, moving away the harsh glare. "With your permission, Lieutenant Kanoa."

"Of course." There might have been a faint lilt of amusement in that deep voice. He leaned back in his chair, placed cigar-thick fingers in a steeple. He studied me, a man in no hurry. But there was nothing tranquil about the silence.

I'd spent a lifetime searching for truth in people's faces. Had my gaze been quite so cold and skeptical?

"I understand you came here to avenge your husband's death." Blunt, sharp, unequivocal.

My answer was swift. "I came here to find out what happened to Richard."

He leaned forward, folded his massive arms on the desk. "What did you find out?"

I felt as if the earth had split in front of me and I teetered on the edge of a chasm.

"Someone in this house killed Richard." Anger flooded through me. I wanted to shout it. I wanted to grab his huge shoulders, shake them, demand that he listen.

I would have as much effect pounding my fists on the trunk of a redwood.

"Mr. Collins died several years ago. Why have you waited until now to come to Kauai—if indeed he was murdered?" His huge head tilted forward attentively.

I was afraid the deck was stacked. But I had to play the hand.

I began with the poster. Once again, I told it all, but this time I repeated my angry conversation with Lester at Spouting Horn, my effort to inform Belle, and Lester's subsequent lies.

Kanoa said lazily, as if it didn't matter, but his eyes were alert and intelligent, "Johnnie Rodriguez. Let's start there." His deep voice had the lilting Hawaiian cadence. For once I wasn't charmed. "You believe Rodriguez knew what happened to CeeCee Burke."

"That's correct." I massaged the tight tendons in the back of my neck.

"But you don't know what Rodriguez said to your husband." His dark brown eyes were bright and interested.

"Richard came here . . ." My voice was weary. "And was pushed off the cliff."

"That's what *you* believe."

I didn't like the emphasis on "you."

"That's what happened."

"You learned of this from a poster. That's very dramatic." And, his tone said, as likely as a personal visit from a menehune.

Yes, it had been dramatic. Life-changing. For me. For, ultimately, everyone at Ahiahi.

"Lester sent me the poster. He was doing his best to protect Belle. Lester for years had refused to believe the kidnapper was one of them. He'd resisted the idea when Richard came. And he'd made himself accept Richard's fall as an accident. Lester didn't face his doubts and fears until Belle's car crashed down the mountain. Even then he waited, wondering and worrying. He waited until it was time for everyone to gather again at Ahiahi. Lester was frantic. Was Belle in danger? What could he do? I know what he did, Lieutenant. He posed me a challenge I could not refuse. He sent me a poster telling me my husband was murdered."

"Mrs. Collins." Those sleepy eyes watched me so closely.

"Yes."

"Where is this poster?"

"I told you." I was so tired. My head pounded. "It was stolen from my room the day I arrived."

"You are very creative, Mrs. Collins." Once again his hands formed a steeple.

"I am telling the truth, Lieutenant."

"You are telling some of the truth. You believe Johnnie Rodriguez and Lester Mackey kidnapped CeeCee Burke and that your husband came here to confront Lester Mackey."

"I know that Richard came here because of what he learned from Johnnie Rodriguez. I know Richard came here to see someone—"

"Obviously Mr. Collins came to see Mr. Mackey." Kanoa was impatient.

"Perhaps. But we know that Johnnie Rodriguez took a walk the night CeeCee Burke was kidnapped. What if he went to the cabin where he and Lester had left her? What if he saw someone in the family there with CeeCee?"

"And Rodriguez kept that a secret from everyone after her body was found?" Kanoa's disbelief was apparent.

"Johnnie was afraid no one would believe him. And he followed Lester's lead when Lester told him to keep quiet. But"—I leaned forward—"it had to be something like that. Why else would Rodriguez call Richard, tell him he had to tell someone the truth about the kidnapping?"

"Because he and Mackey kidnapped her." Kanoa spoke with quiet finality.

"But someone engineered it!" I was angry now. Kanoa wasn't listening to me. He was shaking that huge head, throwing a great pumpkin of a shadow against the wall behind him.

"That's what you claim now, Mrs. Collins." His dark eyes accused me.

I felt a sudden emptiness in my chest, the visceral response to shock.

Because now I understood exactly what Kanoa believed. He had figured it out to his satisfaction. He believed that I had come to Kauai seeking retribution. I found the man who committed the kidnapping, ergo I found the man who had to silence Richard.

"You talked with Lester Mackey the night you arrived."

He ticked off the points on his fingers. "This afternoon you learned that Mackey was seen near the cliff trail the night your husband died. You accused him to Mrs. Scanlon—"

How odd. He meant Belle. I wondered if anyone else had ever addressed her that way.

"—but Mackey convinced her you'd invented the story. So what were you going to do, Mrs. Collins? You had no proof."

"Lester lied because he was trying to protect himself—"

"Exactly." Kanoa looked at me curiously, wondering that I didn't see that I had blurted out a damning truth.

It was frustrating, infuriating. "No. Not that way. Lester didn't intend to kidnap CeeCee. He thought it was a joke, a prank, one of the silly games the children played. When I say he was trying to protect himself, I mean that he didn't want Belle to know he had any knowledge of the kidnapping because he had lied about it for so many years and he was terrified that Belle would turn against him."

"He and Rodriguez took the girl," Kanoa said stubbornly.

"A joke." My desperate, driven litany.

"That's what you claim now."

We'd come full circle. I damned his persistence, his twisted interpretation, though I understood how he had reached his conclusion.

"Mr. Mackey didn't confirm your story." Kanoa's eyes bored into mine. "You were upset, Mrs. Collins."

"I was very frustrated, Lieutenant Kanoa."

"You were asked to leave the premises."

"Yes."

"When did you decide to return here to see Mr. Mackey?"

Nice. He was setting the groundwork for premeditation.

"I had to come back, make another effort. I decided to come back after dark so that I could talk to him. I was afraid for Belle."

"So it was your intention to return from the moment you were ejected. Is that correct?"

He was certainly a persistent devil.

"I was determined to persuade Lester to tell the truth."

Kanoa's expression was especially sleepy as he asked, "Now what did Mr. Mackey say when you talked with him?"

I shook my head. "I had no chance to talk to him tonight, Lieutenant. I was on my way to see him when I met Anders."

"But you left the hotel around eight o'clock, Mrs. Collins." He regarded me steadily.

"Yes. I came directly here. It took me about an hour to climb the hill—"

Something flickered in his eyes and I knew they'd found the jeep.

"—I went around the wall and came in an entrance by the tennis courts. I went straight to my room—the room where I'd stayed—and waited on the lanai until it was—" I almost said past midnight. Careful, careful, careful, Henrie O. "—very late. Obviously, I didn't want to run into anyone. But I did." And I made my tone rueful.

"You went to Mr. Mackey's quarters." Kanoa's deep voice was compelling. "You quarreled. You shot him. You were escaping when you encountered Mr. Burke."

It was eerily close to the truth.

"No, Lieutenant. I came along the cliff path, climbed the steps to the living room and was heading toward Lester's quarters when Anders turned on the light. We went together to see Lester and we found him. Dead."

"Did you touch anything in that visit?"

"I did not. Anders insisted we go to Belle first. I wanted to call the police immediately." Such a good citizen am I.

He looked at me skeptically and I knew we were back where we'd started. I was the intruder. I was the suspect.

"Lieutenant, I did not shoot Lester Mackey."

He inclined his head gravely. "Thank you, Mrs. Collins."

He reached forward, clicked off the recorder, then scooped up his notebook and pen. He heaved himself to his feet. "Our investigation into Mr. Mackey's death will continue. Do not leave the island, Mrs. Collins."

I stood and looked after him.

Do not leave the island, Mrs. Collins.

I took a deep breath. Damn, damn, damn. And yes, I could appreciate the irony. Wasn't I the clever one to rig up a murder scene?

What was I going to do now? I'd counted on Lester Mackey. I'd been sure I could wrest the truth from him, one way or the other.

Think, Henrie O, think!

I was exhausted, confused, threatened. What was—

The soft whisper buzzed like a faraway bee, a sound, yes, but not clear. Then, more loudly, "Henrie O!"

I stepped closer to Belle's desk.

"Henrie O, can you hear me?" It was a faint whisper again.

I looked at the white intercom, bent near it. "Yes."

"Pretend you are searching my desk." My desk . . . It was Belle. "Don't appear to be listening."

Through my fatigue, I understood. Or understood in part. Belle had left on her intercom system so that she could listen to Lieutenant Kanoa's interviews.

Clever.

But Belle Ericcson had always been clever. It gave me a solid spurt of satisfaction to know that she was a jump ahead of Lieutenant Kanoa. And that she knew exactly what had happened to this point in his investigation. She knew, and she wanted to talk to me.

"Search the desk, then go to your suite." A click.

I opened the center drawer of the desk, checked its contents. Did Belle think I was being watched? Or was she merely being cautious? In any event, Belle had accepted the obvious. Tonight someone here committed murder. The murderer had to be afraid, watchful, wary, and was certainly keeping a close track of the investigation.

And of me. Because I was the catalyst.

I opened the side drawers, glanced through folders, then closed the drawers. I sighed and walked slowly toward the garden walkway. Belle wanted to talk to me without being observed. As soon as I was out of sight of her office, I began to walk swiftly.

I flicked on the lights in my suite. I was sharply disappointed to find it empty. I walked into the bedroom, stood there at a loss.

Once again I heard that faint sibilant whisper.

The intercom.

I was savvy now. Just in case I was being observed, I walked to the bed and sat on it, bent my head as if in deep weariness—and listened.

"He's going to arrest you." Belle spoke calmly.

Once again that feeling of emptiness struck me. "Yes, I'm afraid so. I tried to tell him—"

"He won't listen," she said crisply.

"No."

"Then it's up to us, Henrie O. All right, we'll handle it." She didn't wait for an answer. "Here's what we'll do." Yes, Belle had a plan, a gallant, reckless, dangerous plan. Her crisp emphatic words burned in my mind.

"Belle, I can't let you—"

"Meet me on the lanai outside my office." Click.

No ifs, ands, or buts. Belle at her imperious, brave best.

All right. I'd signed on and the ride wasn't over. But if I hurried and if Belle and I were right that the night held watchful eyes and listening ears, I could—with luck—buy a little insurance.

This was a chance I felt I had to take. If a watch had been

mounted on Belle's office, the watcher was very likely on the cliff path. That would provide a vantage point to overhear exchanges in Belle's office. Moreover, it would be difficult to remain unobserved by the police in the garden or the nearby rooms.

So I was going to assume that the killer, if nearby, was on the cliff path and therefore could not observe my actions on the garden side of the house.

I ran up the garden walkway, my goal the third suite from mine, the suite where Stan Dugan was staying.

I reached his open doorway and darted into the dark living room. I tiptoed to the bedroom, using my pocket flash for just an instant.

He lunged up from his bed.

"Shh. Shh. Stan, I need your help—"

A powerful hand gripped my arm.

I whispered fast and prayed he would listen and understand and help us.

"I got it." His voice was low. He released me.

I heard a rustle as he pulled on clothes, then I felt a quick squeeze on my arm. We hurried out into the night. He turned toward the tennis courts.

I headed for Belle's office.

Belle was standing on the lanai outside her office.

And we gave our performance.

"Belle, you have to help me. The police think I shot Lester."

She faced me. "Why should I help you?" Her voice was bitter. "If you hadn't come here, Lester would be alive."

I came up beside her. We stood by the railing. In the heavy stillness of late night, the roar of the falls pulsed loudly.

"Lester protected CeeCee's kidnapper. Will you protect the person who killed Lester—and CeeCee?"

"Never."

I whirled away, faced out toward the valley. And the listening figure on the cliff walk? "Oh, what difference does it make what you do or say. The police won't listen. There's no way to convince them—"

"I can." Belle spoke with finality.

I jerked toward her. "What are you saying?"

"I talked to Lester. Later. After you left." Her voice ached with sadness. "He didn't realize he'd given himself away. But I knew him so well. And after I talked to the police tonight, I thought about everything. And something he said. The pieces fell into place."

"Are you going to let me be arrested for someone else's crime?" My voice rose.

"No. No, I won't let that happen."

I grabbed her arm. "Let's call them now. We can catch Lieutenant Kanoa."

"Not tonight." She shook free. "I want some time alone with CeeCee. Then I'll do what I have to do. But I want you to give me this time."

I didn't answer for a long moment, then, finally, grudgingly, I replied. "All right, Belle. I understand. But in the morning you'll call the police?"

"In the morning." She turned, walked toward the garden, her cane clicking on the tiles. On her way—alone, unprotected, vulnerable—to CeeCee's grave on that isolated, dark, and silent point.

seventeen

I wanted to run after her, but I forced myself to wait. If Belle and I were right, the murderer had listened from the cliff path. If we were right, that person—with murder in his or her heart—would give Belle time to reach CeeCee's grave, then slip quietly along the cliff path to the point—and to Belle.

"Damn." I swore aloud for that hidden listener, venting my unhappiness at Belle's refusal to call back the police immediately. I heaved a quick sigh of anger, then walked, head down, toward the garden.

Once out of sight from the cliffside steps to the lanai, I broke into a light, swift jog.

I passed Belle.

We didn't speak.

There was nothing now to say. Both of us carried with us a lifetime of memories and a determination to put a face to a deadly figure. And to stop the killing.

When I reached the fork in the path, I moved on tiptoe. I edged around the point. The falls thundered. Moonlight silvered the silent ledge, glistening on the granite gravestone. The gnarled branches of the ohia tree made an intricate design against the velvet black sky. Beyond the grave enclosure was the inky darkness of the overhang. I slipped into that black shadow and joined Stan Dugan. He squeezed my arm.

The roar of the falls, so close here, thrummed in my ears, loud, never-ending, forever. Their roar dominated the night, obscuring the creak of the wind-tossed branches.

So there was no sound to signal Belle's arrival. She came around the point, walking slowly, leaning on her cane. She stopped beside the grave and looked out at the falls, the wind molding her gown against her. Then she came to the enclosure, sank down onto the low wall. The moonlight was stark on her face, a face heavy with sorrow.

We waited, the three of us, separate, alone with thoughts we could not share, alone with the burning anger that flames out of injustice, Belle sitting by the grave, Stan and I hidden in the deep shadow of the overhang.

Soon we would know.

I wished I had been able to warn Belle.

Would that have been a kindness?

Or was it better for her not to know until her husband came into view? Perhaps that was kinder. How hard it would have been for me to tell her about Keith and Elise and how hard it would have been for Belle to learn it from me.

It was going to be a devastating blow for her to realize that a man she'd trusted had betrayed her in every way, but at least she would be free of the agonizing fear that one of her children hid death behind a lifetime of laughter.

I was so certain of Keith's guilt that for an instant my eyes denied the reality of the figure that appeared on the path.

Not Keith, that was my first stunned thought.

But I should have realized. The last piece slipped into place. That last Friday morning, CeeCee indeed wanted to warn her mother that her husband was unfaithful. But I should have remembered that it takes two to cheat. That's what I should have remembered. Keith was a womanizer. Elise had not been the first. He'd ruined two earlier marriages with his infidelities. Yes, Keith was being unfaithful, but his lover then was not Elise.

As Gretchen came around the point with a grim and terrible determination, I understood.

Gretchen hated Belle. She had delighted in seducing Belle's husband, the ultimate theft. Gretchen must have enjoyed her conquest immensely, feeling a surge of triumph whenever she saw Belle.

Then CeeCee found out. CeeCee told Peggy it was "rotten" the way Belle was being treated. CeeCee was determined to tell her mother. She almost told Belle early that Friday morning. Instead, CeeCee confronted Keith, quarreled with him.

And Keith must have told Gretchen.

How quickly Gretchen moved, how cleverly she put together her plan. None of it revealed her, none of it could be traced to her. She could back off at any time, let it go.

In the end, it was so easy. Johnnie and Lester did the work. CeeCee played along with the game.

When Gretchen came to the cabin that night, did she slip the crushed powder of the tranquilizer into CeeCee's glass? Or was the wine already poisoned?

So easy.

And so profitable.

Gretchen's hatred was fueled by a lust for money. Maybe in the end, that's what it came down to. Money. There would be no more money if CeeCee told Belle.

Gretchen had to weigh the pleasure she would take in

Belle's knowing about Gretchen and Keith against the grim reality of losing her place in that world.

Gretchen stopped a few feet from Belle.

Belle stood. "Why?" It was a cry of anguish.

"You killed Dad." Gretchen's voice was hard and bitter. "You came and took him away from us. And you made love with him in my mother's room. My mother's room." The words trembled with fury. "I hated you. I always hated you. I should have killed you. But I wanted you to know what it was like to lose somebody. And CeeCee was such a bitch. She was going to tell you about me and Keith."

Belle's head lifted.

"Oh, yes, Keith likes to have fun. I got him. But I was already tired of him. Then CeeCee found out. I had to kill her—or you. I decided to get rid of CeeCee. I even got the money out of the graveyard. You didn't call the police. That was stupid, Belle. But I had fun, driving to Gainesville and sneaking into the cemetery. I spent every penny of it. I took it to places like Mexico where nobody cares about serial numbers. I spent every penny."

"Gretchen—" There was a sob in Belle's voice.

"It was all very clever, wasn't it? Nobody ever thought it was one of us. I knew Lester would keep his mouth shut. He didn't want to think it could be one of us. So he lied and lied. I was safe until Johnnie Rodriguez called that friend of yours. Johnnie was watching the cabin when I came. CeeCee had drunk most of the wine by then. We sat there and kidded around and she got sleepier and sleepier. While she was still able to walk, I led her out to the car. We went to the rowboat and I just got her in before she passed out. I went way out into the lake and pushed her over the side."

Belle buried her face in her hands. Stan grabbed my arm, held it in a viselike grip.

"Your friend came over here. I told him Johnnie was wrong, that it was all a mistake. But I could tell he didn't believe me." Gretchen sounded faintly regretful. "I took the cliff path to his room that night and called up to him and said you wanted to see him. He came down the steps. I let him go ahead of me. Then I pushed him. I had no choice."

Stan curved an arm around my shoulders, held me tight.

I pressed my hands against my lips.

"Oh, Gretchen," Belle said wearily. "Richard. Then you tried to kill me. And now Lester. Gretchen, it must end. It must end now."

Gretchen stepped toward Belle. Her face wasn't quite human, drained of all emotion, hard and bleak as CeeCee's granite tombstone. "It's going to end, Belle. For you." She lifted her arm and an alabaster figurine glittered in the moonlight.

Stan lunged out of the shadow and in two steps stood beside Belle. He held out his hand. "Give it to me, Gretchen. It's all over now. It's finished."

Gretchen stood frozen for an instant, her arm held high. Then she looked toward the path. "Wheeler, is that you?"

We looked past her.

In that instant, no more than an instant, she was running, moving with a wild, crazed swiftness, and she was around the end of the bluff.

Stan pounded after her.

I ran, too.

Gretchen swarmed along the ever-narrowing path, the path that ended alongside the stream flowing to the falls. She passed the warning sign.

I screamed at Stan. "Stop! Stop!"

He skidded to a halt, looked back at me.

I caught up with him, grabbed his arm, held tight. "The rocks are too slippery. We can't go on."

Gretchen reached the edge of the stream. Her feet flailed out from beneath her on the slick rocks. With a long, shuddering, desperate scream, she tumbled into the swift, inexorable water, and, still screaming, plunged over the falls.

eighteen

My plane would leave soon. My bags were packed and stored in the jeep.

Belle and I stood on the lanai outside her office, looking out over the valley. Heavy clouds banked in the north, but a rainbow glistened in the heavy mist of the falls, vivid swaths of orange and gold and rose. The falls thundered down the face of the canyon, their beauty impervious to sorrow.

Purplish shadows accented the deep blue of Belle's eyes. Her skin was chalk-white. She looked older, but there was a fine courage in her gaze, a commitment to life.

We looked at each other across a gulf of pain and loss. I doubted we should ever meet again.

"I'm sorry," I said simply. I had not intended to bring her even greater sorrow.

She gave a quick shake of her head. "You had to come."

Belle was right. I'd had no choice. I had discovered the

truth of Richard's death. Now was the time to discover the truth of his life. And mine.

"Belle—"

The heart hears far more than words say. Or perhaps my voice said it all.

Belle's pale face was grave and thoughtful. "I'll be leaving soon, too. I believe I'll go to London for a while. Keith is going back to Texas. I'll be getting a divorce." Her tone brooked no discussion. This was now and would forever be a closed chapter. She would never speak about the reason this marriage had failed or what Keith's promiscuity had cost her. Or the terrible price she'd paid because of Gretchen's anger.

Then Belle's eyes met mine directly, with no pretense. "I've never been unfaithful in marriage, Henrie O."

Those words were meant for me. I knew that.

She reached out, gently clasped my hand. "We should have been friends, Henrie O. Because we both cared so much for Richard. He was the best friend I ever had." She sighed and looked out into the valley. "I should not have taken advantage of that friendship."

I scarcely breathed. Why had Richard always hurried to her side, whenever Belle called?

She dropped my hand, smoothed back her hair, looked at me steadily. "I saved Richard's life in Vietnam. When our patrol was attacked and we escaped, I grabbed a dead soldier's rifle. Richard and I found an abandoned rubber plantation. We hid there. The next day, when Richard was drawing water from a well, a sniper shot at him. I heard the shot. I took the rifle and wormed my way to the clearing. I killed the sniper. I made Richard promise he would never tell anyone. He kept his promise."

I looked at her with a rush of affection. I understood her request. I'd read her book. This was not a woman who sought attention. She wanted to do her job and leave it at that. If word had got out that she'd saved Richard, there would have been stories, interviews, admiration. Belle didn't want that kind of admiration.

I knew then why Richard had valued her friendship, how much it had meant to him. I knew that he must have wanted to tell me why he felt so in her debt. But being Richard, a promise made was a promise kept.

"I didn't expect him to repay me." Belle looked at me for understanding. "But I'm afraid he felt in my debt. Whenever I asked him for help, he came."

So now I knew.

"Thank you, Belle."

We embraced. Then I turned to leave.

"Before you go," Belle said quickly. She snapped two blossoms from one of the hibiscus shrubs. She handed one to me.

"For Richard," she said quietly, and she threw her blossom into the valley.

I held the bloom against my face for a moment, gave the flower a gentle kiss. I lifted my arm and let go, let go of pain and anger, fear and jealousy.

The pink blossoms drifted on a wind current, down, down, down toward the kukui trees.

Acknowledgments

I am especially indebted to three wonderful librarians who read the manuscript of *Death in Paradise.* My thanks go to Caroline Spencer, Director, Hawaii State Library, Honolulu; Marya Zoller, librarian in the Hawaii and Pacific Section, Hawaii State Library, Honolulu; and Alice Miles, library assistant, Kalihi-Palama Library, Honolulu. I am also indebted to fellow mystery writer Connie Shelton, whose knowledge of and affection for Kauai were of great help to me.

About the Author

An acknowledged master of mystery and spinetingling suspense, Carolyn Hart has written three previous *Henrie O* mysteries: *Dead Man's Island* (an Agatha award-winner), *Scandal in Fair Haven* (nominated for both an Agatha and a Macavity Award), and *Death in Lovers' Lane*. She has also been nominated and has won Agatha, Anthony, and Macavity awards for her popular "Death on Demand" series. One of the founders of Sisters in Crime, Ms. Hart lives in Oklahoma City, Oklahoma.